CRITICAL ACCLAIM
A CRACK IN FOREVER

KT-224-469

'Good Blub of the Week . . . You sniffle and sob and keep eagerly turning the pages'
Daily Mail

'Even cynics will find it hard to read *A Crack in Forever* without wiping away a tear'
Woman's Journal

'Sexual sparks and romance . . . Have the Kleenex ready'
Cosmopolitan

'Mascara is guaranteed a marathon run . . . A *Love Story* for the nineties'
She

'[An] intensely moving love story you won't be able to finish without at least a few tears'
Prima

'An emotionally touching story told with exquisite care'
Booklist

'Part spicy contemporary romance, part tragic love story . . . [A] compelling story'
Publishers Weekly

A CRACK IN FOREVER

Jeannie Brewer

BANTAM BOOKS

LONDON · NEW YORK · TORONTO · SYDNEY · AUCKLAND

A CRACK IN FOREVER
A BANTAM BOOK: 0553 40973 5

Originally published in Great Britain by Bantam Press,
a division of Transworld Publishers Ltd

PRINTING HISTORY
Bantam Press edition published 1996
Bantam edition published 1997

Set in 10/12pt Ehrhardt by
Phoenix Typesetting, Ilkley, West Yorkshire

Bantam Books are published by Transworld Publishers Ltd,
61–63 Uxbridge Road, London W5 5SA,
in Australia by Transworld Publishers (Australia) Pty Ltd,
15–25 Helles Avenue, Moorebank, NSW 2170,
and in New Zealand by Transworld Publishers (NZ) Ltd,
3 William Pickering Drive, Albany, Auckland.

Reproduced, printed and bound in Great Britain by
Mackays of Chatham PLC, Chatham, Kent

ACKNOWLEDGMENTS

I am thankful to my agents, Elizabeth Pomada and Alan Nevins, and especially to Gail Barrick, for belief in me and for perseverance on my behalf; and to my editors—Michael Korda, who has been more than generous with his time, sensitivity, wisdom, and support, and Chuck Adams, for his attention to detail.

For the donation of their consultative expertise, I thank Suzanne Asbury-Oliver for assistance with skywriting passages; Greg S. Labate, Esq. for reviewing legal and courtroom material; Leslie Blackhall, M.D., for her contribution regarding Durable Power of Attorney for Health Care Information; and Peter Katsufrakis, M.D., for valuable comments.

A special thank-you to my friends and family for their faithful reading of early manuscripts and for their encouragement, love, and confidence in me; particularly Rocky Lang, my husband; Neva

Reifsnyder, my mother; her husband, Paul Reifsnyder; Kate Douvan, best friend from the beginning of time; Rita Harmon, writing sister; Peter Jucovy, M.D., educator, mentor, listener, and friend; and Monica Lang, my mother-in-law.

I am grateful to my daughters, Nicole and Erica Lang, for bringing me unbridled joy and for taking long naps.

Finally, I am indebted to Leo Rangell, M.D., my wizard, for helping me to discover my voice.

To Rocky,
the love of my forever

and in memory of

Eric H. Cohen, M.D. (1948–1995), disseminator
of compassion and wisdom; he brandished hope
like a sword.

Albert Kempton d'Ossche (1947–1990), laughter maker;
I warmed my hands by the light of his heart.

John Robert Ware (1955–1994), gentle artist and
visionary; he taught me beauty and showed me bravery.

CHAPTER ONE

I feel my hands and they're slippery with blood. Heavy, warm blood, like scarlet gloves drawn to my elbows. I scream, but no sound comes from my throat, constricted by anguish. Now I can see it's not blood on my hands, but sweat; my own sweet, sticky sweat.

It's hot. The musty, wood-scented air in the church is waved into a breeze by heart-shaped bamboo fans. There are a lot of us, but it doesn't look that way. We're dwarfed by the cathedral ceilings, the somber, polished wood, and the peaked stained-glass windows whose brilliant colors cast rainbows over our breathing bodies. We are tiny and helpless, swept along by happenstance and a careening will to survive, to go on living despite sorrow beyond description, despite the desperation that is life.

Suddenly I know that it isn't sweat that coats my arms and hands, and soaks my spirit, but tears; my entire body cries. How do I absorb the loss of a twenty-seven-year-old man, the love of my forever? Maybe, like this body heat, it is unabsorbable.

Words are spoken at this gathering, the funeral service, but they are of no comfort and have no meaning. And why should I join the rest of these mourners? Just so that they may know I am not ashamed, that I did love him? I feel no need to express that here. My feelings are my own, existing as an unwavering spike driven deeply from one side of my soul to the other. Words will not change them.

Finally it is over and I clutch a wad of damp tissues in my hand, sliding dark glasses over my puffy face, covering grief as strangers shuffle by. They whisper about the service, how beautiful it was, how reassuring; about how Eric, so young a man, is now in God's hands. It is only with effort that I keep my rage inside, holding an expanding bubble high in my chest. It feels so large that if that bubble explodes, this whole church will rock and fall, crushing us all.

By the time I am able to leave the church,

clusters of people are spread about on the lawn, chatting, hugging, even laughing. Purged by the service, they ease back into their lives, making me wonder: What is a life? Is it merely water running through our fingers, impossible to grasp or cling to? Does it leave a trace, like salt from seawater? Or does it simply vanish, invisible, transformed into vapor without our notice? Does it evade description? Yes, yes, yes, and yes.

I wipe slick moisture from my forehead. It's humid, mid-July, that prickly, wet hot that Midwest cities brew. Once Eric and I found it steamy and sexy, now it's pure misery. Eric no longer sweats. Soon he'll be desiccated to fit into an urn: dry, powdered, and compressed.

His parents see me as I hesitate on the front steps, and they turn away hastily, scrambling into a glossy black car, accelerating out of my life. I stand on the cement stairs in stark sunlight. Grief-stricken describes this feeling perfectly. I feel like I've been struck over the head with a big club. The blow turns everything in view a watery gray.

CHAPTER TWO

When I met Eric, I drew for a living. It wasn't much of a living, but I liked the work. And I was good at it. I could make bodies look on paper like they looked in real life, and that was a talent in demand. I was hired mostly by advertisers to do fashion illustrations, but occasionally I was called by medical or professorial types who needed realistic illustrations for textbooks and such.

That was how Eric appeared on my Philadelphia doorstep six years ago, a model and medical student; cute, sassy, and dangerous.

I opened my front door. 'Mr. Moro?' I asked.

'Yeah, no *w*. But my name's Eric, with a *c*.'

'I see. I'm Ms. Dublin. Come on in.'

I watched him as he entered, walking smoothly on the heels of his scuffed cowboy boots. There was a red bandanna tied around the ankle of one.

'I thought you were a med student,' I said, unable to hide my skepticism, sparked by his long, jet black hair and the three delicate silver hoops piercing his left earlobe.

'I am,' he responded, and smiled, more intimately than I was prepared for. I shut the door and walked away; I could feel his eyes hot on my back. He stayed where he was and went on. 'Kolpinski, the art history professor, advertised for models. I got picked.' I turned around to look at him and he shrugged.

'We'll be working over here,' I said from my drawing corner. Sectioned off from the gloom and dust, it was the bright spot in that studio apartment. Cramped would be an understatement for those working quarters, but I didn't need much room; Eric Moro was, for my purposes, a still life.

He joined me. 'Do I strip now?' he asked.

I met his eyes. They appeared solid black, with no hint of brown, no separation of pupil and iris. I had been drawing nudes for four years, since I was twenty, and Eric was the first model that made me nervous. I didn't usually draw people in my apartment either, but had made the exception for this project with Kolpinski. He hired models exclusively from the med school, sent them to me, and I sketched various features of their bodies. His book was something only an academic press would touch: *The History of Sculpture and Its Relation to Surface Anatomy in the Twentieth Century*.

'Haven't you done this before?' I asked.

'What, taken my clothes off for a beautiful woman?' He flung me a half-smile, one of many I would come to know. It was just a twitching of the delicate skin around his lips, meaning nothing, perhaps meaning everything.

'Actually,' I said, 'the more interesting question is, have you taken your clothes off for a woman you don't consider beautiful?'

His half-smile broadened into a full grin. 'Can't say that I have,' he admitted. But before I could comment he added, 'All women are beautiful.'

Despite my efforts not to, I smiled. 'Anyway, Mr. Moro, the actual question I intended was, have you modeled for a drawing before?'

'I told you my name's Eric—'

'I know, with a *c*—'

'What's your name?'

'It's still Ms. Dublin.'

'I know, but what's your name?'

'I said, Ms. Dublin. Why don't you have a seat?'

'Is that what your boyfriend calls you?'

'That's none of your—' The half-smile stopped me, mocking, gentle, accusing. It made my mind stumble. 'Take your clothes off,' I said. 'Let's get started.'

'Okay.'

'There's a screen over there.' I pointed. 'You can get undressed behind it.'

'Why? You're gonna see all of me anyway, aren't you?'

'Well . . . yes. Do what suits you; I just want you to be comfortable, that's all.'

'Oh, I am,' he said, perching on the stool and twisting his boots off. I noticed he didn't have socks on.

I walked away, toward the kitchen. 'Tea?' I called.

'No thanks.'

'Beer?'

'No thanks.'

'Anything?'

'Thanks, but no. I'm ready whenever you are.'

I nodded as I filled the teakettle at the kitchen sink, placed it on a crusted burner, and lit the flame beneath it. I stared at its blue heat.

Changing my mind, I switched the stove off and returned to the brightly lit corner. He wasn't there. I glanced around, a little blinded by the lights. Then I saw him. He was naked, wandering around the apartment, looking at my possessions.

'Who are they?' he asked, pointing to a picture I had taped to the wall near the bathroom.

I walked over to him. 'My kids.'

'Kids?'

'That was the group I worked with this summer. It's part of an antigraffiti art program I started a few years ago.' The picture showed ten teenagers that I had painted 'Outdoor Art' with.

'What's the program?'

'They make art around the city, on retaining walls, sides of buildings, things like that.'

'You teach them?'

I laughed. 'More like they teach me. This city has some great young artists. There just aren't many people telling them that.'

'But you are.'

'I don't have to. You can see for yourself.'

'They painted you?'

He was looking at another picture. I smiled. 'That was our session on "living art." It was their idea.' I had worn a bikini and they had covered me with paints of every color. My hair was green for a week.

Eric seemed particularly fascinated by this picture; he touched it with his finger, which was long and surprisingly graceful. 'What'd it feel like?' he asked.

'It was a little cold, but mostly it tickled and itched. They got quite a kick out of it.'

'Will you paint me?'

He looked at me, imploring, like a little boy. My breath caught for a moment, the reaction startling me. 'Uh . . . my job is to draw you,' I said.

'Maybe next time?'

'Why don't you have a seat on the stool by the lights,' I said. 'I'll be right there.' I turned toward the bathroom, entered, and closed the door. My heart was beating urgently, and in the mirror I saw my chest was flushed red. I ran the water, washed my hands.

When I emerged, there he was, twirling wildly on the stool, comfortable and amused.

'Hi,' he said, dragging a bare foot along the floor to stop the spinning. He faced me. 'Are those yours, or your boyfriend's?' He pointed upward to where several airplane models hung suspended from the ceiling.

'Mine,' I said. 'But you aren't getting paid by the hour, so we might as well—'

'How about taking me flying?'

I had never learned to fly, but his request brought back a longing to, one I had had since childhood. 'I don't think so,' I said, shaking my head. 'Anyway, for the drawings we'll be focusing on your torso, back, and hip area, starting with the left side.'

'Okay.'

'Your muscles are being featured,' I said, and looked at him, his body. I could see why he had been picked; he would be easy to draw. Even relaxed, his muscles were defined, fluid, dynamic, shaped like the books said they should be.

'To answer your question, no,' Eric said.

'Excuse me?'

'I haven't modeled before. I just started med school—'

'And you're broke.'

'Well . . . ' He shrugged and I watched his lats, traps, pecs.

'All right,' I said, 'just listen, don't talk. Move only when I tell you.' He nodded. 'I need to see your left side,' I added as I got up, 'like this.' I twisted the stool. 'Put your left hand on your left knee—what's this?' I took a step back.

'Is that a problem?'

'A tattoo?'

He looked down at it, then up at me, smiling

sheepishly, proudly. 'Living art,' he said.

'Right.' I laughed.

There was an unbalanced silence while I inspected it, intrigued. 'It's not a problem,' I said, 'but what is it, a magician?'

'Wizard.'

We were both staring at it. I had grasped his left arm by the elbow and twisted it upward, to better see the design. It was over his deltoid, a wizened man with a long yellow beard, a tall, pointed hat, and flowing purple robes decorated with stars and crescents. The wizard's right arm was lifted, and his fingers, their nails sharpened into miniature daggers, cradled a crystal ball. I rubbed my finger over the picture embedded in his skin; it was firm and smooth.

When I looked up, Eric was watching me and our faces were close; I could feel his warm breath. I stepped back.

'It's magnificent,' I said. 'Who's the artist?'

'A blonde in New Orleans,' he answered, looking down at the wizard with a touch of melancholy. 'She was a brilliant artist.'

Was? I wanted to ask, but instead I said, 'Put your hand here, bend your leg with your foot up on the rung of the stool. Good. Like that.' I went to my chair and easel, but remained standing, assessing. 'I need more of your back. Twist a little to the right. There! Perfect.' I sat.

I had a series of drawings of the male torso to do, but my initial subjects were his left arm, upper back, and left chest, all in profile. I proceeded to trace his body, angles, curves, concavities, with my charcoal pencil, shading, enhancing, contouring, shaping for hours.

It may be that there is something inherently sexy about drawing nudes, the focus on a naked body, the intimate details. But for me, drawing had never been tactile in a sexual sense. That evening was different, however; it was as if my pencil were running over Eric, not my paper. I could sense his body heat, smell his skin, feel him quiver in response to my light touch. Or maybe it was my body I sensed, suffused with a tingling awareness in response to his reckless sensuality.

The front door clicked open after I had been drawing—and Eric sitting—for two and a half hours without a break.

'Peter, hello,' I murmured, looking up.

'Excuse me,' Peter said. 'I thought you'd be done.'

I looked to Eric; he hadn't moved his body with this interruption, just his face, and he seemed intrigued to be naked under the circumstances.

'Uh . . . right,' I said, standing up, ashamed without reason. 'Eric—Mr. Moro—you can get dressed.'

Eric didn't move. 'Are you sure you're done?' he asked. 'I can stay if you need me.' He was looking directly at me, unembarrassed.

'Thank you,' I said. 'But no, that's enough. I'm done.'

'I can leave . . . ' Peter offered.

'No,' I said.

'May I see your sketches?' Eric asked, ignoring his nakedness and pulling his body into a languid stretch before walking toward me. Peter remained in the doorway with the door open.

'No!' I said, snatching the pad from the easel. 'I mean, I'd rather you not.' I felt caught between the two men, pinned by their silent, waiting gazes.

'Please, get dressed,' I said to Eric, and relaxed a little when he shrugged and reached for his jeans. He must've been poor: no socks, and no underwear, either.

Peter and I waited while Eric dressed. He didn't go behind the screen and it was hard to figure out where to look, so I switched off the lights in the corner, cloaking his body in purple-gray shadows. The moment was quiet, and very long.

'Thanks, Ms. Dublin,' Eric said as I saw him out.

'Thank you, Mr. Moro,' I said. 'You were great.'

He grinned and winked. 'Be seeing you.'

I closed the door, stood staring at it.

'Ms. Dublin?' Peter asked.

'Name of the day,' I answered. I didn't turn around; my hand was on the doorknob. I had an incongruous urge to go with Eric, to wherever med students wearing cowboy boots with no socks went after dark.

'Seems like a nice guy,' Peter said.

I examined the cheap brown grain of the door. 'He's just a model,' I said.

'Sorry I interrupted. I thought . . .'

I turned around. Peter was standing near the end of the folded sofa bed, which was faded red and threadbare. He looked small somehow, diminished and vulnerable. I felt a stab of pity cross my chest. I walked over and embraced him. 'How could you think you interrupted?' I asked. 'You live here.' I kissed him.

He smiled. 'I love you,' he said.

'I love you, too.'

He held me for a moment and then I watched him walk into the bathroom and close the door.

I waited, sitting on the arm of the sofa, and thought. Peter and I had been living together for two years, two solid, steadfast years. He was faithful and devoted, a good companion. I thought of him as my anchor, keeping me even and straight. Still, I often felt the cord to that anchor straining, threatening to break loose and send me bobbing away. Even in our work, there was a distance between us. Peter was studying to be an architect, and spent his days drawing inanimate objects, creating ceilings and walls, building firm structures. I spent my time doing who knows what—sketching hunks like Eric, drinking espresso with too much sweetener, laughing with strangers at bus stops. My subjects moved, breathed, and got up to pee; his dared not budge. Discipline, control, and organization were his strong points; mine were ephemeral, transient. I needed him.

When Peter came out of the bathroom, I went to him, held him, and said, 'Let's make love.'

'I'm hungry.'

'Then we'll have oral sex.' I laughed, and he joined me.

His face was dark, thin and alluring, like his body. It was dim near the bathroom but his sharp teeth gleamed in the light slanting toward us from the kitchen. I kissed him and we made love like a million times before, pressed against the abrasive carpet, our movements smooth, flat, practiced.

As I came, I clutched his back, two bony shoulder blades under my grasping fingers, a yellow, blue, and purple wizard winking in my mind's eye.

CHAPTER THREE

'Hello?' I said, grappling with the phone that had been ringing through my dreams for what seemed like hours.

'Ms. Dublin?' a man asked.

'What time is it?' I squinted at shafts of sunlight bursting from beneath the shade covering the only window in the apartment.

'Uh . . . let's see,' he said. 'Sorry, I don't have a watch.'

I looked at the clock: 9:30 A.M.

'Ms. Dublin?' he said again.

'What are you selling?' I asked.

I heard laughter, inviting, sensuous. I was about to hang up when I realized Ms. Dublin had been my professional name from the day before. Was this the model? I sat up in bed. 'Is this Mr. Moro?' I asked.

'Please, call me Eric.'

'Did you forget something?'

'Nothing I didn't know to begin with. Like your first name.' I hesitated and he went on, 'Or should I continue calling you Ms. Dublin?' I paused, and he repeated, 'Ms. Dublin?'

'Listen,' I said, 'I haven't even had coffee—'

'I'm buying. Meet me?'

I sighed, considering. Overeager, bad sign. Med student with a tattoo, questionable sign. Treated my work with respect, good sign. Exceptionally sexy—good, bad, and questionable sign.

'Ms. Dublin?' he said again. 'Tell me where, I'll be there.'

'Alex. My name's Alex.'

'Alex . . .'

It took me three minutes to get ready. I had told him to meet me at the Bookstore/Coffeehouse, near my side of the city; he didn't question the location. He arrived before me, looking a little rumpled in jeans and a white T-shirt, the wizard's robe peeking from beneath the short sleeve covering his left shoulder.

I paused at the door of the shop, studying

him before he saw me. He was sitting at a scarred wooden table by the window, sipping from a small white cup and reading the morning paper. White, autumn light grazed the right side of his body, illuminating him obliquely. Across from him sat an empty chair and a cup of espresso, covered by a saucer to keep it warm.

There was an intensity to him as he read, a determination that betrayed genuine intelligence. Suddenly he smiled, and everything changed, making him appear innocent and young, alarmingly cute. It was difficult to stop watching him, but he had seen me. Apparently, I was the reason for the smile, and he was waiting.

'Sorry if I'm late,' I said as I slid into the chair across from him.

'You're not late,' he said. 'I'm here to meet you and here you are.'

'Is this mine?' I asked, pointing to the cup in front of me.

'I ordered it for you. But if you'd like—'

'Espresso, just what I need.' I uncovered the cup and reached for the sweetener. 'Thanks. How'd you know?' I looked into his face for the first time since I had entered; even with the sun hitting them, his eyes were still the deepest black. I looked away, ripping open a fourth pack of sweetener and emptying it into my coffee.

'Only a guess,' he said. 'Espresso suits you. I never would've guessed about the sweetener, though.'

'I get a lot of shit about it, but I like it that way.'

'Next time I'll know.'

I sipped through my smile. I didn't know if it was his presence or the caffeine, but something was making my heart pound.

We looked at each other, me from behind my cup, him forthright in bare sunlight, before he asked, 'What are you doing today?'

'Having coffee with you.'

'And later?'

I shrugged. 'We'll see when later comes.'

'I wish I had such freedom.'

'Freedom's just a pretty word for unemployment.'

We laughed. That was followed by a little silence. Then he said, 'I like your laugh.'

'I . . . well . . . ' I stammered.

'I didn't mean to embarrass you—'

'Not at all . . . I . . . just . . . aren't you supposed to be in school?'

'I'm supposed to be having coffee with you.'

'Exercising *your* freedom?'

'A pretty word for cutting class.'

We laughed again.

'What made you decide to become a doctor?' I asked.

'You want the med school interview answer or the real one?'

'What do you think?'

'Okay. Blood and guts.'

I laughed. 'Lovely. That must be the interview answer.'

'So the real answer must be "I want to help people."'

'Do you?'

He paused and looked at me, making me wonder, could what I wanted him to be be true?

'You can discover that for yourself,' he said.

'Or you can tell me.'

'But it'd be more fun to let you discover it.'

My espresso was finished; I was on the fence about another. 'It'd take more time,' I said.

He raised his eyebrows; they were dark, independent. 'Just a minute,' he said, and got up to walk to the counter. He came back with another espresso for me.

'Thank you,' I said.

'Anytime.'

'Is it real?'

'What?'

'The tattoo. The wizard. Or do I have to discover that for myself too?'

'Here,' he said, scraping his chair across the warped wooden floor to my side of the table. 'Feel it.' He pulled his T-shirt sleeve up and bunched it around his shoulder. The colors of the tattoo were rich and dazzling in the light, the detail exquisite; it was definitely real. I didn't touch it this time.

'What does it mean?' I asked.

'Mean? It's art.'

I blushed and cursed myself for it. The light was bright by the window and he was so close. I felt exposed somehow. 'Well,' I said, 'permanent art, you know, I thought—'

'Permanent!' He laughed. 'As permanent as I am, that's all.'

Our gazes held for what seemed a long time.

'Your eyes are golden,' he said finally. 'Your hair matches them.' He reached out and gently grasped a handful of my hair, running his fingers down its length. It was long and silky-straight, down to the level of my midback. His touch did not solve my blushing problem. Instead, it sent a quick, tantalizing shiver from my scalp down my neck and into my spine. I gave into it, letting my head fall back. Then I pulled away.

'I'd better go,' I said.

'That program with the kids, how'd you get it started?' he asked.

'The antigraffiti art?'

'Uh-huh.'

'Do you really want to know, or are you just trying to get me to stay?'

He smiled; it worked.

'Well,' I began, 'I started by going around to kids I saw spraypainting public property and asking if they were interested in doing murals.'

'Strangers?'

'I guess you'd call them that.'

'Guts, Alex.'

'Half of what you became a doctor for.'

He laughed. 'Then what?'

'A bunch of them wanted to do it, so I took a proposal to the city. I told them how good it would look, literally and politically, and they bought it.'

'Why'd you do it?'

'Why? Because I wanted to help people.' I realized, too late, I had echoed him.

'Did you? Help them, I mean.'

'I don't know.'

He drank his coffee and examined me. I glanced away. 'Are you drawing today?' he asked.

I turned back to look at him. 'Why do you ask?'

'Vicarious pleasure.'

'It's not all pleasure,' I said with a smile,

thinking about the night before. 'I do work.'

'I know. What I meant was vicarious pleasure with respect to your model. I wouldn't presume to know what pleasures you.'

'Oh . . . well, I should go—' I stood.

'Please don't. I'll tell you about the wizard.'

I was poised to squeeze past his chair and leave. 'What about it?' I asked.

'What it means. About the girl in New Orleans.'

'Girl?'

'She was just a kid.'

'Thanks for the coffee, but I'd better be on my way—'

'Things weren't always so great in this land. They weren't always about pleasure, fun, happiness—'

'What?'

'Once there were people who would hurt children in ways that couldn't be undone, making the children something other than what they were born to be: playful, mischievous, enthusiastic. The wizard was created to—'

'So that's what you're talking about!'

He nodded and I sat. He stared out the window now, his eyes distant. 'The wizard's purpose, his quest, was to mitigate that harm, to lift those children away from that land to a place where happiness and truth were allowed—no, *cherished*.' He stopped and looked directly at me. Instantly, it was there again, his intensity the way I had seen when I entered the coffeehouse, raw, revealed.

'The wizard's like a good fairy?' I asked.

He shook his head. 'The wizard allows what should happen to happen. He allows life.'

'He's a guardian angel?'

'He just is. He is what he is.'

'He's anything and everything?'

'He's hope, Alex. Hope where there's a need.'

'And what is it you hope for?'

'For us.'

My face was suddenly hot, and I stood. He didn't stop me. 'I have to go,' I said.

'Your leaving won't stop me from hoping.'

'Hope is harmless.'

'I hope so.' He smiled.

'Good-bye.'

'I hope not.'

I walked down the block in a direction that was simply *away*. I didn't look back, but I was convinced he was following me, ready with his charm, intelligence, beauty. I needed to think. I wanted to kiss him. I needed to walk, run even. I wanted to curl up next to him in a warm space. I needed to be free of him. I wanted to be part of him.

I stopped and turned around. He wasn't there, and a little sound came out of me, almost a whimper.

I headed for home.

That afternoon I tried drawing, reading, yoga. My concentration was poor, so I went out. Back at the Bookstore/Coffeehouse I browsed the bookshelves, thumbing over dog-eared used books that I couldn't believe anyone had read the first time: 10,000 Tricks for Your Parakeet, Floral Arrangements Made Simple, Building a Better Employee Work Space, Skywriting for Beginners—I pulled this last one off the shelf, flipping through the discolored pages; they blew a scent of musty chalk toward my nostrils, their thin edges crumbling. The book was older than I, but it was only a buck fifty, so I bought it; it helped get my mind off him.

I sat on a park bench at the side of a busy thoroughfare where buses puffed dark exhaust toward me. A low beam of late afternoon sunlight flickered across my face and down the angle of my book as I read.

My eyes must've adjusted to the dusk, because by the time I had finished the paperback it was evening, and I had contorted myself into an uncomfortable position to best utilize the light from the streetlamp. That's when I knew what I had to do: start flying lessons to become a skywriter. I would make sky-art.

'A *what*?' Peter said when I arrived home and told him my plans. 'I thought you were going to become a lawyer.'

I wiped my nose; I had gotten chilly on the bench. 'I know, but this is more exciting,' I said.

'Excitement isn't what's important.'

'What is?'

'Long-term stability, a solid future—for starters.'

I wiped my nose again.

He came closer, studying me. 'What's wrong?' he asked. 'Are you crying?'

'No. I was reading outside.'

'It's after eight. Aren't you cooking dinner tonight?'

'Is that all you have to say about the skywriting?'

'It would make a good hobby. Expensive, but different.'

I tossed the book on the bed, still unmade from the morning. I didn't need a hobby, I thought as I looked about, but I did need to start a life.

'What would you like for dinner?' he asked.

'I'll take care of it.'

He came over and held my chin, gazing at me sympathetically, which was exactly the wrong thing to do. 'I love you, Alex,' he said. 'I only want what's best for you.'

I almost laughed; I almost cried.

I made dinner in my usual fashion: I picked up the phone and ordered Chinese, or Thai, or Vietnamese, or something equally Eastern, still thinking of Eric and imagining him living on the east side of the city, in an apartment devoid of the problems of missing socks and dirty underwear.

Peter and I ate sitting on the sofa bed, watching a PBS documentary on his little black-and-white TV. He didn't like network TV with its poisonous commercials, so I sneaked it during the day, watching *Oprah*, *Wheel of Fortune*, soap operas. In the evenings, though, I deferred to his 'I'm-ten-years-older' status and watched what he wanted.

Our tongues were still spicy-hot when we began kissing, the blue TV-glow blinking on the ceiling, the romantic lighting of our generation. I watched it undulate along with us and concluded that our union had been distilled down to that purest of forms, a 'relationship,' where order, discipline, and reason surround brief episodes of sex.

Peter slept as I practiced skywriting in the darkness, swirling and dipping in a plane visible only to me.

After that night, I couldn't find my sky-writing book. It must've fallen beneath my solid, stable future.

CHAPTER FOUR

For a time, I tried to put Eric out of my mind, concentrating on living with Peter. We had started dating when I was fresh out of college and he had just returned from living in Europe for four years. We had art in common, and had met at a local seminar, given by a realist. Painter, that is.

Across the room we were opposites, he dark and tall, me petite and pale, but together we worked. He was mature, gentle, and wise; I was unpredictable. I was attracted to his remarkable equilibrium and loyalty, drawn to a promise of security, flattered by what I interpreted as single-minded desire. We joined our households after we had known each other for what Peter deemed an appropriate amount of time, a year, and we began preparation for our 'future.'

Despite my efforts not to, in the weeks after I had met Eric, I thought of him often. He had become a powerful fantasy, a pulsating urge in my chest every time the phone rang, or I traced an outline with a charcoal pencil, or emptied sweetener into espresso. But I didn't try to contact him, and he didn't call.

I was riding the bus the next time I saw him. It was around lunchtime, and there he was, suddenly, like an apparition, standing outside a small cafe. His booted foot was up on the seat of a white wrought-iron chair, his long, straight black hair dangling over the face of an olive-skinned beauty as she smiled up at him. I looked away.

One evening, a few days later, I waited for Peter in our apartment at the round card table, my elbows resting on the white sheet that served as a tablecloth, hypnotized by candlelight from two red tapers. I had squandered the early afternoon shopping for delicacies and the late afternoon arranging them; I had even bought wine.

Peter arrived home at seven o'clock, as always, having spent the day at the university and the early evening at the library and gym.

'Hi,' he said. 'Hey, what's up?'

I peeked up at him through my hair, worn

seductively long over my eyelashes. I noticed him taking in the diving neckline of my clinging Lycra minidress, my spike heels. 'Hi, honey,' I purred.

He leaned over and kissed me. 'You look great, what's the occasion?'

'I wanted to surprise you. I cooked dinner.'

'You're incredible.'

'Why don't you sit down and I'll serve,' I said, getting up and teetering on my heels. He grinned, setting his gym bag down and encircling my waist with his arm. We kissed; he tasted of hunger.

'I'm famished,' he said. 'How about oral sex?'

I smiled and hugged him. 'Sure, but first let's eat the food. I made a special meal for you.'

'Whatever makes you happy,' he said, taking off his jacket, laying it across the couch, and returning to sit at the table.

I busied myself in the kitchen, navigating without a map, and returned with the first course: a cold tomato–and–cucumber soup. 'Ta-da!' I said.

'Wow. My favorite.'

'I know.'

He slurped a little from his spoon as I returned to the kitchen for the wine.

'It's good,' he said.

I came back, poured two juice glasses of Merlot, and lifted mine in a toast. 'Here's to our future, the architect and the lawyer!' I declared.

He smiled and said, 'No skywriting?'

'No skywriting.'

We toasted our future, a concept I didn't fully understand. That distant life seemed hazy and slippery, something I couldn't quite get my arms around. I counted on Peter to know.

We finished dinner and dessert, Peter contented and full, me hoping that some of his happiness and confidence would slosh onto me.

'I love you,' he said, standing and leaning over to kiss me. 'Thank you for dinner.'

I rose and embraced him; we headed for the couch. Peter was a gentle lover, and sweet.

By 1:00 A.M. I was munching pecan pie in bed, with Peter asleep beside me. Our communication was good—it always had been—and he was a good man. But was 'good' the pinnacle, the end? When would the future arrive, and why did a different dark-haired man with sparkling black eyes, naked beneath his jeans, gallop through my mind during intimate moments with Peter?

Why did I think of the wizard so often, it somehow more real than what should have been reality?

When my pie was done, I swept the crumbs out of the bed, got down on the floor, and did as many push-ups as I could: four. I resolved to start an exercise program.

CHAPTER FIVE

Another month passed and I was in terrific shape. I now ran five miles a day and met Peter at the gym virtually every evening, where I lifted weights, struggled with computerized stair and rowing machines, and bopped around in a shiny black leotard with other aerobically fit women. I felt better, I looked better. But I wasn't better.

Peter and I remained on the same plateau, and, although I was comfortable, I can't say I was happy. Still, the busier I got, the easier it was to forget my doubts. I was taking a few political science courses at a local community college during the day and teaching drawing at night, as well as continuing my freelance work.

Being occupied felt good; I was strictly off espresso.

'I'm off to teach my drawing class,' I said to Peter one evening as I leaned down to kiss him good-bye. He was sitting at his drafting table, immersed in a project due the next day.

'Okay. Bye, honey,' he responded, looking up and kissing me. His mouth was dry.

'I'll be home around nine-thirty,' I said from the door.

'Be careful.'

I closed the door and headed for the bus. Teaching drawing was something I had just started. I was amazed at how much I loved it, watching all those earnest people putting pencil to pad, looking to me as the expert.

'Hey, Jackie,' I said as I entered the drawing studio. She was one of my students, always the first one there.

'Hi, Alex,' she said. 'What's the assignment tonight?'

I shrugged and responded, 'I'll check in a minute,' pulling my scarf and jacket off and walking toward the instructors' area in the back. There on the bulletin board was our list of assignments; I had lost my own copy just days after I had received it. I ran my finger down the dates: Tuesday, October 5: 'Human Form, Live Model.'

Sitting in my cubicle, I heated water for tea in the hot pot as I waited for my students to assemble. I could hear them gathering and conversing. Then, over the assembling noise, I heard, 'Alex Taylor?'

'Yes?' I looked up and my heart lunged into my throat.

'Oh, hello, Alex. Alex Taylor.' He extended his hand; it was Eric.

I stood, startled, and robotically took his hand. It was supposed to be a handshake, but it was stimulating, as if a little electric pulse passed between us. I prayed he couldn't tell how nervous he was making me.

'I'm your model,' he said as I pulled my hand from his.

'Model?'

'For the class tonight.'

'Oh, right. Of course.' Inside my body, I was having one of those fight or flight responses, neither of which appeared warranted under the circumstances.

'You look good,' he said.

'So do you,' I mumbled. 'What are you . . . how did you . . . I mean, why are you my model?' I asked.

'You thought I was a Kolpinski exclusive?'

'Well . . . I . . . '

'I answered an ad, and here we are.' He

shrugged. 'Hey, maybe the wizard . . .'

'The wizard . . .'

'Should I strip here or out there?' he asked, flipping me his half-smile, the one I had fought to forget. It flooded me with him and every image I had had of him in life and dreams. 'I don't know the etiquette for so many people,' he added.

'Right. Well—'

He grabbed my hand. 'I missed you,' he whispered.

'Not now, Eric,' I said, twisting my hand out of his. I was flustered, confused. For six weeks he had been made real only by my imagination; now, suddenly, he was so three dimensional.

'Later, then?' he asked. When I didn't answer, he said, 'Alex, I want to see you again.'

I looked at him, and his pleading expression made me smile, which helped. I said, 'I have a class to teach—'

'I'll stay after school . . .'

'Strip in here,' I said, indicating the cubicle, and left.

Strange would not be an accurate description of how it felt to have Eric as my model that night. Even bizarre and surreal don't adequately sum it up. I hadn't forgotten him by a long shot, but he wasn't a part of my life. I had put our brief encounter and my crazy desire for him into a private place, neatly wrapped, just mine. Now suddenly he was with me, the object of my most secret fantasies, exposed and inspected for artistic and instructional purposes.

Finally, after two interminable hours we were finished, and the students were gone, leaving Eric and me alone. I retreated to my cubicle.

'I turned it off for you,' Eric said, following me.

'Turned it off?'

'The hot pot. It could've caught on fire.'

'Oh, that. Thanks. I always—'

'Should I get dressed?' he asked.

My eyes fixed on his; I was painfully conscious of his nakedness. 'I think that'd be appropriate,' I said.

'As you wish.' He slipped black jeans over his smoothly muscled legs. The jeans had a hole in the right knee and his foot kept getting caught in it, making him hop around.

'Would you like to sit down?' I asked, laughing.

'No, thanks. This is how I get my exercise.' He jumped around some more.

'I have to go,' I said, quickly putting on my jacket, gathering my things.

His jeans were on in no time; he zipped

carefully. 'Not that again,' he said, walking toward me.

'What do you want, Eric?' I asked.

'An hour. Give me one hour, that's all.'

'An hour . . . '

'To be with you.'

'I have a boyfriend. I live with him—'

'I know, but does that mean we can't have a drink?'

I hesitated, briefly. We went to a local pub, one of those places frequented by students: dim, with sodden carpets reeking of rotted beer. I ordered a Samuel Adams at the bar.

'Good beer,' Eric commented, and ordered one too. He insisted on paying, grasped our bottles, and headed for a table. We sat across from each other.

'You're an excellent model,' I said.

'Thanks.'

'Do you get bored?'

'I have my mind to keep me entertained.'

'What do you think about?'

He paused, then laughed and tossed his head back to clear the hair out of his eyes. 'Well,' he said, 'on the stool at your place I concentrated on not getting a hard-on.'

'You're kidding!'

'Was I successful?'

'That area wasn't featured,' I said.

'You mean sometimes it is?'

'We'd better change the subject.' I sucked on my beer. I hadn't been drinking for the past month and the alcohol was starting to charge through me, shaking me loose; I was fighting it.

'I've made you uncomfortable,' he said. 'I'm sorry.'

'Uncomfortable?' I shook my head. 'The human body's no problem for me.' That wasn't a lie; I was comfortable with the human form. Eric's human form, however, was another story.

'Our work is similar,' he commented, taking a swig of beer. 'We're both in the business of examining bodies.'

I laughed. 'But I keep my hands clean. My eyes and pencil do the work.'

His look was that wayward smile that spoke of mischief. It made me lose my place for a second.

'I . . . I was wondering something . . . ' I said, tapping the dark bottle lip gently against my front teeth.

'Yes?' he said, raising his eyebrows.

'Well . . . your story about the wizard . . . '

'Yes?'

'Did you make it up just for me?'

'All my wizard stories are for you.'

I downed the last of my beer while I searched for what to say. 'Why do you say that?' I finally managed.

'Because you asked about its meaning.'

'I thought that was a dumb question.'

'Not dumb, revealing,' he said. I watched him speak, saw his soft tongue, and noticed we were leaning over the table toward each other. There seemed to be something pulling me, making my breath shallow and quick, drawing me to examine every detail of his lips as they moved together and apart, their pink borders flowing smoothly into pale skin.

'I'll get us more beers,' he said, and was up and gone to the bar while a draft of air rushed over me, a vacuum created by his abrupt absence.

'Here,' he said when he returned, setting another bottle in front of me before sitting down. 'You did want one, didn't you?'

'Yes, thank you.'

'You intrigue me, Alex.'

'I don't think you know enough about me to be intrigued.'

He leaned over the table toward me. I concentrated on his eyes, afraid of his mouth. 'I've got a challenge for you,' he said. 'You up for it?'

'Sure.'

'I bet I know more about you than you do about me.'

'That's unfair—'

'Then you take that side and I'll bet I know less about you.'

'But you'll lose. You've been in my apartment, seen my pictures—'

'Is it a bet?'

'No, let's make it even,' I said. 'I bet you don't know twice as much about me as I know about you.'

'Okay. If you win, if you know at least half as much about me as I know about you, then you get to ask me any ten questions you want and I promise to answer them honestly. Vice versa if I win.'

'You're on.'

'Let's subtract for incorrect information, to eliminate wild guessing.'

'Okay.'

'You start, beautiful Alex.'

'Don't distract me,' I said, and began. 'Your name is Eric Moro, you're a first-year medical student. Are you keeping track?'

'Yes.'

'Write it down.'

'I'll remember. Or don't you trust me?'

'I trust you. How many do I have?'

'Two.'

'You're trustworthy. You have a good memory.'

'Four.'

'You're Italian.'

'Lucky guess.'

'But it counts.'

'Five.'

'You have a tattoo that you got in New Orleans, designed by a blonde. You're an exhibitionist.'

'Eight.'

'Uh, let's see, you're smart—'

'It sounds like you're done, darlin'. That's not knowledge, that's flattery.'

'It's true.'

'Thank you. Nine.' He smiled and sighed. 'Do you want to keep embarrassing me or are you done?'

'There's another one. You never get embarrassed.'

'Now you're wrong.'

'I am not.'

'No arguing. The listening party has the final say.'

'Is nine a good score?'

'That depends on what I get. Are you done?'

'I guess.'

'Then I'll start. Your name is Alex Taylor, but your full name is Alexandra Taylor.'

'Lucky guess.'

'You use false names because you like to maintain distance with strangers, especially in professional settings—'

'You're still guessing.'

'You're living with a man, but you're not sure you want to keep living with him.'

'That's too personal!' My ears grew hot.

'And his name is Peter.'

'But—'

'We can stop if you want.'

'No, I can take it. Go on.'

'It's supposed to be a game, Alex. If you're upset, let's forget it.'

'No, you're right. You're right about everything so far.'

'I think we should quit.'

'I think we should continue.'

'You're sure?'

'I'm sure.'

'Okay, I have seven points. I need more than eighteen to win. You're a good teacher and you love to teach almost as much as you love dark-haired men—'

'Lucky guess!'

'Educated guess. You get up late, drink espresso with four packets of sweetener, and you're trying to decide on a career—'

'This you couldn't know.'

'So, I'm right. That's six more points, thirteen total. You dedicate yourself to projects you believe in, no matter how big the battle. You enjoy working with kids. You build plane models, but you don't fly—'

'I didn't tell you that.'

'But I watched you when I asked if you'd take me flying. You seemed wistful.'

'That could've been for a million reasons—'

'But it wasn't.'

'You're right, but how . . . '

'I'm not a mind-reader, if that's what you're thinking. I observe people I'm interested in, that's all. I also take the risk of being wrong.'

'But so far you haven't been.'

'I'm lucky tonight.' His eyes flashed, reminding me how little I knew about him, making him seem dangerous and exciting. 'I need two more points, darlin',' he said.

'I have no doubt you'll get them.'

He smiled. 'You don't have much money and you don't care.'

I laughed. 'You win.'

'Oh,' he said, smiling, 'and one more for good measure. You're the most sensuous woman I've ever met.'

He stared at me so frankly, I blushed, something I normally did infrequently—yet so far, very frequently with him. I shook my head in an attempt to cool it, which didn't work. 'That's an opinion,' I said. 'You don't get a point for that.'

'I know, but I couldn't help it. You are.'

'Now you're embarrassing *me*,' I said.

'What about the bet?'

'Ask me whatever you want.'

'Beers first,' he said, and got up.

I watched him move toward the bar. The place was packed and loud, something I hadn't noticed until then.

He returned. 'The questions,' he said, setting the bottles down on the table.

'I'm ready.'

'Don't forget to answer truthfully—it's part of the bet.'

'Got it.'

'Do you want to kiss me?'

I gasped. 'You mean you can ask that kind of question?'

'Any ten, that's the bet.'

'And I have to answer?'

'You don't have to do anything.'

'I know . . . yes, I want to kiss you.'

'Why haven't you?'

'That's question number two.'

'You're right. Why haven't you kissed me?'

'Because I don't know you.'

'Do you want to know me?'

I sighed. 'Are all the questions going to be like this?'

'I only have seven left.'

'Yes, I want to know you.'

'Have you thought about me since you last saw me?'

I paused. He was looking at me unflinchingly. 'Yes, I have,' I said, 'but—'

'What have you thought?'

'You're good at this, aren't you?'

'That's a question, not an answer. What have your thoughts been about me?'

I looked at him. There were two swatches of pink high across his cheekbones, painted there by excitement, anticipation. His stare didn't waver. I looked down and answered, 'I've thought about wanting you to be who I hope you are—'

'I've thought that about you, too.'

I glanced up and searched his eyes. 'You have?'

'Yes. Go on.'

I could feel my body flush, tingle, like my skin was standing at attention. 'I've thought about . . . feeling your hands on my body.'

'I've thought about that, too.'

Our hands linked across the table. I could sense my chest moving with each breath, lifting

my breasts, my nipples firm against my bra.
'Eric—'

'If you had to pick one area, only one, of your body for me to touch, where would it be?'

My hand was hot in his and it took all my effort to keep from running it up his bare arm. 'Only one?' I asked.

'Only one.'

'Then it'd be my inner thigh—can I have both sides, or do I have to choose?'

'I'll choose.' He smiled. 'What have your fantasies been about me?'

I sighed, taking my hand from his and running it through my hair. Prickly sweat broke out over my back, between my breasts. I stood up. 'I can't do this,' I said.

'Then I'll tell you my fantasies.'

'That wasn't the bet.'

'Screw the bet. Please stay.'

I sat.

He said, 'I fantasize about drawing you.'

'Drawing?'

'Running my pencil over your delicious body; around your desire, tracing your profile—'

'I've got to go,' I said, standing again and looking at my watch. 'Dammit, it's eleven!'

'Trouble with Peter?'

I put my jacket on and started for the door. He followed; I felt his warm, strong hand on my shoulder as I exited and a current of cold air hit me. It felt good.

'Alex, I'm sorry—'

I turned to face him. 'About what? I'm responsible for getting home on time.'

'Can I draw you?' His expression was sincere and hopeful, his breath a puff of white steam against the night.

Impulsively, like stepping over a brink, I kissed him, inhaling his air, his lips skimming lightly across mine, a lick of warm satin. His hand feathered through my hair, gently cradling my head as he pulled me close with his other arm, his palm firm between my shoulder blades. That kiss was at once sheer translucence and dark beyond light; while not seeming quite real, it somehow defined what was.

He pulled away. 'Is that yes?' he asked, still holding me, his sweet mouth revealing white teeth that I longed to trace with my tongue.

'I have to go,' I whispered, backing up, pulling out of his embrace. 'I shouldn't have done that.'

'Why do you pretend to have doubts?'

'I'm going.'

'Do you want me to call?'

'No . . . yes . . . during the day.'

'I understand.'

We stared at each other from about two feet apart, and I knew if I touched him again there would be no going home to Peter. I wasn't ready for that. I turned quickly and ran.

My mind was still reeling from the beer, and from Eric, but the cold night air and the exercise helped clear my head so I could think. I thought about how the games I played with Eric were daring, honest, and exceptionally erotic, about how he made my body forget gravity.

What would I tell Peter?

'Hi, honey,' I said as I entered the apartment. Peter was still sitting at his drafting table.

'Where have you been?' he asked, looking up and then glancing at his watch. 'I was getting worried about you.'

'Out with some friends,' I said casually, removing my jacket and scarf and stuffing them in the closet. The lie. The first.

'You couldn't call?'

'Sorry, I lost all track of time.' I went to him, kissed him on the forehead.

'It's okay,' he said. 'Hey, you smell like a brewery.'

I laughed, too loud. 'We had some beers.' I moved away, picked up the morning paper, and sat on the couch.

'I missed you,' he said.

'I missed you, too, but I knew you were busy. I thought I'd stay out of your hair.'

He stood and stretched. 'I don't ever want you out of my hair. I'm almost done here, anyway.'

'Good.' I got up and crossed to the bathroom, closing the door behind me. I stared at myself in the mirror; my eyes had changed from gold to green and my cheeks were flushed, partly from Eric, partly from running, and partly from lying to Peter.

'Eric Moro,' I breathed to my reflection, 'who are you?'

When I emerged from the bathroom and began to unfold the sofa bed, Peter asked, 'Would you like me to give you a back rub?'

'No thanks,' I said, flattening the sheet and picking my pillow up from the floor. 'You work on your project.'

'It's no problem, Alex. I'd like to.'

'Really, no. I just want to go to sleep.' I got into bed.

'This early?' he asked, now settled again at his drafting table behind me.

'I'm tired.'

'You must be. I've never known you to go to bed before two.'

'I'm so, so tired.'

'All right, then. Good night, honey.'

'Good night.'

I lay there, not the least bit tired, with Peter drawing at my back and Eric flaming through my mind and body. I reworked the kiss Eric and I had shared a thousand times, and finally fell asleep to the rhythm of his imagined hot breath.

CHAPTER SIX

Eric called four days later, in the morning.

'Hello,' I answered.

'It's great to hear your voice, Alex. It's Eric.'

I paused, trying to still my heart. Its sudden excessive beating seemed to rock my body. 'Hi,' was all I could manage.

'I have an invitation for you,' he said.

'An invitation?'

'You like bodies, right?'

I laughed, relaxing a little. 'That depends on whose.'

'It's no one you've met.'

'I'm listening.'

'I thought you might be interested in coming to gross lab with me this afternoon.'

'Gross?'

'Not too bad.'

'No, I mean, what is it?'

'Gross anatomy, cadavers—'

'Right.' Was he trying to judge my repulsion factor? I swallowed. 'Okay, when and where?'

I knew I shouldn't do it, but I canceled a model that afternoon so I could go with Eric. We met outside a gray concrete building on the periphery of the university campus. I saw him waving as I walked up to the entrance. He was dressed in his usual casual fashion, but his clothes were covered by a shapeless, long white coat, and his hair was pulled into a ponytail.

'Hi,' I said as I neared him, suddenly feeling very unsure.

'Al, my pal,' he said, throwing an arm across my shoulders. 'I'm glad you could come.'

'Where are they?' I asked.

'The bodies?' He raised his eyebrows. 'Come on.' He took my hand and led the way up some steps and into a large tiled hallway, lined by brown lockers. Med students were everywhere. 'Here, put this on,' he said, handing me a white coat like the one he had on.

'Why?'

'So you won't get "juice" on you. And so you'll blend in.'

I put the coat on. 'I don't think I'll ever blend in, Eric.'

'Then think of it as a costume.' He watched as I straightened my lapel, pulling my hair out from beneath the collar of the coat.

'I told the instructor you're a premed,' he went on, 'and that you're an out-of-town cousin. So do your best to act cousinly.'

'Okay, but do I have to act like a premed, too?'

He laughed and shook his head. 'Even I can't do that.'

'Is one of your fantasies that I'll become a med student?' I asked. 'Is that why you invited me here?'

He smiled. 'No, but one of my fantasies is that you'll be a part of my life.'

I felt that sudden surge of passion for him again, but before I could speak, he said, 'It's time,' and gently pushed me forward toward a set of double doors. As we entered, I smelled the preservative; it made my nostrils sting and my skin itch. Then I saw the bodies, gray-brown and stringy, partially unwrapped from soaked rags and plastic by students who were picking at them.

'This one's ours,' Eric said, as we came up beside a cadaver.

'The arm muscles,' I said, immediately

captivated by the dissection of the right arm. 'So that's what they look like.'

'Ssshhh,' Eric whispered, and I looked up. The instructor was at the front of the room, near a blackboard, writing out the assignment for the day. I watched Eric. His focus forward was instant and complete, his eyes unblinking, his lips moving back and forth over his teeth ever so slightly. The other students mumbled, shifted, and talked among themselves, but Eric was unwavering, totally absorbed. Then the instructor was finished, and almost as if someone had snapped him out of a hypnotic state, Eric turned toward me and grinned.

'Let's do it,' he growled in my ear. My arms were instantly covered with goose bumps.

'Okay,' I whispered back.

'You don't have to whisper,' he said. 'SHOUT IF YOU WANT! RIGHT, PARTNERS?'

One partner shouted back, 'YES, PARTNER!' Several neighboring groups looked over and scowled.

'This is Alex,' Eric said. 'Alex, meet Julie.'

I shook the gloved hand of the woman who had shouted. She was petite and blue-eyed. 'Welcome, Alex,' she said.

'Nice to meet you,' I answered.

'And Alex, this is Danny. Danny, Alex.'

'Hi,' I said. Danny was strikingly pretty, tall and olive-skinned. I recognized her as the woman I had seen Eric with from the bus, outside the cafe.

'Hello,' she said, but didn't offer her hand; she was dissecting already. 'Let's get to work,' she added. 'We have a lot to cover.'

'Danny's the serious one,' Eric said, and tickled her on the ribs. She twisted away.

'Someone's gotta be,' she said, and went back to work. 'Where's that damn insertion?'

'Okay, Danny, we'll work,' Eric said. 'Why don't you two take that arm, and Alex and I will take this one?'

Danny looked up. 'Who is she, Eric? Is she a med student, or what?'

I flushed as Eric said, 'Are those the only two possibilities?'

'Forget it,' Danny said, 'do what you want. Come on, Julie.' Julie winked at me, smiled, and joined Danny. I exhaled.

'Alex, Alex, Alex,' Eric chanted. 'Let's see what we have here.' He uncovered the left arm of the cadaver; it hadn't been touched. Apparently, they had been working exclusively on the other side. 'Put on these gloves. Here's your scalpel,' he said. Then we sat on stools and looked at the arm. His eyes sparkled as he glanced at me, rubbing his hands together in anticipation. 'Which muscle would you like first, darlin'?' he asked.

I pointed to the deltoid and he sliced the skin, peeling it away, all the while showing me the proper technique and then letting me try. He pointed out various structures: nerves, vessels, tendons, and named them. I thought of all the models I had sketched, of how I had studied their form and movements, and now I could see first-hand why and how they worked. After this, bodies would never be the same for me.

Eric was teaching me, but because he treated me as an equal, I didn't notice. It wasn't until later that I realized how immersed we had been, forgetting our attraction for each other, abandoning our game playing, and simply working together.

I also didn't notice how quickly he was dissecting. It didn't take long before Eric had caught up to where his partners were. 'I'm there,' he breathed, and Julie looked up and over to our arm.

'Jesus, Eric!' she exclaimed. 'Look, Danny. How does he do it?'

'Julie, concentrate,' Danny responded, not glancing up.

I watched Eric; a shadow of pain crossed his

face before he turned to me and smiled. 'Want more?' he asked.

'How long does that usually take, what you just did?' I asked.

'What *we* just did,' he corrected me and began dissecting again.

'He's incredible, Alex,' Julie said. 'It took us four days to get this far.'

'Speed isn't everything,' Danny commented.

'True,' Eric said, and showed me where to make the next cut.

Later, as we left the lab, I asked Eric, 'You're a genius, aren't you?'

'You won't get a point for that.' He smiled.

'Games aside. Your dissection was brilliant.'

'I'm good at dissecting, I'll grant you that.'

'Why?'

'I'm the one who won the bet. The leftover questions are mine.'

'But I'm the one who needs answers.'

'About what?' His smile faded.

'Nothing,' I said. 'Forget it.'

He took my arm and pulled me close. 'Will answers make you have dinner with me tonight?'

'I'm not sure.'

He backed up a step, releasing my arm. 'I see,' he said. 'That depends on the answers.'

'I didn't mean that.'

'What did you mean?'

'Nothing.'

'It's about Peter, right?'

'I live with him—'

'Is that going to change?'

'It's not so easy.'

'What does that have to do with it?' His intensity had returned; it was like a contained power.

'I have to go,' I said, and started to take off the white coat.

'You're not doing that today.'

'What?' I handed him the coat.

'Running away from me. You're braver than you're acting.'

'I don't know what you mean.' I watched him take off his coat and unfasten his ponytail.

'Are you really like this, or are you just torturing me?' he asked.

'Torturing?' I laughed. 'I hardly think I'm capable of—'

He grabbed my arm, squeezing it tightly above the elbow. 'You're capable, believe me,' he said.

'And so are you.'

'Is that what we're doing? Mutual torture? Because if so, I'm willing to be the first to stop.'

I pulled my arm away and stood facing him, silent.

'You're in me, Alex,' he said, 'and there's nothing I can do about it.'

'Is that the torture?'

'No.' He turned away and started pacing. 'The torture is not being able to call you at midnight, or give you piggyback rides, or eat Oreos in bed with you.'

'Yes, that's the torture.'

He looked toward me and abruptly stopped pacing. 'But you can have me,' he said, coming over and grasping both my hands.

I was lost momentarily, but then I spoke, softly. 'So it's Peter that's keeping us apart?'

He nodded.

'You're not seeing any other women?'

'None worth mentioning.'

'So you are.'

'I'm not a virgin, if that's what you mean.'

'You know that's not what I mean.'

'There may have been others in my bed since I met you, Alex, but not in my heart.'

'And my heart is full of you.'

He pulled me close. 'Come with me. Please.'

'Where?'

'Anywhere. Everywhere.'

I looked into his eyes, bottomless and riveting, encompassing a world I had not yet known. Then I kissed him, sealing my body, my fate, to his. There would be no turning back.

When we finally resurfaced into the world, into that hallway lined with student lockers outside the anatomy lab, I found pulling away from him cold and unnerving, even more so because responsibility was there to meet me. I felt its rigid hand on my throat.

I breathed in deeply. 'I know I have to leave Peter,' I said, 'for a lot of reasons—'

'Don't involve me in it. I'll wait for you.'

'Help me, Eric.'

He shook his head. 'You don't need me for that.'

'But—'

'No.'

He was right. I was avoiding doing a hard thing—something I had become expert at—and it was time to confront it.

I never could get Eric to admit it, but he was a genius.

CHAPTER SEVEN

'Peter?' I said one evening, a few days later, days spent in a state of both dread and anticipation.

'Yes?' Peter said, turning from his drafting table.

'We need to talk.'

'Oh?' He glanced up. 'About what?'

'About us.'

He smiled. 'Okay.' He stood and walked over to me, sitting beside me on the couch. 'I'm glad you brought this up,' he said.

'Really?'

'I've been meaning to talk to you. Well, actually, I've been trying to figure out how to say this . . .'

My heart began to hammer.

He continued, 'But . . . well . . . here.' He handed me a gray velvet box he had pulled from his jacket pocket. Then he said, 'Will you marry me?'

I tried not to gasp. I shouldn't have been surprised.

'Aren't you going to look at it?' he asked, pointing to the as yet unopened box.

'Yes, of course.' I peeked inside.

'Do you like it?'

I had rarely seen him so eager, so excited, and it made being honest so much harder. 'Uh . . . uh . . . yes,' I sputtered. 'It's beautiful.'

'Well?' he asked.

I stared at the ring, a large, solitary diamond glittering up at me, mocking. 'Well . . . '

'I love you, Alex.'

'I . . . I love you, too. I . . . I'll think about it,' I mumbled, snapping the box shut.

'You don't like it, do you? I can get another, or have it reset.'

'No, I love it. Really.'

'I want to spend my life with you.'

'I . . . I know. It's just so . . . so sudden. I . . .'

'Sudden? We've been living together for over two years.'

'Yeah . . . but marriage. It's a big step.'

'Of course it is. But we're ready. We're right for each other, Alex.'

I looked at him and nodded slowly, a numb-
ness settling over me, weighing me down, as he
began to pace, making his case for why we
should get married, why now. He had all the
answers; the blueprint of our life together was
so clear to him, the logic of our union as clear
and as sparkling as the diamond in that ring.
Yet, as Peter talked, what I thought about was
Eric, how the light glowed behind his eyes, how
his hands, cool and pale, would feel on my
body, how I wanted to be the only woman in his
bed, in his life. As much as I didn't want to hurt
Peter, I couldn't imagine going on without
Eric. A tear of indecision and tension trickled
down my cheek; Peter saw it.

'Why are you crying?' he asked, stopping to
kneel on the floor in front of me.

'It's so much at once.'

'I'm sorry if I'm pressuring you. I don't
mean to. We can wait if you'd rather.'

'I just need to think,' I said.

'Whatever you need is yours,' he said, taking
my hands in his. 'I can wait forever, as long as
you'll be my wife.'

I pulled him close so he wouldn't see the
shadow of betrayal on my face.

*   *   *

That night I didn't sleep. I listened to Peter's slumbering breath for a long while, and at about three in the morning I got up, got dressed, and went outside. I sat on the front steps of the building and watched the street. The moon was crisp, not full, but clear and radiant. I didn't think when I stood, I simply started walking, then jogging, and finally running. I was trying to pretend I didn't know where I was headed, that I was just running to release tension. But it wasn't so; I was going to Eric's apartment near the university, to where I had walked him home that day after lab.

·I rang his bell, panting heavily, my face hot. I rang again. 'Eric, Eric,' I whispered.

'Who is it?' I finally heard through the intercom.

'Me, Eric. Me.' He didn't ask; he buzzed me in.

He lived in a three-story walk-up. The hall-way leading to his apartment was dark, the carpet worn. Eric stood silhouetted in his door-way, dressed in navy blue sweatpants. We embraced, holding each other tightly; his chest was bare, comfortably secure, firm and smooth. 'Hello, "me," ' he said, and smiled, leading the way into the apartment and closing the door behind us.

He looked down into my eyes. 'Tears?' he said. 'You're crying?'

I felt my face; I hadn't known. 'I miss you,' I said, hugging him close again.

'I miss you, too. What happened?'

'Peter proposed.'

'Congratulations.' He grinned; I pulled away.

'Maybe I shouldn't have—'

'No, Alex, you should have.' He took my hand and led me to a sagging green couch against one wall. We sat. 'I'm glad to see you.'

'It's so late, and—'

'Talk, darlin', talk.'

And so I did. It would be the first of thousands of times I would lay my problems at Eric's feet, drawing on his strength, his wisdom. When I was finished, he asked, 'Do you love yourself?'

'Love myself?'

He nodded.

'Of course.'

'Who do you love more, Peter or yourself?'

That question pierced me, sharp and clean, like a needle. Finally, I answered, 'Myself.'

'Then do what's best for you.'

'I don't want to marry him, Eric.'

'Don't tell me,' he said, chuckling and standing up. 'Tell him.'

He stood there, watching me, and I sensed it was time to leave. Still, I wanted to be with him, damn the consequences.

'Good night,' I said, hoping he'd ask me to stay.

'Good night, "me," ' he said. 'I'll call you a cab.' He kissed me and I left.

Peter hadn't noticed my absence, and he snuggled against me as I crawled into bed, like a guilty sneak, at 5:00 AM. Yet I didn't feel guilty, I felt cleansed, and for the first time in many months, at peace. I watched the sky lighten behind the window shade and then heard Peter stirring beside me.

'Good morning,' I said when he opened his eyes.

'You're awake already?' he asked.

'I didn't sleep.'

'Thinking it over?'

'Yes.'

'Good. Take all the time you need.' He began to get out of bed. I felt tears sting my eyes, watching his slender back, dark and supple, so familiar. He started toward the bathroom.

'Peter?'

He turned around. 'Yes, hon?'

'I love you.'

'I love you, too,' he said with a smile. I thought he might hop back into bed, but he ran his hand through his hair and headed toward the bathroom.

The blood pounded through my aching head, blurring the words in my mind. Still, somehow I blurted, 'I can't marry you.'

He stopped and hesitated before turning around. 'What?' he said.

I took a deep breath; tears began to fall quietly, quickly, from my downcast eyes. 'I'm sorry,' I said.

He walked over to me and sat beside me on the bed, wiping my tears away with his thumb. 'No, Alex,' he said, '*I'm* sorry. I know I pressured you too much last night. Let's just forget about it for now. Take your time.'

'Peter,' I sighed, beginning to sob, 'I don't want to hurt you. I do love you. You're a good man, you'll make a great husband for someone . . . just not for me.'

'You don't know what you're saying, Alex. You shouldn't make decisions when you're upset. Wait a few weeks, calm down.'

I looked up and swallowed my tears, waiting for the shaking in my chest to subside, trying to replace it with courage. He smiled and took me in his arms, which is where I was when I said it, practically a whisper in his ear, 'I'm in love with another man.'

His withdrawal from me was abrupt, his shock radically apparent across his face. 'You're what?'

'I'm sorry. I can't help it.'

'You're in love with someone else?'

I nodded.

'Since when?'

'Just recently. I was going to tell you . . .'

He stood, suddenly stiff, recoiling. 'I would hope so.'

'Peter, it doesn't mean—'

'What's important is what it does mean.'

'It means I can't say yes to marrying you.'

He paused, then sat, thinking, measuring. 'Alex, I know how you can be,' he said. 'This sounds like an infatuation, an impulse.' He looked at me, hope chasing hurt away.

'I . . . I . . . you could be right.'

'I'm talking about a life together, not some fling.'

'I know.'

'I can give you stability, a future.'

'I know.'

'What is *he* offering?'

I shrugged. 'Something else, I guess.'

He examined me, saw doubt, indecision, and gained strength from it. 'Who is he?' he asked.

'That's not important.'

'It is to me.'

'Why?'

'Because I love you!'

'This isn't a competition. It's just something that happened, someone who came into my life. And no matter whether anything works out between him and me, it's made me realize that marrying you just isn't right for me.'

He stood, straight and upright. 'How can you be so sure?'

'I'm not . . . but I'm sure I can't say yes.'

'You'll regret this,' he said. 'And I can't guarantee I'll be around when you change your mind.'

'I know.'

He picked up the gray velvet box from where it sat beside the sofa bed and clutched it in his hand, marching to the bathroom, closing and locking the door behind him.

I lay down in bed, covering my head with the sheet, crying softly. I didn't feel free, or elated, or relieved; I felt tired and unsure, but mostly despicable.

CHAPTER EIGHT

It took me three weeks to move out, three weeks filled with doubts, longing, regret, tears, hope. It was hard and lonely. Peter stayed late at the library most nights; we slept with our backs to each other.

It seems incredible, but I lived in my new apartment for two weeks before Eric and I saw each other. He was in the midst of exams, and I could never seem to catch him at home. And I stayed busy too, doing anything to avoid thinking. Those early months, from the time I met him until we finally got together, free of encumbrances, were like extended foreplay, prolonging while anxiously anticipating the inevitable.

'Eric? Is it really you?' I said into the receiver.

'Yes, darlin'.'

'What have you been up to?'

'You wouldn't believe the hell I've been through. But not seeing you is worse torture than exam week.'

'I've had my own kind of hell.'

'I can only imagine.'

'Do you want to see me?'

He laughed; it vibrated down the phone line and into my ear, through my existence. 'I'd like to see all of you,' he said. 'Let me draw you.'

'Okay.'

'I'll be right over.'

I was frenzied preparing my apartment for Eric's arrival. Not that there was much for me to do; I owned practically nothing except my art supplies, some books, a card table and chairs, the stool for my models, and a foam rubber pad covered with a sheet that I had been using as a bed. Fortunately, I was at no loss for art—my own, naturally; it gave the place a wall-papered look.

The bell rang. The sound of it petrified and agitated me at the same time. It rang again and I opened the door. There was Eric, beyond handsome, beyond desirable, in fact, beyond my own ridiculously exaggerated fantasies about him, smiling a half-smile that I knew was all for me.

We clutched each other in that doorway and stepped out of time, kissing like two hungry puppies, licking, giggling, panting, groping. It was Eric who finally pushed us inside and closed the door.

'God, it's good to see you,' he murmured, rubbing my hair, kissing my ears, forehead, eyes and nose. 'I could eat you up.'

'Please do,' I whispered.

'No,' he said, stepping back. 'I'm an artist. I came to draw you.'

The thought of sitting naked and still for him sent a lightning shiver of excitement through me. I grabbed him, opening his sweet lips with my tongue. He moaned, but then pulled away.

'Be a good little model,' he said. 'Strip for me.' Although my breath quickened, I didn't move. He looked at me, waiting for me to comply.

'Ms. Taylor,' he went on, taking me by the hand, 'I know this is your first time, but you'll need to take your clothes off.' He held my face for a moment, staring into my eyes. 'Don't be shy,' he said.

I felt an urgent heat between my legs while I did what he asked, feeling his eyes on me. I took off my sweater and T-shirt, then my bra. My nipples were hard, my breasts begging to be stroked, and he looked at me, not speaking, but silently telling me to continue. I pulled off my jeans, then hesitated, clad only in panties. I was incredibly aroused, but I waited. We locked eyes.

'If you hadn't worn them, this wouldn't be a problem,' he said.

I couldn't help smiling; the panties were off in seconds. I stood before him naked, ready.

'Lie down,' he instructed. 'There.' He pointed at the pad I used as a bed. I lay on my back, staring at the ceiling, breathing hard, waiting.

'All right, since you've never modeled before,' he began, '"just listen, don't talk. Move only when I tell you."' My breath caught; these were my words from the night he had modeled for me. 'Stretch your arms above your head,' he said. 'Close your eyes.' I did. Suddenly, I felt heat through my eyelids.

'Open your eyes, Ms. Taylor,' he said, and I did. He had arranged the lights over me—brilliant, powerful, and hot. They lit me completely. He was sitting on a chair about five feet away, still fully clothed. He had set up my easel and drawing pad in front of him, and he tilted his head to look at me, assessing. His eyes traveled my body slowly as I watched them, felt them, caressing my chest, breasts, belly, hips, thighs, all the way to my toes. He smiled.

'Put the pillow under your upper back,' he said. I reached for it, positioning it between my shoulder blades; it tilted my breasts upward and made my head fall back, chin up. He murmured his approval. 'Arms above your head again,' he said. 'There. Perfect.' He began to draw.

My desire to be touched by him had turned into an ache that roamed my body, moving from my scalp, to my nipples, to deep between my legs. That ache made me writhe. I felt I might die from desire.

'Ms. Taylor?'

'Yes?' I said in a soft pant. I was moist with sweat, my breath rapid.

'I need you to stay still. Move only when I tell you.'

'I can't. I can't,' I said, twisting.

'Concentrate,' he said.

I tried. The sensation I was experiencing was remarkably similar to the one I had had the night I had drawn him, but exaggerated a millionfold.

I couldn't see his drawing, but his arm moved in a sketching motion. And his eyes. They lingered on each part of my body, roving it, exploring every aspect of it, making me feel both exposed and admired, vulnerable, yet powerful.

Finally he got up and walked over to me, standing above me. Then he switched off the hot lights and knelt down, close to where I was, so close it hurt. He had one of my charcoal pencils in his hand.

'Eric, touch me,' I breathed.

'Ms. Taylor,' he said, shaking his head, '"I keep my hands clean. My eyes and pencil do the work."'

My words again!

'Close your eyes, princess,' he said. I did. Then I felt it, the blunt end of the pencil; he was tracing my body with it, teasing. It was cool, light, skimming down my forehead, along the profile of my nose, my lips, gently, slowly. I arched my neck and there it was, running over my chin, down my breastbone and then over to my left nipple, circling it, my body curving up to meet it; then it was gone, over to the right nipple, where it lingered, observing my response to it, almost like a magnet, drawing me upward, my back no longer in contact with the pillow. It was gone abruptly, reappearing along the midline of my belly, tickling its way across the hair covering my mons, making my pelvis flex upward, searching for relief, finding none. It inched along the inside of my right thigh, traveling downward, across my knee, my calf, then to my toes, each individually outlined, making them curl and stretch, and on to the other side, tracing the left foot and leg, again to my pelvis. I had been softly moaning and breathing hard, every nerve in my body upright, awaiting the next sensation. I groaned when I realized the pencil was at my forehead again, starting over, and then over again. Each successive exploration of my body brought me closer to climax, and as it continued, my mind and body blended into a powerful urge that included nothing else in the universe—not Eric, not me, just focused ecstasy. When I came, it was bare and pure, intense like never before, into air, against nothing. He had not yet touched me.

When I opened my eyes, Eric was naked. His body was fluid, moving without effort or seemingly without thought, simply with a glistening energy. He lifted me; I was limp, utterly relaxed, but still passionately aroused when he kissed me, so tenderly it was as if I hadn't been kissed at all. Then he gently eased himself down to the pad, holding me tightly to him so that he lay down beneath me and I felt the length of his body underneath my own. I could not stop kissing him, yearning to fill a craving that opened wide within me, a primitive and absolute need to fuse with him. I felt his hands, silky sparks along my spine, and saw his eyes, dark and penetrating, as I sat up, drawing my hair across his face before throwing it back over my head and settling against him, pelvis to pelvis. I could feel him behind me, stiff against my lower back, and I reached around to stroke him with my fingers, from base to tip and again and again. I watched as the effects of my touches raced across him, making him twist, his muscled arms over his head, clutching one wrist tightly in his other hand, his face almost savage with fierce longing.

I continued stroking and watching as Eric writhed, wrenching his head from side to side, now groaning, almost snarling. I imagined that I witnessed a battle, not between Eric and me, but between Eric's will and his body. More powerful than lust, hunger, pain, or thirst, was Eric's tenacity against practically insurmount-able odds; I was seeing it for the first time.

I thought he wasn't present, that he was deep inside himself, unaware of me or our surround-ings, but he surprised me by reaching over for a condom, ripping open the package, and slip-ping it on. Then, unexpectedly, he stood, lifting me off my feet and onto him, my legs encircling him, my head thrown back. I didn't know it at the time, but we made love in this position for almost an hour, his sweat slick against my own, his climax held for my pleasure, pleasure that went on and on, pleasure that I couldn't and wouldn't resist. I thought I would pass out from orgasms, but Eric kept going, sustaining my weight, and waiting. Finally, when I was on the precipice of exhaustion, he lowered me to the floor and, as I lay under him, exploded into orgasm, the violence of which I'd never beheld. His body contracted and convulsed while he growled and wrestled with what appeared to be a demon that had finally overtaken him. It was eerie to watch, formidable and frightening, but compelling.

When he was done, he opened his eyes and looked into me. Sucking air through closed teeth, he inhaled deeply and then exhaled, his body shaking with a shudder of release. He smiled. 'So that's what it feels like,' he said, sighing.

'You don't expect me to believe you've never done that before,' I whispered into his ear. I kissed each of his three earrings and he shivered again.

'Not that I care to remember.'

'Me neither,' I agreed.

He rolled onto his back beside me and I snuggled under his arm. We were silent for a time, our breathing slowing, warm together.

Finally he said, 'Are you scared?'

'Scared?'

'Yes.'

'Are you?'

He pushed himself up on an elbow, looking at me. 'Alex, you're the person I thought I'd never find. Now I'm frightened, because for the first time I know what I could lose.'

'But you won't lose me.'

'I hope not. But hope seems a little flimsy sometimes.'

'Hope is good.' I kissed the wizard.

Eric smiled.

'But,' I said, 'hope won't keep us from being scared.'

'What will?'

'Time, I guess.'

'Time . . .'

We were quiet, and I studied him, those brilliant black eyes, that shining body, and in that moment, I made friends with being scared.

I lost track of how many times we made love that first night; I know I was sore the next day, although that could have been from what happened next. Around three in the morning, Eric suddenly jumped up. 'Let's go for a ride,' he said, and started getting dressed.

'A ride?' I asked.

'Yeah, on my bike.' His jeans and boots were on in seconds; he threw me my pants and shirt.

'As in motorcycle?' I asked.

'You want to?'

'Can I drive it?' I asked, wiggling into my clothes.

'Can you?'

I shrugged.

He laughed. 'After what I've just been through, I have no doubt you can handle a Harley.'

'Me neither.'

We started out the door. 'That's it?' I asked. 'You're just wearing that jean jacket, no shirt?'

He smiled.

'Eric, it's November.'

He snatched me, rubbing his bare chest against my coat. 'I like to feel life,' he said. 'I want it next to my skin.'

I laughed, pulling away, and we ran down the stairs and out to where his motorcycle was parked. It was spare, just the rugged basics, black and chrome. He handed me a helmet.

'Where's yours?' I asked.

'You're wearing it.'

'What about you?'

'The other one got totaled.'

'Better it than your skull.'

'Yeah.'

'Here, you take it,' I said, handing it back.

He shook his head. 'I'm not taking you riding without it.'

I put it on, reluctantly, and said, 'I think you should wear one.'

'I'll pick one up tomorrow. Get on.'

I straddled the bike while he watched. I had driven minibikes before, when I was younger, but this was a real motorcycle, heavy, and hard to keep upright. I struggled and he smiled, finally getting on in front of me and starting it up.

'It's not easy,' he said, turning his head to yell over the sound of the engine.

'I guess not.'

'How 'bout if you take me flying instead?'

I laughed. 'I'm not making any promises.'

I gripped his waist and off we went, racing over glossy, deserted pavement, the late-night streetlights blinking a pure red or yellow. My hands searched his muscled chest, which was cold, covered with goose bumps. I rubbed it, scraping my fingernails over his nipples and down his belly.

After a time, we stopped at a light and he turned to me. 'You ready to drive?' he asked. I shook my head. 'Come on,' he said, urging me off and holding the bike while I got back on in front of him. 'I'll help,' he added.

I felt his gloved hands on mine, gently, just for support, as I took that machine's brazen, deafening energy and made it mine. It was bone-grating and leg-numbing, a frigid and windy ride. Finally, we pulled in front of my apartment building and he turned off the bike.

'See, there's nothing you can't handle,' he said.

'You might be the test of that.'

'That's one test I wouldn't mind taking.'

We climbed off the motorcycle and he removed my helmet, holding it in his hand and tilting his head to watch me. His skin looked brittle white and cold, making his ebony hair and eyes seem beyond black, extravagantly dark. I kissed him deeply, with complete openness, feeling whatever was solid beneath me fall away.

As long as I knew him, it never came back.

CHAPTER NINE

The following day was Sunday. The sun rose orange through the frosted panes of my apartment window before we snuggled into a contented sleep.

Eric awakened me around noon, bearing croissants and cappuccino to the bed. 'Good afternoon, darlin',' he said.

'Hi.' I smiled. 'Did you carry this stuff on Shadow Blaster?'

He laughed. 'Is that what you named my bike?'

'You like it?'

'It's perfect . . . you're perfect.' He kissed me.

'How'd you carry this stuff?' I asked.

He shook his head. 'I have no idea.'

I gobbled three croissants before I touched the cappuccino, which was blissfully strong. When we were done eating, we started kissing; he tasted of steamed milk. His hands began stroking my breasts, my body, bringing tiny beads of sweat to my forehead and between my shoulder blades. Suddenly, he lay back and looked up. 'Sorry, Al,' he said, 'I'd love to, but I'm sore as hell.'

I erupted into laughter before he did. When we had recovered, I said, 'I guess that was more than you're used to.'

'You're more than I'm used to.'

He was infinitely more than I was used to, and I had never been so sore before, but I didn't admit it. Let him wonder.

He stood and began to dress. 'I'd better study today,' he said, 'I'm behind in gross.' He looked down at my naked body, gracing me with a smile. 'You're so beautiful,' he said.

'And you're beyond beautiful.'

He knelt down beside me, removed one of his earrings, and poked it into the second hole I had had pierced some years before in my left earlobe. He held my face and kissed me. 'What are you doing today?' he asked.

'I have a model coming late this afternoon. I'm finishing that project you modeled for, the one for Kolpinski.'

'Are your drawings gonna be in his book?'

'That's what he says. But he uses some for his research.'

'Maybe you'll be discovered.'

'I doubt that. It's one of those academic books.'

'I'll buy it.'

'You're in it.'

'Not me, just my torso, sans wizard.'

We stood up and I rubbed my bare body against his rough clothing, embracing him. 'How do you know I didn't include the wizard?' I asked.

'I don't. You never let me see the drawings.'

'I guess you'll have to wait for the book. By the way, where's your drawing of me?'

'You don't remember?'

'I mean the one before that.'

'On your easel. Call me later?'

'Of course.'

We kissed, lingering, fighting the stretch of time, and then he was gone. I went to the window, letting my nipples touch the cold glass, and watched him climb onto his motorcycle, start it, and zoom away. He didn't look up, but he raised his hand in a wave as he drove away. I waved back.

I found myself smiling, still aroused after all

we'd been through, despite my soreness. I walked over to my easel.

The paper was blank.

My model arrived at 4:00 P.M., promptly. 'Hello,' she said when I opened the door. 'I'm Daniella Carvacchi. But of course, we've met.'

She was right. It was Danny from Eric's lab group. 'Alex Taylor,' I said. 'Please, come in.'

She did, slipping out of her brown suede jacket and looking around briefly. 'Nice place,' she said. 'Where should I put this?' She indicated her jacket, which was exquisite.

'I'll take it.'

She handed it to me. 'Is this where we'll be working?' she asked, wandering over to the area with the stool, lights, and easel.

'Yes,' I called from the closet, where I was struggling with her coat and a lack of hangers. 'Would you like tea, coffee, soda?' I asked.

'No, thanks.'

I joined her; she was seated on the stool, waiting.

'Have you modeled before?' I asked.

'Yes. Fashion, mostly.'

'Photographs?'

'Um–hmm.'

'I guess Professor Kolpinski told you he wants a drawing of the female torso, from the front, including the breasts and abdomen. Any problem with that?'

'Not at all.'

'You can get undressed behind that screen.' I pointed to it and she got up.

I waited, busying myself in the kitchen with nothing.

'Ready,' she announced.

I turned and went to my easel, settling myself behind it, to look at her. She faced me, watching as I appraised her. Her figure was exceptional, one of those slender but provocatively voluptuous bodies that seem to exist only in magazines.

'Hands by your sides, please,' I said. 'Twist a little to the left. There. Fine. Thank you.' I started to draw.

'I need to go to the bathroom,' she said after about thirty minutes.

'It's by the door.'

She got up and sauntered across the room. She moved beautifully; her skin was smooth, her hair and eyes black.

After about five minutes, she emerged. 'How much longer will this take?' she asked.

'Probably half an hour. Is there a problem?'

She was back on the stool, repositioning

herself. She smiled. 'Gross anatomy. I'm behind.'

I nodded, resumed drawing, quickly. My phone rang. 'Excuse me,' I said, and picked it up. 'Hello? . . . Oh, hi . . . Yeah, sure, that'd be great . . . Yes, she's still here . . . About thirty—better make it forty—minutes. Yeah, I'll be done in forty minutes . . . See you then . . . Me too . . . Bye.'

She was staring at me; I glanced at my watch and began to sketch furiously. After twenty minutes she was off to the bathroom again; I started to pace, looking at the clock about every thirty seconds. Finally, she was out and resettled on the stool. I wasn't done after another ten minutes, but I said, 'I guess that's enough. Better get you to the library.'

'Oh, that,' she said, waving a delicate hand. 'It's okay. I hate libraries anyway.' She laughed, the sound thin and high.

'Really,' I said, 'I'm finished.'

'If you say so.' She stood as I heard Eric's motorcycle pull up outside. I directed her back to the screen. Surprisingly, she was dressed quickly, and I handed her her jacket.

'Thank you,' I said.

'Anytime,' she responded, and turned to leave. 'Nice earring,' she murmured as she disappeared down the stairs.

Five minutes must've passed before Eric knocked.

'Al?' he called through the door.

I opened it. 'Hi,' I said.

'Hi.' He kissed me, then closed the door behind him. 'I see Danny was your model,' he said.

'Yes.'

'That's a curious thing.'

'What?'

'She's rich. She doesn't need to do this.'

'She said she'd modeled before.'

'For big money, fashion stuff.'

'Oh.'

'She must've come to check you out.'

'Me?'

'She was pissed that day I brought you to the lab—'

'Because she knew I wasn't a med student?'

'No.' He paused, looking away.

'Oh. You slept with her.'

He nodded. 'It was around the time you came to lab that I broke it off. She wasn't happy about it. When she asked how I knew you, I told her I modeled for you through Kolpinski.'

'So she came here for what, to make me jealous?'

'Probably to assess the competition.'

'Is that what I am?'

'Not to me.'

I studied him. He was sincere, even a little nervous. 'This isn't a game to me, Eric,' I said.

'Nor to me.'

'But she thinks it is.'

'I'll set her straight.'

'You know,' I said, 'it's scary enough without people like her.'

'I know.'

'She's quite beautiful.'

'She's not you.'

I pulled back and looked at him, wondering.

'Alex,' he said, 'nothing is more beautiful than you.'

I smiled, relieved, believing him. Eric Moro was new to me, but already so precious, so dangerous.

CHAPTER TEN

Less than two weeks later it was Thanksgiving. Eric had the romantic idea of heading into the country and staying at a bed and breakfast, of donning pilgrim hats and eating turkey legs in bed. But my family expected me at home, so I reluctantly declined his offer and invited him to my parents' house, just north of the city. He accepted with enthusiasm.

It was early afternoon on Thanksgiving Day when we headed over to my old neighborhood on Shadow Blaster. The late autumn had sucked the moisture and color from the foliage, leaving behind curled brown skeletons rustling in the brisk wind, a wind that painted our cheeks a bright, cool pink above our smiles.

We arrived at fifteen after two. I strained to

look through Eric's eyes at that plain, untrimmed yard, that little house, its wood siding in need of fresh paint, where I and my three siblings had grown up, where my parents had lived forever it seemed, where almost everything that mattered in my life until now had happened. That house held history for me, but what I saw through suddenly critical eyes was a random sloppiness, a shabbiness that was not sweet or even acceptable, a neighborhood without ambition or style. What Eric saw was a home.

'Mom, Daddy, we're here!' I called from just inside the front door.

'She's here! They're here!' my mom shouted from the kitchen.

'They're here! They're here!' reverberated throughout the two-story house.

'Come on,' I said, leading the way to the kitchen. I noticed Eric looking around, and it made me shrink a little, reminding me of high school days, when friends from the wealthy Main Line neighborhood would come over to visit, shocked that I didn't have my own TV, let alone my own room, that my mom took the bus to work, that we served tuna casserole for dinner. Their reactions revealed that for some, life wasn't the struggle that it most likely always would be for me. Then as now, nothing in the house matched; it had remained garage-sale patchwork: the orange carpet, gold sofa, green armchair, lamps from God knows where . . .

'Hi, Mom,' I said as we entered the kitchen. It was steamy, and smelled of things delicious and familiar, making nothing else matter. My feeling of security and affection at seeing her there at the stove, just like a thousand memories of her, with her blond hair escaping from its bun and her blouse invariably stained from her efforts, brought tears to my eyes. I hugged her before she had a chance to put down her spoon.

'Sweetie, sweetie,' she repeated. 'We've missed you. It's been weeks.'

'I know. Sorry.' I released her and took Eric by the hand. 'This is Eric, Mom. Eric, my mom, Wilma.'

'Hello, Eric,' Mom said, placing her spoon on the stove and wiping her hands down her apron.

'It's my pleasure, Wilma,' Eric said, extending his hand.

She took his hand and held it between both of hers, looked into his eyes, and pulled him into a hug. When she released him, they stood for a moment, studying each other, and then she turned back to the stove, picking up her spoon, stirring and stirring.

'Mom coaches the girls' basketball team at the high school,' I said, hooking my hand around Eric's waist and pulling him close.

'Did you coach Alex?' Eric asked.

'Coach?' Mom said with a laugh. 'The girl's uncoachable.'

'Mom!'

'Really?' Eric said, kissing me on the cheek.

'Good thing for her,' Mom added, 'she didn't need much. Great natural talent.'

'Thanks, Mom.'

'All my kids are—'

'Hey,' Harry, my younger brother, said, joining us and giving me a sound hug, demonstrating his strength. 'Who's the guy, Alex?'

'"The guy" is Eric, Harry. Eric, my brother Harry, the youngest.'

'Now what'd you have to go and say that for?' Harry said. 'Hey, Eric.' They shook hands, something I'd never seen Harry do before.

'Nice to meet you, Harry,' Eric said. 'You're a sophomore?'

'Yeah, at Westchester High. Wanna toss a football?'

'We'll be eating in forty-five minutes, Harry,' Mom said.

'Okay. Come on, Eric.'

'What about me?' I said.

'Like, you gotta be invited, right?' Harry said, and laughed.

Eric winked at me and we followed Harry outside. We still had our coats and scarves on.

We threw the football around for a few minutes before Cynthia, my youngest sister, a senior in high school, came running out, her hair flying behind her, eyes wild, agonized that she'd missed a few minutes of fun, that Harry had gotten to Eric first.

'Wait for me, you guys!' she called, pulling on a sweatshirt and gloves.

'Hi, Cindy,' I said. 'This is Eric.' I hurled the ball at him. He caught it, held it.

'Hello,' she said, approaching him, her arm outstretched with self-conscious sophistication. 'I'm Cynthia.'

'Hello, Cynthia. Pleased to make your acquaintance,' Eric said, taking her hand and kissing it through her glove. Cindy blushed.

'Eric,' I said, 'toss me the ball.' He did. Soon we were all over the yard, charging through dense heaps of leaves piled against the curb, crashing through neighbors' hedges, and finally tumbling to the ground, all of us in one big mound, weak with laughter.

'Oh, shit,' I gasped, 'you're crushing me. Get up, get up!'

'Not until you hand over that football,' Harry said.

'Get up!'

'Dinner!' It was Mom. Suddenly, the weight lifted and I was free. Saved by turkey and stuffing. I lay on my back and looked up at the trees. What I saw was Eric, standing over me, his dark head framed by the brilliant blue sky, his smile just an outline in shadows. What I felt was love.

'Here,' he said, holding his hand out to help me up.

I took it and got up, hugging the ball and laughing. He picked the leaves from my hair as we walked toward the house.

'Wash up, kids,' Mom said when she saw us. I could hear Harry and Cindy in the upstairs bathroom, arguing as Eric and I ascended the stairs. It was dark and familiar in the stairway, and we stopped to lean against the wall, drawn into a kiss, our lips confirming what our hearts already knew: that love unspoken is still love.

When we went back downstairs, the family was seated, with Daddy at his place, standing beside his chair, waiting for us. His face and the top of his head, under the few brown hairs he vainly combed over his bald spot, were polished pink from scouring and his clothes were starched, wrinkle-free.

'Daddy,' I said as he captured me in a hug. He smelled of Old Spice, the only aftershave he'd ever used.

'You're thin,' he said, releasing me and looking me up and down.

'I'm fine,' I responded. 'This is Eric, Daddy. Eric, my Daddy, Milt.'

'Hi, Milt,' Eric said. Daddy hugged him too, which seemed to take Eric by surprise.

'Welcome, Eric,' Daddy said. 'Please, sit down.'

'Thank you,' Eric replied, and we sat. Cindy and Harry shared the blessing, but I didn't bow my head. Instead, I watched them. What I saw was Daddy inspecting Eric from the edge of his vision, summing him up. It made me smile.

'Amen.'

'Amen.'

'Carve the turkey, Eric?' Daddy asked.

'Daddy, I—' I began.

'I'd be honored, Milt,' Eric said, and rose.

I couldn't imagine that anyone else's family would ask a guest to carve, and it startled me a little, but it didn't seem to bother Eric, who portioned the bird expertly, while answering a slew of questions.

'First-year medical student, are you?' Daddy asked.

'Yes, just three months in,' Eric answered.

'Good grades?'

'Daddy . . .'

Eric smiled. 'So far.'

'He's at the top of his class,' I said.

'Dark or white, Wilma?'

'Dark, please. Thank you. What a beautiful job you're doing, Eric. Do you think you learned that from gross anatomy practice?'

'Gross!' Harry said.

'I think it's cool,' Cindy said. 'You get to carve bodies.'

'We're a little more careful than this in lab,' Eric said. 'White or dark, Harry?'

'White.'

'Eric's great at dissecting,' I said. 'I've never seen anything like it.'

'I wouldn't think so,' Daddy said.

'You saw the bodies?' Harry asked.

'I went with Eric once.'

'So, you're planning on being a surgeon, then?' Daddy asked.

'That's my hope.'

'There's a lot of training in that, I hear,' Daddy said. 'Years and years of schooling. Not much time for anything else.'

Eric was nodding. 'Light or dark, Alex?'

'Dark, please.'

'You've heard right, Milt,' Eric said.

'How do you handle working nights?' Mom asked.

'It's pretty hard during training, but it gets better. I plan to be on staff at a hospital someday, where I can share the work.'

'Will you have time for a family?' Daddy asked.

'Daddy, don't—'

'It's okay, Al,' Eric said, 'it's a valid question. That's one reason I wouldn't want to be in a private practice and on-call all the time, Milt, so I can always put my family first.'

'It sounds like Eric has a good plan, Milt,' Mom said.

'It sounds like the plan won't begin until sometime in the next century, Wilma,' Daddy said.

'He's right,' Eric said. 'Milt's right. Any woman who's willing to marry me will have to be patient. And when I make that commitment, I'll have to make some compromises.'

'Sounds fair,' Daddy said.

'I want to be a veterinarian,' Cindy said. 'Will I have time for anything else?'

'You're too young to think about marriage,' Mom said.

'Veterinary medicine is great,' Eric said. 'Light or dark, Cynthia?'

'Light, please. I can't wait to get to do some of the stuff you're doing, Eric.'

'Like carving turkeys?' Eric said.

'Right.' Cindy laughed.

'Actually, I started dissecting when I was about your age, Cynthia,' Eric said. 'My dad made arrangements for me with local butchers, then the humane society, and, when I was in college, with a medical school in Chicago.'

'He must really want you to be a surgeon,' Daddy said.

'Yes, he does,' Eric said. 'Light or dark, Milt?'

'Dark, please. I'll take a leg.'

'Okay.'

We were silent for a moment. We had been passing the other dishes while we talked: sweet potatoes with marshmallows, green beans topped by canned fried onions, stuffing, mashed potatoes, gravy, rolls, cranberry sauce. Only Eric's plate was empty.

'Please, start,' Eric said. 'I'll help myself.'

Eric sat and we began to eat as he served himself.

'Your father's a surgeon?' Daddy asked.

'Businessman. Automotive supplies. But I think if he'd had the chance, he would've been a doctor.'

'Why didn't he have the chance?' Mom asked.

'His parents moved the family to Chicago from Italy when he was ten. They had to struggle to make things work.'

We continued eating, pausing only to exclaim over how good everything was.

Finally, Daddy said, 'We've been blessed with healthy and happy children. Now all of them are growing up.'

'Alex is our oldest,' Mom said, 'and such a brilliant artist. We always knew she had that talent—'

'Mom, don't exaggerate,' I said.

'I know you're modest, honey,' she said, 'but it's true. You have the ability to do whatever you put your mind and efforts to. And to do it well.'

'I agree,' Eric said.

'If it's true, I owe it to Mom and Daddy,' I said.

They smiled proudly.

'Harry has a good dose of that same talent,' Daddy said.

Harry beamed. 'I'm gonna do art,' he said. 'Or football.'

'Art,' Daddy said.

'Then we have our two scientists,' Mom said, 'Cindy and Linda—'

'Linda?' Eric asked.

'My other sister,' I said. 'She's in a graduate psychology program at Columbia.'

'She stayed in New York for Thanksgiving,' Daddy said.

'Why, a new boyfriend?' I asked.

'I don't know about any boyfriend—'

'A boyfriend? Must be serious—'

'To miss Thanksgiving with the family.'

'I haven't met him. What's his name? Why haven't I met him?'

'Is there something wrong with him—'

'A problem?'

'Couldn't be, Linda would've—'

'But to be missing Thanksgiving—'

And on it went, a circle of truncated ideas, a family together, finishing each other's sentences, anticipating each other's thoughts and dealing with uncertainty through exaggeration, what was real shrinking in comparison to what was imagined. I looked at Eric. He was bewildered, his eyes jumping from one speaker to the next, as if following a bouncing ball. We all spoke, but it was as if we were one entity, and that's when I realized all families aren't like mine.

I dropped out of the conversation, something no one noticed, and watched with Eric as the rest of them kept eating and talking. I was used to this kind of family exchange, but seeing it as if for the first time, with Eric there as an uninitiated guest made me feel giddy, proud of them and excited by the prospect that Eric might some day be a part of this.

Gradually the circle subsided, and we began to lean back in our chairs.

'Dessert?' Mom asked.

We were full, but we nodded, and everyone rose to clear.

'Alex and Eric, sit down,' Mom said. 'We'll take care of this.'

'Okay,' we agreed.

We were alone in the room when Eric said, 'That thing your family does—'

'The circle.'

'It's like a sentence symphony, without a conductor.'

I laughed. 'I never thought about it that way.'

'It works, doesn't it?'

I nodded.

Cindy and Mom walked back in and gathered more dishes, carrying them back to the kitchen.

'You have a good family, Al,' Eric said, leaning over to kiss me.

'I know. Doesn't your family miss you when—'

'I should help with the dishes.'

'You're a guest. Enjoy it.'

'I am.'

'Here we are!' Mom declared as she led the way from the kitchen holding a pumpkin pie. Daddy followed with pecan and Harry with apple, practically a half pie per person. Excess—the key to a good Thanksgiving.

By the time it was all over, I couldn't move. I swore I'd never eat again. I don't know how Eric did it, but he got up, followed Mom and Daddy to the kitchen, and began doing the dishes with them. I groaned at the thought of standing. Harry, Cindy, and I crawled to the living room and lay on the floor.

It reminded me of so many times after big dinners when we were little. We'd lie like the spokes of a wheel, our heads at the hub, talking, laughing, watching the ceiling. It was a game for us, making up sections of stories, passing the baton on to the next in line, each embellishing, enhancing, adding her or his brand to the tale.

We were telling a story like that—although it was different now that we were growing up and Cindy preferred science fiction, I liked adventure, and Harry was into horror—when Eric, Mom, and Daddy came into the room. I tried to get up as my parents settled into their places on the sofa, but before I could, Eric lay down beside me. When it was his turn to join in the story, he began to spin a fascinating tale of intrigue, mystery, and romance, too intricate for our simple game. Several times he tried to hand it over to us, but we made him continue, and eventually we sat in a circle on the rug, staring at him, mesmerized. Even Mom and Daddy were listening.

It was dark and starting to snow when we left. They wanted us to stay the night, but we declined. As much as I adored my family, I wanted Eric to myself that night, and as far as I could see, for every night to come.

Eric drove carefully on Shadow Blaster, the streets slick, made deceptively benign by the beauty of fresh wet snow, treachery beneath our wheels. We rode to my apartment and he parked the bike. As we removed our helmets and started for the stairs he grabbed me by the arm and pulled me against him.

'You're a lucky woman,' he said.

'I'm lucky to have you.'

'I meant your family. There's so much love and warmth there . . . and honesty.'

'Of course.'

'Not "of course," Al. It's rare.'

I looked at him and could see he meant it, but I didn't know what he meant, so I laughed. 'Thanksgiving makes you sentimental,' I said.

'Isn't there something in turkey that does that? Something they feed them?'

'Maybe,' he said, and kissed me.

'Whatever it is,' I said, 'it makes me want to drag you to bed.'

'No dragging necessary, my pal.'

He was right.

CHAPTER ELEVEN

If I had to pick one word to describe the first month of my relationship with Eric, it would be breathless. That's the romantic word for it, anyway. Gasping, panting, winded, air-hungry would also describe it. Maybe we didn't come up for air much, but I know we breathed hard a lot.

We didn't share an apartment, but we spent each night together, whether at his place or mine, slurping late-night chop suey, dancing midnight tangos to the tune of our hot laughter, and making love in the blue glow of streetlamps angling through our windows. And Eric studied.

'Al, my pal?' he called to me from his bedroom one night in mid-December.

'Yeah?'

'I hate to ask, but could you help me memorize these parasitology life cycles for my exam tomorrow?'

I went to the bedroom door and looked at him. He was naked except for sweatpants, and he lay splayed across the bed with papers and books covering all surfaces. It was finals week.

'Life cycles?' I asked.

'Sometimes they live in snails or fish or something before they get to humans.'

'Oh. What do you want me to do?'

'I need to say them out loud as you follow along on the paper and check me. This is gonna be boring as hell.'

'But you have to do it.'

'You don't mind?'

'No problem.'

He handed me the papers and I sat on the bed with him. 'I hope I can pronounce this stuff,' I said. 'Here goes. The life cycle of *Toxo*—*Toxo*—*plasma*?'

'*Toxoplasma gondii.*'

'Is that how you say it? *Gondii*?'

'Yeah.' He looked at me.

'Am I that bad?' I asked.

He took the papers from my hand. 'It's not that. You were sketching and I interrupted you for this—'

'I want to help you,' I said, snatching the papers back. '*Toxogondii* is my buddy.'

We stared at each other. 'Then let me give you a massage while we do it,' he said.

I smiled. 'You know more ways to get my clothes off than anyone I ever met.'

'And you know more ways of making me smile during exam week than anyone *I* ever met.'

He aced his exams.

CHAPTER TWELVE

I was making linoleum block prints, my idea of Christmas presents, when Eric burst into my apartment and asked me to spend Christmas with him. 'It'll be great,' he said. 'We can get a little tree, with ornaments—you can make some—and we'll bake cookies—'

'On our own?' I asked.

'Why not?'

'What about our families?'

'Aren't we family, Al?'

The beauty of his face, still pink from the cold wind, made my chest tighten. I said, 'Don't your parents expect you to come to Chicago?'

He walked toward the window and looked out, his back to me, resting his palms on the sill, his forehead on the frozen pane, and sighed. The moment was broken, fractured by something that was suddenly with us in my small studio.

'What is it?' I asked.

'Nothing. You're right. We should spend Christmas with our families.'

'Eric.' I walked toward him, embracing him from behind, red, green, and white paint sticky-wet on my hands, his black leather motorcycle jacket cool through my smock. 'I want to spend Christmas with you,' I whispered into his ear, 'more than anything.'

He turned to face me, his smile sudden, and took my face in his hands, kissing it all over.

'I've never spent Christmas away from my family,' I said.

'So we'll spend it with them. I like them.'

'But what about your parents?'

'I'd rather be with you.'

'Why don't I go to Chicago with you?'

Again, he turned away, escaping from our embrace and walking to my work area. He picked up a print and pretended to inspect it.

'What's the deal, Eric?' I asked. 'You hardly ever talk about your parents, you never call them when I'm around, and now you don't want to take me home. Are you ashamed of me?'

His head whipped around and his stare was one of astonishment, bordering on anger. 'Of course not!'

'Then why won't you take me home?'

'Why can't we stay here?'

'We can, but that doesn't answer the question.'

He didn't walk away this time. He put the print down gently and took his coat off, motioning for me to sit next to him on the sofa. I did.

'My family is complicated,' he said.

'All families are.'

'Not like mine.'

'You saw mine, Eric. Mighty weird.'

'Loving.'

'And yours isn't?'

He paused. 'Not like yours.'

'But you said your father—'

'He's helped me out, that's true, and in some ways he's like you, fighting like crazy for what he believes in. He built his business from scratch. Hell, he didn't even speak English until he was eleven.' He stood and began to pace. There wasn't much room, and his turns were quick; he didn't look at me, but at the rug, his boots, something imaginary.

He went on. 'There were lots of times my father didn't get what he wanted, what he deserved. He had an accent, his hair and eyes were too dark. He was foreign.'

'Foreign?'

'Uh-huh, but he was accepted in the Italian community when people recognized his intelligence and determination. From there he began to build.'

'His business.'

'Right. But making it outside . . . that was harder. He doesn't like to talk about it much. His mom, my grandma, told me most of it.'

'What happened?'

'He wouldn't give up. He went door to door, talking to people, getting to know them as a trusted friend. His way of advertising.'

'That's a good story.'

'But that's not the story.'

'Oh?'

'He was almost beaten to death by some rivals in a neighboring community.'

'How horrible!'

'But it didn't work. He was out of the hospital and back to it in less than a month.'

'He went back to the same place?'

'He has courage . . . and pride.'

'Or foolishness.'

Eric stopped pacing and looked at me, then grinned. 'I guess,' he said. 'He was beaten twice more.'

'My God!'

'And he went back three more times.'

'He's still alive?'

'His business is, too.'

'They just gave up after that?'

'What choice did they have?'

'They could've killed him!'

'But they didn't.'

'How did he know they wouldn't?'

'He didn't.'

'Guts.'

'Yeah, and blood.'

'Tell me more.'

'He did it to prove he could, but also to build something for his future, for his family.'

'It sounds more brave than complicated, Eric.'

'He's an admirable person. He has compassion, too. He knows what it's like to be the underdog. He supported his employees' unionization, even though it cost him money.'

'That's unheard of.'

Eric nodded. 'He's rare.'

'I can see that. But I still don't get what this has to do with Christmas. Is there a problem with your mom?'

'No.' He began to pace again. 'Mama's great, no problem.'

'I want to meet them, Eric.'

'My father is a brilliant, powerful man . . . '

'And?'

'He has high expectations, like any man of his caliber would—'

'Meaning, he wouldn't like me.'

'No!' He stopped and stared at me. 'No, not at all. He has high expectations of his children.'

'Obviously you live up to them.'

It startled me to see sudden tears in his eyes; he blinked urgently, resumed pacing. 'He's a hard man to impress,' he said.

'But you're in one of the best med schools in the—'

'You think that's enough?' he asked, turning and looking directly at me, almost accusingly.

'Yes,' I said, 'it's enough. Besides, that's not what makes you impressive.'

'What does, Al?'

I looked into his eyes. He was several feet away from me, but I was close enough to see he was sincere. I stood and went to him, pulling him close. 'You, Eric,' I said. 'Just you.'

We remained that way for several minutes, silent, both clinging to something that reached beyond holidays, family, memories, traditions. When I looked up, I expected to see him crying, but instead, he bore a faraway look, one that spoke of troubles he wasn't ready to reveal. I didn't press him.

Finally, he said, 'Come home with me for Christmas.'

'It's okay—'

'I want you to know I'm not ashamed of you.'

'Eric—'

'No, we'll go to Chicago for Christmas and you'll meet him. He'll love you, probably more than he does me.' He smiled, like it was a joke, although I could tell it wasn't. It was fear cloaked in levity—which was why I had to go, to prove him wrong.

CHAPTER THIRTEEN

We were on the plane, headed for Chicago on Christmas Eve. It was crowded; shopping bags brimming with presents in shiny wraps of silver, gold, red, and green outnumbered the passengers. I had packed a linoleum block print of a Christmas tree and a framed sketch of Eric's torso for his parents.

I was excited about the trip, but Eric was uncharacteristically quiet, making me wonder if we were doing the right thing, making me nervous. We sat in one of the side rows, with three seats; an enormous man occupied the aisle seat, his breathing a musical whine.

'Will it be cold in Chicago?' I asked Eric.

'Probably.'

'I hope they like the presents I—'

'They will.' Eric looked out the window.

'We don't have to go, you know,' I said. I could feel the man on the aisle glance toward me and shift, reminding me we weren't alone.

'Don't you want to go?' Eric asked, looking at me.

'I think so.'

'You'll have a fine time, Al.' He kissed me on the forehead.

'But will you?'

'Sure.'

The plane began to taxi down the tarmac and it was suddenly too late to back up. 'Here we go,' I whispered, and Eric smiled, taking my hand in his.

About twenty minutes of silence passed between us while we took off and reached cruising altitude. Then I asked, 'What does your father think of the wizard?'

Eric looked at me, surprised. 'I don't know,' he said.

'You got a tattoo and he didn't have an opinion?'

'We never talked about it.'

'Are there other things you don't talk about?'

He didn't look uncomfortable or sad, just distant. 'Yes,' he finally said.

'You don't have to tell me,' I said, squeezing his hand.

He turned to face me and said, 'But I want to, Al.'

I waited.

He said, 'When I was little, my father boasted about me to his friends. He'd tell them about my batting average, my good grades, about how I was a miniature him.' He looked at me and smiled the faintest of smiles, then went on, his demeanor growing somber. 'I was twelve when he lost interest in me.'

'I don't believe that—'

'It's true. He stopped liking me.'

'That can't be.'

'But it is. And when I turned sixteen, I left home to go to college at Stanford. I've hardly seen him since then.'

'Did you ever ask him what was going on?'

'He refused to talk about it, and eventually I stopped telling him things.'

'Like about the tattoo?'

'Yeah, and about Tiffany, the blonde I met in New Orleans the summer after my freshman year in college. She was my first serious girl-friend.'

'You never brought her home, did you?'

'Never.'

'Why'd you break up with her?'

'I didn't. The truth is . . . well, it's awful.'

'What is it?'

'As awful as it is, it gave us pain in common, and neediness. I needed to save her; she needed unconditional love.'

'And you gave her that?'

'I tried.'

'What was the awful truth, Eric?'

'Her pappy fucked her.'

'What?'

'Fucked,' Eric repeated. 'She's dead now.'

'Dead? How?'

'She sucked the muzzle of a gun, like she was givin' it head. It came in her mouth.'

I gasped. He looked at me with his half-smile, but it was different than before, stretched to cover a profound anger and sorrow.

'It wasn't your fault,' I said.

'I know, but that doesn't keep me from feeling guilty.'

'Survivor's guilt.'

'Maybe. But I'm glad I survived to meet you.'

'Me too.'

We held hands for a moment; mine was sweaty, his dry and cool.

'So I guess your father doesn't know about any of that,' I said.

'I didn't want to give him any more reasons to dislike me.'

'He wouldn't have approved.'

'Not by a long shot.'

'Still, he's your father. He'll love you no matter what, Eric.'

'We don't talk about love much.'

'But he does love you.'

'I suppose.'

I could sense the large man listening to us, and it made me want to climb into Eric's lap and whisper with him. Then the drink cart came.

After a few minutes, the man said, 'Merry Christmas,' and raised his plastic glass as the flight attendant set two ice-filled glasses and two miniature bottles of Johnnie Walker Red in front of Eric and me.

'What?' I said, turning to look at the man, for the first time noticing him, his face, his eyes, something beyond his enormity.

'Merry Christmas,' Eric responded, raising his glass in return. 'Thanks for the drink.'

I looked between them, unsure, reluctant, when the man said, 'Sounded like you could use it.'

We laughed. He was a stranger, an eavesdropper, but a friendly one. 'Merry Christmas,' I murmured as I twisted the top off the tiny liquor bottle.

The drink would help chase away thoughts of Tiffany, incest, suicide and stern fathers, at least for a while, and I was grateful. As we flew, I fell asleep against Eric's shoulder, against the wizard.

We took a limo from the airport, courtesy of Eric's father, and thanked him by quietly making love in that spacious, dim backseat, on red velour. The driver didn't seem to notice, or if he did, we didn't notice him noticing. Merry Christmas.

The Moros' house was in a Northside suburb, a grand brick colonial draped in wreaths, bows, and holiday cheer, surrounded by exquisitely trimmed bushes covered by a dusting of snow. Shafts of yellow light split the darkness, spilling onto the lawn from sparkling windows.

We thanked the driver and got out. The air was a dry cold, still and quiet.

'Here we are,' Eric said, taking my face between his hands and kissing me on a different part of it as he spoke each word: 'I love you.' It was the first time he had said it to me. I kissed him greedily on the lips, wanting to make love again, right there on his parents' frozen yard. When I pulled back, anxious to respond in kind, he had turned away.

'Hello, Mama,' he said, waving.

Mrs. Moro was at the door, framed by light, a crisp green apron with red scalloped trim tied around her tiny waist, her black hair sprayed into submission. She waved back and called, 'Come in! It's cold.' She spoke without an Italian accent, having been born and raised in Chicago, but both her parents had immigrated from northern Italy, and, although she rarely spoke it now, Italian had been her first language.

'Mama, this is Alexandra Taylor,' Eric said as we approached the house. 'Alex, this is my mama, Patricia Moro.'

We shook hands. Her fingernails were manicured the same bright red of her apron trim. 'Nice to meet you, Mrs. Moro,' I said.

'The pleasure is all mine, dear,' she responded. 'How are you, Eric?'

'Fine, thank you, Mama.'

'Good.' They kissed each other's cheeks and we entered, with Mrs. Moro closing the front door behind us. 'Malcolm?' she called from the foyer as we shrugged off our coats.

Eric whispered, 'That's my father.'

We waited.

'Bro!' Eric exclaimed as a striking, dark-haired teenager came bounding up.

'Bro!' the young man responded. They hugged.

'Jerry, meet Alex Taylor,' Eric said. 'Alex, this is my kid brother, Jerry.'

'Hi,' I said.

'Hi,' he responded. Then, to Eric, 'Fox, bro, as usual.'

'Malcolm!' Mrs. Moro called. When there was no answer, she said, 'Jerry, go find your father,' and he ran off.

'Now,' Mrs. Moro said, 'let's get you kids settled.' She led the way up a flight of stairs; the carpet was beige, wall-to-wall. Eric carried our suitcases.

'Eric, dear,' she said, 'you're in your room, of course.' She switched on the light in a room we were passing, illuminating Eric's boyhood. It contained a single bed covered by a lime green bedspread with blue boats printed on it, a bulletin board meticulously arrayed with papers, and an assortment of models, toys, trophies, and books.

'And Alexandra,' Mrs. Moro said, continuing down the hall as we followed, 'you'll be in here, away from the boys.' She showed me into a girl's room, pink-white, frilly, and canopied in lace.

'This must be Pammy's room,' I said. Pammy was Eric's sister, twenty, now living in France.

'This is a guest room,' Mrs. Moro said.

'I trust you'll be comfortable here.'

'It's lovely,' I said, and went in to get unpacked and washed up. Eric set my suitcase on the bed and left. His mother followed him back to his room and then continued down the stairs.

After a few minutes, Eric joined me. 'Welcome home,' he said, closing the door and pinning me to the bed with his body. I giggled.

'I'd like to make this canopy shake, how 'bout you?' he asked.

'Your mom put us in separate rooms.'

He rolled onto his back and looked up. 'Catholic,' he said. 'What did you expect?'

'I didn't know you were Catholic.'

'I'm not.'

'But—'

'I was raised Catholic, that's all.'

There was a knock on the door, loud, impatient. Eric jumped up and cleared his throat. 'Come in,' he said, opening the door.

'Alexandra?' Mr. Moro asked. He was tall, his coloring darker than Eric's, and impressively handsome, heart-catchingly so. His voice was deep, his Italian accent faded, but present, arresting and exotic. I lost my breath for an instant.

'Yes?' I answered.

'Dad, this is—'

136

'Malcolm Moro,' Mr. Moro said, shaking my hand firmly. His suit was wool, blue pinstripe, and he smelled of aftershave mixed with tobacco, a hint of something murkier beneath, like back-room authority. 'Welcome to our home,' he added, then nodded to his son, and we followed as he led the way to dinner.

The Moro house did not look lived in; it was immaculately pale and neutral, with flawless country accents and tasteful holiday decor. It was difficult to imagine how three children had been raised there.

At dinner, Mr. Moro sat at the head of the table, serving onto plates that were passed around to the rest of us. We ate prime rib, baked potatoes, asparagus, and a mixed green salad in portions he deemed appropriate.

'Alexandra. You draw?' Mr. Moro asked.

'Yes, I do,' I said.

'And what is it that you draw, dear?' Mrs. Moro said.

I swallowed a mouthful of wine. Why had I never thought how to phrase it? Naked bodies? Nudes? Surface anatomy? 'Uh . . . I draw humans,' I said.

'Humans,' Mr. Moro mused, pausing in his serving to look at me thoughtfully. 'Well, that is quite interesting. Quite. We would love to see your work.' He went back to dishing and passing, something between a smile and a grimace twitching on his face.

I said, 'Did Eric tell you he's at the top of his class in—'

'Do you exhibit your work?' Mr. Moro asked me.

'No. I'm working on the illustrations for a book, an academic one.'

Mr. Moro nodded, finished serving, and the family bent their heads to pray. Jerry said grace. I was surprised to see Eric mouthing the words, after what he had said upstairs.

When the blessing was over and we raised our heads, I said, 'Mr. Moro, I understand you have an automotive business.'

'Yes, I built it myself, working my way up from nothing. I own a chain of stores now—'

'Moro's Automotive Parts,' Jerry said.

I nodded. Eric sliced his prime rib, began to eat.

'I worked hard,' Mr. Moro said. 'That's what it's all about. Work, work, and more work. The key to success. That and values.' He paused to chew, to savor his wine, and I saw him looking at Eric, almost disdainfully, while Eric studied his plate.

We continued eating. The conversation turned to my drawing again, my family, Philadelphia, the weather on the East Coast.

Soon dinner was over and Mrs. Moro began clearing.

'I'll help,' Eric volunteered.

'Sit down,' Mr. Moro said.

'Let me,' I said.

'If you'd like, Alexandra,' Mrs. Moro said.

While we cleaned the kitchen, I chatted with Mrs. Moro about her china and silver patterns, and after that about Chicago, Jerry, Eric. When I mentioned Pammy she changed the subject. We were finished in about forty-five minutes, and I went to the living room, expecting to see Eric there, talking with his father and brother by the fire, but he wasn't. Mr. Moro was alone, reading. He looked up when I entered.

'Where's Eric?' I asked, glancing at my watch.

'Upstairs, I believe. Come tell me how you became an artist.'

I sat down next to him and looked into the fire. He was drinking brandy or scotch, I couldn't tell which, and he periodically swirled his glass, causing the ice cubes to clink and glimmer in the firelight. We began to talk, and by the time I looked at my watch again, an hour had passed, with no sign of Eric.

'Well,' I said, 'I guess I'd better see if Eric—'

'Are you Catholic, Alexandra?'

'No.'

'But you will accompany us to Midnight Mass.'

'When?'

He laughed. It was like a gift, generous and warm, adding a twinkle to his handsome maturity and forcing a nervous laugh out of me. 'Tonight,' he said. 'Christmas Eve Midnight Mass is tonight.'

I nodded and stood.

'You'll learn,' he said.

'Thank you,' I mumbled, and turned toward the stairs, practically tripping over a lamp on the way.

Upstairs, I knocked on Eric's door and entered his room. He was lying belly-down on his bed, reading.

'Hi,' I said.

'Hey, darlin'. Come on in.'

I sat next to him and he turned onto his back, pulling me to him and kissing my eyes, my hair. 'My father corner you?' he asked.

I nodded. 'Where were *you*?'

'Right here.'

'And Jerry?'

'In his room, probably.'

'This is family togetherness?'

'I told you, we don't talk much.'

'Your father talked to me plenty.'

'I knew he'd love you. Why wouldn't he?' He began kissing my neck.

I pulled away. 'He's interested in me because of you,' I said.

'Did he bring up Midnight Mass?'

'Yes.'

'Did you tell him you'd go?'

'Not exactly, but we are going, aren't we?'

'Not me.'

'Why not?'

'I told you, Al, I'm not Catholic.'

'Me neither.'

'So don't go.'

'I think we should.'

'I'm not going.'

'We're visiting for the holidays. Can't you make some concessions?'

'You think that'd help?'

'I don't know, but why not humor him?'

'Freedom of religion.'

'God, Eric.'

'Exactly, Al.'

We left for Mass at eleven. Eric stayed at the house, while Jerry and I accompanied Mr. and Mrs. Moro. I made small talk and forced a smile as Mr. Moro drove the large blue

Mercedes to the church, but I felt off-balance, thrown sideways by Eric's uncharacteristic hardheadedness.

The cathedral was radiant. Tremendous stained-glass windows lit brilliantly from behind—topaz, aquamarine, blood orange—towered over our heads. Bundles of fragrant evergreen looped by stiff red velvet ribbons festooned the pews. Candles, opaque white with purity, flickered in front of the altar and at the side chapels, where statues of saints and the Virgin Mary smiled benignly in their recessed havens. Near the altar was a nativity scene. Poinsettias, a sea of bold red punctuated by white, erupted from around the altar and the sides of the pews.

The enormous space was choked with parishioners. They genuflected before entering the pews, bowing their heads slightly and making the sign of the cross, mumbling, 'In the name of the Father, and of the Son, and of the Holy Ghost,' and although they were reverent, dressed formally, they smiled, even waved, in what appeared to be a vast outpouring of community spirit and goodwill. For those rare moments we were urban strangers, cocooned into one beneath arched ceilings, embraced by massive architecture, dramatic history, and near oppressive beauty. For that instant, we represented a single pinnacle of faith and hope, raising a collective voice to God in song.

When the caroling ceased, a priest with a bare, shining head and layers of white brocade robes bordered in gold began to speak. He uttered words startling in their simplicity and depth, extolling the birth of the son of God, celebrating his coming to save man from his sins, his timeless legacy of mercy, charity, and grace. But above all, the priest spoke of love, a love that by Jesus' life, death, and resurrection, he had bestowed upon humankind as its savior for all eternity, a love far beyond the reaches of human comprehension, a love worthy of every sacrifice.

The ride home was quiet. For me, silence was the product of fatigue, tinged with awe. For the others, I could only guess. We reached the house, exchanged our 'good nights,' our 'Merry Christmases,' and climbed the stairs to bed. When I passed Eric's room, the door was closed and it was dark; I didn't knock.

Eric came to me early Christmas morning, before anyone else was up. He knelt by the side of my bed and kissed my hand, still limp with sleep.

'Merry Christmas,' he said when I opened my eyes.

'Merry Christmas, love,' I murmured.

'Are you Catholic yet?' he asked.

I smiled. 'Can they do that without your knowing?'

'You'd be amazed at what they can do.'

I propped myself up on an elbow and looked at him. 'I wanted you with me last night,' I said.

'You should've come into my room.'

'I meant at Mass.'

'Oh.'

'It was so beautiful, Eric.'

'The service?'

'The cathedral, the spirit.'

'I remember that.'

'Will you try again with your parents?'

'About the Catholic thing?'

'About everything. None of you are trying for family cohesiveness.'

'Maybe we're not capable of it.'

'Maybe not, but you're capable of more than this.'

'I love them, whether I show it or not. They know that.'

'Are you sure?'

'Of course.'

I sat up and took both of his hands in mine; they were warm and smooth. I turned them palm up and looked at them. 'Please,' I whispered, 'tell them.'

'That I love them?' He pulled away and stood up. I rose and held him.

'Eric, it's Christmas.'

'It is.'

We kissed, our mouths sticky from early morning awakening. We walked downstairs.

Eric made us cocoa with mini-marshmallows, and we settled into the breakfast-nook window seat to watch the sun rise. The sphere was practically colorless as it edged over the frigid green-gray water of Lake Michigan.

'Do you want your present now?' Eric asked.

I nodded and he handed me an envelope, which I opened. 'Plane tickets?' I said.

'We leave tomorrow morning.'

'Eric!' I grabbed him around the neck and kissed him. 'This is perfect. Thank you.'

He laughed and tickled me. 'New Mexico, darlin'. Skiing at Taos.'

'But I don't have any equipment.'

'We'll rent.'

'Won't your parents be disappointed that we're leaving so soon?'

'They've known all along we'd only be here for two days. I told you we were staying longer to surprise you about the trip to New Mexico.'

'A whole week?'

'A whole week in Taos with my baby. I've got the best life in the world.'

'No, I do.'

'Good morning, children.' We looked up; it was Mrs. Moro. 'Did you sleep well?' she asked. 'Did you sleep?'

'Yes, thank you,' I said.

'Merry Christmas, Mama,' Eric said.

'Merry Christmas, dear. Get your brother.'

Eric stood and headed for the stairs.

After breakfast, we gathered around the tree, coffee mugs held on our laps, sedately opening presents, the way adults do, without joy, without anticipation. Eric's parents gave me a nightgown, a pair of gold, heart-shaped earrings, and note cards with cats on them. I suspected his mother had done the shopping. Eric received new skis and boots, a ski jacket, and what was for him a lifetime supply of underwear and socks.

Finally, only the gifts from me to Mr. and Mrs. Moro remained unopened. 'Here,' I said, handing his mother the print and his father the sketch.

'Thank you,' they said, practically in unison.

Mrs. Moro opened her present. 'Will you

look at that!' she exclaimed. 'It's a Christmas tree.'

'Beautiful,' Mr. Moro said, taking it from her and examining it. 'How is it done, linoleum block?'

'Yes,' I said.

'Exquisite.'

'Thank you.'

'Shall I open mine now?' Mr. Moro asked.

I nodded. He unwrapped the package and looked at the sketch, at first unsure, examining, appraising.

'It's me,' Eric said.

Mr. Moro's jaw tensed and he mumbled, 'Um-hmm, very good.' He placed the framed sketch on the floor near his chair and stood. Everyone was quiet. 'I almost forgot my gift to Alexandra,' he said, walking around to the far side of the tree. He reached under it, emerging with a rectangular package, obviously wrapped by an upscale store, and handed it to me.

'Thank you,' I said, accepting it and glancing at Eric, who smiled. I started to unwrap it carefully, preserving the elegant silver bow, when we heard it, a sharp crack that could mean only one thing: broken glass. The sketch of Eric's torso, my gift to his father, was shattered, stepped on by a paternal foot in an Oxford shoe.

We all watched as Mr. Moro stooped to pick it up.

'Oops,' he said.

'It can be re-framed,' I said quickly, my heart pounding.

'It's ripped,' Mr. Moro said. He handed it to me.

I took it gently, the black wooden frame splintered, the glass in a starburst of shards, one clear stiletto slicing the drawing through the upper chest.

'I'll draw another,' I said.

'Open your gift,' Mrs. Moro urged.

I lay the ruined sketch by my side and opened Mr. Moro's gift to me. Inside lay a leather case of impeccable design, housing a set of the best drawing pencils money could buy. I was speechless; never before had I owned materials of such quality, such perfection. I looked up at Mr. Moro and we shared a smile. Then I reached for Eric's hand and turned to him, consumed by delight and possibilities. What I saw wiped the smile from my face, the laughter from my heart; I had never seen him so sad.

It was early afternoon by the time Eric and I escaped to his room. We sat on the bed and he started kissing me, snaking his cool hand under my blouse, over my breast. I gently pushed him away.

'Are you okay?' I asked.

'Sure. Why?'

'It's been hard for you coming here, hasn't it?'

'It's okay.'

'Quit being brave. I saw how you looked downstairs when we were opening presents.'

'I got some good shit.'

'Eric, stop it.'

He sighed. 'What do you want, Al?'

'The truth.'

'I thought they taught you that in church last night.'

'Why are you acting this way? Ever since we arrived here you've been avoiding real conversations with me. I feel like we're so separate. '

'I'm sorry.' He put his arm around me and pulled me close. 'I didn't mean to do that.'

'Why were you sad downstairs?'

'It doesn't matter.'

'It does to me.'

'I can't talk to him,' he said, standing and beginning to pace. 'I was thinking about what you said about family togetherness and I was trying to make it that way. But it just doesn't fit.'

'I can help you,' I said.

He stopped and looked at me, walked over to the bed and knelt before me, taking both my hands and kissing them. 'You have, Al,' he said. 'You mean so much to me. I love you.'

'And I love you. But I mean I can help you with this, with them.'

'He doesn't listen, he turns away . . . I love him, though. I can't help but respect him.'

'You want him to like you, Eric. That's not so hard to understand.'

'But he doesn't seem to like who I am.'

'Maybe that's because you haven't shown him you.'

'You mean I should tell him the stuff I've done?'

'No. Just be Eric. Be the Eric I love.'

He looked skeptical.

I said, 'I have an idea. After Christmas dinner, we'll sit in the living room and talk. We'll all be there so there won't be any pressure on just you two. Then, when you say good night, you can tell them.'

'Tell them?'

'Like this: "Good night, Mom. Good night, Dad. I love you."'

'Okay . . . if that's what you want.'

'I want you to be happy. I want us to be a family.'

'So do I.'

'Good.'

He sat next to me and for many minutes we remained like that, side by side, silent.

Christmas dinner was rich, delicious, and filling. The red wine made me talkative, fuzzy, hazing both my surroundings and the passage of time. Looking back, I realized Mr. Moro and I did most of the talking.

After dinner, Jerry suggested a game of Scrabble, which they played well. Apparently, they'd done it a lot. They laughed, they argued; through the front window they would have looked like a normal, happy family. The game lasted two hours. Mr. Moro won.

'That was great fun,' Mrs. Moro said as she and Jerry put the game away.

I glanced at Eric. He nodded and said, 'Dad, you doing any ice fishing this year?'

His father looked at him, surprised. 'I haven't been ice fishing in five years.'

'Oh.'

'Why not?' I asked.

'Too much trouble for just some old fish you could buy in a grocery store.'

There was a pause, then Eric said, 'I really think surgery will be right for me.'

'I would hope so, after all the effort I've made on your behalf,' Mr. Moro responded.

Jerry got up from his chair. 'Good night, you guys,' he said.

'Good night,' we all said. He headed for the stairs and disappeared. We listened to his footsteps on the carpet.

My heart pounded, my palms grew sticky, as Mr. and Mrs. Moro stood, ready to retire for the night.

Eric rose. 'Good night, Mama,' he said.

'Good night, dear.'

'Good night, Dad.'

'Good night.'

Mr. and Mrs. Moro started for the stairs. I looked at Eric; he was staring after them.

'I love you,' he said. I heard it, clear and even, three syllables representing a courage that brought tears to my eyes.

His mother turned slowly and said, 'Of course, dear,' then turned back to the stairs. His father kept walking.

I whispered, 'He didn't hear you, Eric. Go after him.'

Eric walked toward the stairs, toward his father's back, and his look was one of determination and pain. He stood at the bottom of the staircase and said, 'I love you, Dad,' loud enough for anyone to hear. I couldn't see Mr.

Moro, but I could see Eric's face and it told me what I feared most: Mr. Moro had not looked back.

I watched as Eric reached into the hall closet and put on his jacket, his hat and gloves, and walked out the front door. I jumped up. 'Eric!' I called, grabbing my own coat and following him. He was walking slowly down the driveway, staring up at gray smudges of clouds against velvet midnight, a Christmas sky.

'Hey,' I said, catching up to him.

'That felt shitty.'

'I know.' I bit my lip in an effort not to cry, but the tears ignored my will and began to flow. 'I love you,' I said, embracing him.

'Let's walk,' he responded.

'Okay.'

'When I was a kid, I used to walk along the lake at night in winter. It's got a certain feel.'

We arrived at the shore and I knew what he meant. The lake's darkness was cold, yet vital, harboring life, undulating and constant. The wind against our faces was biting and harsh, but it dried my tears.

'I'm sorry,' I said.

He smiled and took my hand as we began to stroll along the shore. 'Don't be,' he said. 'I meant what I said. I do love him.'

'He loves you too, Eric, I know he does. It's just hard for him to say it. Some people are like that.'

'It's hard for him to show it, too.'

'Maybe he shows it by giving you money.'

'But he doesn't.'

'I saw the gifts they gave you.'

'I let them give me gifts, but not money, not since I was twenty. I need my independence.'

I nodded.

'I pay for trips, school, everything, with money from work and loans, or shit I've pawned.'

'I didn't know.'

'It's not important. Are you cold?'

'No. You?'

'No.'

'I was wrong to pressure you to come here for Christmas,' I said.

'I decided we should come.'

'But you'd rather have stayed in Philly.'

'They're my parents, Al. But it isn't always easy.'

'I can see that.'

'And I wasn't sure what you'd think of all this.'

'I think it's amazing you love your father like you do.'

'Really?'

'He's not exactly warm and affectionate toward you.'

He stopped walking and I turned to face him. We stood staring at each other under the shifting silver-white moonlight.

'You're right,' he said, 'and he hasn't been for a long time. But look at how strong he is. I admire him. And I want him to admire me, the way he used to.'

'When you were a kid playing Little League?'

'Back then he was more affectionate. I told you he has high expectations—I just haven't met them.'

'Why should you have to?'

'I want to, Al. Maybe you can't see it, but he's a compassionate man. He knows what it's like to suffer, to inch your way up from the bottom. You don't know this, but every Christmas he gives ten thousand dollars through the church to support shelters for the homeless, toys for poor kids, stuff like that. I grew up seeing his generosity.'

'But not receiving it,' I said softly.

He took both my hands in his and kissed them gently, avoiding meeting my eyes. Still, his shone with tears as we turned and headed back. I had known Eric for only a short time, attracted by his easy laugh and smooth body, intrigued by his sensitive intelligence and fondness for games, his irresistible charm and radiance. But as we walked, I glimpsed a different part of him, a place where a sad, confused little boy lived, a little boy who felt true love for a father he honored but could not reach.

I wouldn't know until much later the unfathomable horror that had produced such sadness and alienation, and even then, it would not come from Eric's lips.

I slept little that night. Eric and I had snuggled into his bed until early in the morning, when I had arisen quietly and left for my room, only to toss and turn, trying to untangle the mysteries that entrapped this family.

I waited until a reasonable hour, about six, before heading down to the kitchen for coffee. Mr. Moro was already there, pouring a cup for himself, the *Tribune* under his arm. It was too late to back up; he had seen me.

'Good morning,' I said cheerfully.

'Morning,' he responded.

'Just getting a cup of coffee.'

'I see.' He remained standing between me and the coffeemaker. Then he set his coffee mug and newspaper on the counter, crossed his arms, and said in a deep, level voice, 'Tell me you did not commit an act of sin with my son last night.'

'Excuse me?'

'An act of sin, young lady, is to have sexual relations with an individual who is not your husband.'

'Oh.'

'Tell me this did not happen in my house, that you did not betray my trust, God's trust.'

'Uh . . . uh . . . ' I could feel shame heat my face as he glared at me with eyes fiercely black. 'Uh . . . no,' I stammered.

'It is a sin to lie,' he said.

'I know . . . I know that, sir. I'm telling the truth. No, we didn't betray your trust.'

'Good. God sees the truth.' He picked up his cup and his newspaper and left for the living room.

I gasped for air and leaned against the counter, my armpits suddenly slippery with sweat. 'Shit,' I said softly to myself, and wondered what I would have told him if 'yes' had been the true answer.

I didn't want to walk by Mr. Moro to go upstairs, so I stayed in the breakfast nook until Mrs. Moro arrived in the kitchen at seven. Then I excused myself and hurried away to plunge into a very long, very hot shower.

Eric and I left at ten-thirty, after breakfast, without much fanfare, just 'good-byes' and a few scattered 'thank yous.'

We took a cab to the airport, relieved to be alone. I didn't tell Eric about the episode with his father that morning. They seemed to be in equilibrium, and troubled balance though it was, I didn't want to tip it by crossing Eric's loyalties.

After about fifteen minutes of silence, Eric asked, 'So, what'd you think of my family?'

'It's complicated,' I said.

He smiled. 'All families are.'

I smiled back and shook my head. 'Not like yours, Eric. Not like yours.'

'Not like mine,' he agreed. He kissed me, easing the taste of apprehension and exhaustion from my lips, and arousing that inexhaustible craving that only he could fill.

After Chicago, and seeing Eric with his family, New Mexico was like bright air, and each mile we crossed toward Taos served to diminish a bit of the disquietude that had seeped into that Christmas Eve and Day.

We stayed at the bottom of the mountain in a hotel that was luxurious in a southwestern way. It must've cost a fortune.

'What did you pawn?' I asked after the bellhop left.

Eric winked. 'You like it?'

'I've never stayed in a place like this.'

'It's about time you did.'

'But the money—'

'Forget it.'

'Okay.'

He lay back on the bed. 'Shall we . . . '

'I have a present for you, Eric. I didn't want to give it to you in front of your parents. Here.' I handed him a box. I had wrapped it in scraps from sketches I had made.

He sat up, took the box, and opened it, smiling radiantly when he saw what it was. 'Shadow Blaster!' he exclaimed. I had built a replica, a model that I had had to piece together from several sets, his bike was so, well, unique. 'I love it,' he said. 'It's the best present ever. Thank you.' I smiled. He kissed me.

'I have another gift for you,' I said, 'but I have to give it to you when we get home. And not right away.'

'What is it?'

'That ride I never promised you. In a plane.'

'Really?'

'I'm taking flying lessons as soon as the weather's better.'

'That's fantastic.' He kissed me again, still

holding the little Shadow Blaster. 'Life is great, isn't it?' he asked.

I kissed him back and began to unbutton his shirt. I didn't answer, but I didn't have to. We both knew: it was.

Eric was a dynamite skier, miles above my level, but he stuck with me, grinning at my ill-matched secondhand ski clothes that were constantly covered with snow from my most recent tumble. I wasn't terrible, I had skied before, but I was trying to stretch beyond my skill, which left me on the ground most of the time.

At the end of our last day skiing, we met at the bottom of the mountain.

'One last run?' he asked.

'Do we have time?'

'A minute, hurry.'

We scurried to the lift just as they were pulling the rope across the line.

'Sorry, dude, we're closed for the day,' the lift operator said. Eric looked at him and nodded with a smile, but as we started to turn around, the guy beckoned us back and let us pass.

'Thanks, dude,' Eric said as we got on the

near-empty lift. The operator waved a gloved hand.

Halfway up the mountain, Eric turned to me and said, 'Now for flying,' and jumped off the lift.

I almost screamed until I saw how close we were to the ground, about four feet, and that he had landed okay, laughing. Then, against all my better judgment, I joined him, briefly 'flying' and landing a short distance from him. The trip down was great fun, almost worth the broken ankle.

CHAPTER FOURTEEN

By June, Eric's first year of medical school was finished and my ankle was healed. I had started flight school, which stretched my budget no end, forcing me to increase my teaching duties, do more freelance projects, and begin a waitress job that paid better than the other two combined. Meanwhile, Eric toiled in a surgery research lab at the university. On weekends we were let loose, I with ten paint-splattering teenagers, and Eric as a Little League coach.

The summer months that first year with Eric were characteristically blistering, and we rarely made love indoors. Sometimes it was grass, or sand, or asphalt beneath us, sometimes a rubber-bellied swing in an abandoned playground, but always with the dark and windy sky above us, nature to nature. The heat was close and dense, wetter than lust; wrapped in it we tensed and strained against, and finally with, our desire.

In August, we escaped for a week to Cape May, where New Jersey extends itself in a final southern stretch, cleaving the Delaware Bay from the ocean. There we baked on the sand, sticky with salt from the sea and ourselves, slick together, with humidity curling our hair. The Atlantic Ocean spun a breeze in the evenings as we walked along the boardwalk, hands linked, our faces shiny and pink-hot. As I think of Eric, I remember mostly those times, like our last days of childhood, before crushing responsibility and realism came to roost.

One evening, after playing idiot video games for hours following a cheap fish dinner, we decided to go down to the beach for a midnight swim. It wasn't allowed, so we stripped out of sight, near a rough cement and rock breakwater, our bodies suddenly white contrasts to the night. It was cool in the water, darkly mysterious and sensuous. Predictably, we ended up on the beach, in the posture of a million romantic movies, with sandpaper knees and elbows, and passion easing the grittiness of our efforts.

It wasn't until after we were finished making

love that Eric saw him, the man in the water. Instinctively, I grabbed my top, and just as instinctively, Eric ran, naked, to drag the man onto the sand. Eric started CPR; my heart bumped in my throat.

'Get help!' Eric shouted as he pumped on the man's chest. I plucked my shorts from the sand and ran, pulling them on and stumbling along the way. Back at the video arcade, the proprietor called an ambulance as I bolted back to Eric. He was still at it, alternately breathing into the man's mouth and heaving on his chest; the victim looked about eighteen.

'They're coming,' I said. 'Can I help?'

'Signal them,' he said, puff, puff, 'when they come,' pump, pump, pump, and I was off again.

When I came back with the ambulance crew, lurching over the sand with their stretcher and emergency box, I saw two silhouettes against the beach.

'Eric!' I yelled.

He waved. 'Here!'

We approached and Eric stood, talking softly but quickly with the paramedics. As he did, I watched the young man lying on his side on the sand; I could hear his sputtering breath. Then, abruptly, we left, just walked away, to gather the remainder of our clothes.

'That was dramatic,' I commented as we headed back toward our hotel.

'He lived,' Eric said.

'You saved him. Take some credit.'

'I don't want credit.'

We had reached the hotel, newly painted turquoise for the season; its neon sign blinked a bright orange over us. I sighed and we went inside, to sleep against rough hotel sheets, our bodies softening their anonymity for a night.

Our morning started the next day around noon, in a restaurant serving thin coffee in thick cups, slimy eggs with crunchy hash browns and toast, already buttered from the kitchen.

I was sunburned, so I stayed under an umbrella when we finally landed on the beach. There I read a fat paperback and watched as Eric played volleyball with an assortment of tanned, casually muscled teens.

When they broke, allowing other youngsters to play, Eric joined me on our towel, his skin glossy with sweat, combing his wet hair back from his face with his fingers.

'Hi, darlin',' he said, collapsing on his back and squinting skyward. 'Look.' He pointed.

I glanced up. The blue and white sky read 'I LOVE YOU' in puffy letters that threatened to dissolve before the last word was yet written, the name 'TARA.'

'I wish I'd thought of that,' Eric said.

'I've thought about it,' I said.

'I've heard it's expensive.'

'I mean doing it. For a living.'

'Now, that's a career.'

I scanned him for signs of sarcasm, but there were none. We studied the air above us, the first three letters already gone to the atmosphere. It seemed such a frivolous thing. 'I LOVE YOU' quickly dissipated, like so many things that should be permanent, like goals, futures, plans.

'It's kind of the opposite of a tattoo,' I said.

'I think it's like a tattoo,' he said, 'memorable to those it affects directly. If someone wrote to you in the sky, don't you think you'd remember it?'

'Yes.'

'And if your name was in a tattoo . . .'

I laughed. 'I'd remember it.'

We looked up, shading our eyes with our hands, watching 'I LOVE YOU' disappear.

Although we never talked about it, every day after that I waited for the tattoo with my name, while Eric searched for his message in the sky.

CHAPTER FIFTEEN

Eric was a couple months into his second year of medical school when we moved into a new apartment together, consolidating our meager belongings.

Two weeks later I took him flying. I had my pilot's license and a little confidence, so into the sharpness of a blue autumn Sunday we blasted on his bike, heading for Alta, a small airport west of the city.

As I inspected the outside of the flight-school rental plane, doing my preflight, Eric trailed me. Then he followed me inside the cockpit, where I went over my list, checking and rechecking, listening to static bits of language from the radio.

'Here's your headset,' I said, handing it to

him. 'So we can talk. But don't press that button, that's to the tower.'

'Okay, captain,' he said, putting the headset on and trying it out. 'Hey, darlin',' came a metallic whisper into my ear.

'Hey,' I answered.

Then I spoke to the tower: 'Alta tower, Cessna zero-four-five fox-trot requesting taxi from northeast parking with information victor.'

'Cessna zero-four-five fox-trot cleared to the active, winds two-seventy at five. Contact departure one-twenty-two point seven. Good day.'

'Thanks. Good day, four-five fox-trot.'

Within minutes we were airborne, our stomachs lifting, the power of soaring held between my small hands. The first time I had flown, with my instructor beside me, was like a sudden sucking, a visceral paradox of surging force and absence of solid earth, maneuvering along currents of air rather than road. Even then I had longed to dip and twirl, defy and test, twist my name and triumph across the sky.

'Can I talk to you now?' Eric asked.

'Sure,' I said.

'Look at the trees, Al, the colors.'

'I know.' I looked out to my left and down: shades of green, orange, red, slick yellow. Eric loved summer, the sizzling heat forcing everything to the surface, but autumn was my favorite. It wasn't just beautiful, it was hope: the plants blazing and then folding for the winter, unafraid, confident of spring and rebirth, like the young. Like us.

'Let's fly over Cape May,' I said. 'We can see where we stayed last summer.'

'Can we go that far?'

'We're in a plane.'

'Right. Amazing.'

We flew over the beach where we'd made love, run, swum, and frolicked. The air was cold, but the brilliant sun and our distance disguised that, the lateness of the season betrayed only by the strand of hibernating hotels and the boardwalk, shuttered for the winter. We soared out over the water, choppy indigo laced by pearls of white foam.

'We should come back here,' Eric said.

'We will.'

'I mean soon, like next weekend.'

'It's closed.'

'A couple hotels stay open all year.'

'But it's cold.'

He was silent and I looked at him. He winked, making me remember our walk along Lake Michigan at his parents' the Christmas before, the icy darkness, beauty frozen.

'Okay,' I said, smiling. 'Next weekend.'

I dipped the plane low, then up and around, back toward the city, going home. He threw up as we turned, twice, into an airsickness bag.

'Are you okay?' I asked.

He nodded. I handed him a plastic bottle of water; he drank deeply, then said, 'That didn't have anything to do with your flying.'

'Are you sure?'

'Helicopters sometimes do that to me, too.'

'Sorry.'

'Don't be,' he said. 'I wouldn't have missed this. My stomach will learn to adjust.'

I took the landing slowly, as gently as I could, sensing Eric's fragility for the first time.

CHAPTER SIXTEEN

Our plan was to take a rental plane to Cape May the following weekend. Despite his queasiness, Eric loved to fly, especially with me. But thunderstorms loomed, so we borrowed a car.

'Are you sure this is the best weekend to go?' I asked as we packed on Friday afternoon.

'Why not?'

'It's going to pour.'

'I know, but this is what we planned.'

'We could go next—'

'No, we need to go this weekend.'

'Okay,' I agreed, wondering. He was rarely so adamant.

My poverty meant I was poorly prepared for weather, the requirement for the big-ticket items like good boots and raincoats beyond me, and cheaper things, umbrellas and galoshes, bought but forever missing. So I packed canvas sneakers and big plastic garbage bags, relieved we weren't camping.

The traffic out of the city was thick, and the storm hit on the way, so we didn't arrive at our hotel until after dark. It was away from the beach, forlorn and drenched. We were the only occupants.

The rain hadn't gotten Eric down; he had chattered continuously on the way and was wide awake when we got to our destination. I flopped face down on the bed.

'Let's go for a walk!' he said.

'What?'

'A walk. Come on.' He put on his slicker and waited for me to move.

'Eric, it's dark.'

'Darlin', it's life.'

I hesitated, but he had that wonderful half-smile on his face, so I dragged myself up, put a garbage bag over my head, and ripped holes for my arms and face. 'I love you,' he said.

'I love you,' I answered.

It was the kind of coastal rain that exerts pressure, making your head ache. And the noise; we could barely hear each other over the liquid hammering that surrounded us. The beach was barely visible, its only illumination the faint glow from scattered streetlights. Still, Eric's dancing laughter was infectious, lifting me out of physical discomfort and into joy. We ran along the sand, stumbling and giggling, to the spot where we had made love the summer before.

Eric had stopped walking but was still beside me when I bumped into something solid. It was a man. He stood shivering in a dripping tuxedo, his hair running with water. But odd beyond words was what he carried atop one hand, like a waiter: an exquisite silver filigree tray, over-flowing with rainwater.

'Eric!' he yelled, and I turned to see Eric, now behind me, laughing. I looked back to the man and realized he was there for us.

Suddenly, Eric was kneeling before me in the sand, blinking his eyes against the rain, my black garbage bag whipping about him in the wind, and he said something.

'What?' I said, bending down.

'Will you marry me?' he yelled.

'Marry?' I asked.

'Yes,' he said, and his smile was like sunshine soaked in rain, a human rainbow.

'Yes,' I said, and started to cry. 'Yes.' I said it softly, but he knew, and we stood.

The man in the tuxedo had bent over us,

straining to hear, and as I stood, my head knocked the tray from his hand. It landed upside down in the sand. 'The ring!' he cried and stooped quickly to retrieve it, scrabbling in the wet sand. We dug for a while, but it was hopeless, the storm and darkness combining like midnight over our eyes.

Finally, Eric thanked the man, who turned out to be a friend from school named Ray, and we walked him to his car. We invited him to stay the night, to at least take a hot shower, but he refused, assuring us he had dry clothes in the car, and telling us he needed to get back. We waved until his headlights were out of sight, then headed back to our hotel.

'The ring,' I said, shaking my head.

'Maybe we'll find it tomorrow,' Eric said.

'What'd it look like?'

'It was just a thin gold band, no jewels.'

'But beautiful.'

'I had it engraved. It said "Together Forever."'

'Eric . . . ' We stopped walking and faced each other in the white–blue glow of a drowning streetlight.

'It's true, isn't it, Al?' he asked.

'Yes,' I breathed, 'even if we never find the ring.'

We didn't.

*   *   *

It poured the rest of the weekend, solid walls of rain, blasting sideways with gusts of wind off the ocean. We walked, ate, played, stayed in bed a lot, and a couple of times went and tried to find the ring. But daylight was gray with rain, and the tide had come and gone, like an eraser on the sand. Still, we were right. 'Together Forever' was ours, with or without the ring.

Back then, we thought we knew what forever meant.

CHAPTER SEVENTEEN

We celebrated Christmas Eve that year at my family's house. Eric had arrived before me.

'I'm here!' I yelled, slamming the door behind me and kicking off my shoes.

'In the kitchen!' Mom called.

'Hi,' I said, sliding over the linoleum in my socks.

'Hi, sweetie,' Mom answered. 'Merry Christmas.'

'Merry Christmas. Where's Eric?'

'Downstairs with Daddy.'

I started down the stairs. I heard Daddy and Eric talking before I rounded the corner to Daddy's studio, where he did his drawing, sketching cartoons.

'Milt, this is the greatest, the one with the egg,' Eric said.

'You like that?'

'Uh-huh. Look.'

I peeked around the corner; their backs were to me and I watched as Eric drew something for Daddy. It took him a few seconds, then they howled.

'Hey,' I said, approaching. They turned.

'Darlin'.'

'Sweetie.'

I came forward, wedging myself between their shoulders, and looked. The table was scattered with their efforts, some mere scribbles, others more detailed.

'I didn't know you could draw, Eric,' I said.

'You still don't,' he responded with a laugh.

'He's good,' Daddy said, standing and stretching. 'I'd better get cleaned up for supper.' He kissed me on the cheek and smiled before disappearing up the stairs.

'Sit down,' Eric said.

I sat in Daddy's chair and Eric and I kissed, long and luscious. When we paused to breathe, I looked down at the sketches they had made. 'I've never seen you draw,' I said.

'I don't do it often.'

'You're good, Eric.'

He shrugged.

'You could've been an artist,' I said.

'My father would never have allowed it.'

'How could he stop you?'

'He disapproved. That was enough.'

I watched him; his eyes were sadder than I'd seen since his father had given me that exquisite set of drawing pencils the Christmas before. It was only now, a year later, that I understood the tip of that sadness, born from years of wishing for such a gift from the man he most admired, the gift of permission to be simply who he was.

We were quiet as I looked over the drawings, suddenly recognizing something in them. 'The wizard,' I said. 'You drew it, not Tiffany.'

'You're right. But she was with me when I got the tattoo.'

'The wizard's the art your father didn't allow.'

'Yes.' He paused. 'But I wouldn't trade being a doctor, Al. I'm thinking about becoming a plastic surgeon.'

'And doing face-lifts?'

He laughed, cupping my chin in his strong, slender hand; its softness always surprised me. 'Not cosmetic surgery,' he said, 'reconstructive. Like patching burn victims together and repairing kids' faces, things like that.'

I nodded; it was closer to art than skywriting. He kissed me, his lips warm, and we walked upstairs hand in hand, into the bosom of Christmas.

Later I cursed myself for not saving even one of those drawings. But then I thought there'd be so many more.

Eric and I slept by the fireplace that night, exploring the newness of each other's skin by firelight, the Christmas tree shimmering silver in the darkness. We played a game with our fingers, never lifting them off the other's body, yet not missing an inch, not speaking a word, nor moving in response, except to turn as a hand crept over the edge of a belly or back. It took Eric fifteen minutes to make me crazy enough to beg for orgasm. I never got him to.

'Haven't you had enough?' I whispered, licking the inside of his ear. His body was still, but the effort that took flickered across his face and his breath came swift and warm.

He shook his head gently. 'Give me more.'

I did, with fingers, lips, and tongue, picking the spots I knew would produce the most intense response: behind his knees, between his toes, at the top of his neck, along his lower spine and that soft area just above his scrotum. I made progress, I even got a moan out of him, but he didn't give in, even after an hour. Finally, I took him in my mouth and watched as he delivered himself to me.

As always, delicious.

CHAPTER EIGHTEEN

Eric and I had announced our engagement to my family at Christmas, but my little sister, Linda, married first, on the following April 28, a Saturday.

The wedding was black tie at the Plaza in New York, and I was the maid of honor. Linda and I were sisters that day in the best sense of the word, wanting for the other what we ourselves had: happiness, joy, love, futures with brilliant careers and a pack of smiling, messy-faced children fathered by handsome, fruitful husbands.

Eric was in the wedding party, trimly handsome in his black tuxedo. He watched me coming down the aisle, and his face glowed, as if I were the bride and he and I were alone in that vast, crowded hall. It would be an hour before we could talk, kiss, or laugh, and in that hour my little sister became a wife.

Eric and I danced every dance that night, except when he took me by the hand and said, 'Come on.' I followed him through lobbies and hallways, up a staircase. It was metal, and the openings in its grating kept catching my heels, spiraling their silk-satin coverings.

'Here,' Eric said, reaching a hand back to help me over the lip of a doorway.

'Wow!' I exclaimed. We were on the roof.

We walked over tar paper and pebbles to the edge, bordered by a short wrought-iron fence. Below, darkness and distance had thrown a blanket over New York's big-city grime, leaving glitter, brass, and diamonds twinkling through.

We looked at each other and smiled. Then we danced, me in floor-length peach taffeta, he in a rented black tux beneath which the wizard burned. We made love on the exposed roughness of that space, with cool New York on my back, and warm Eric against my belly.

When we were done, we stood and started toward the door to the stairs. But before we descended, I turned, flinging my shoes, one by one, to the adjacent rooftop.

That was the only time I remember seeing

Eric stunned, if briefly; then he laughed. I shrugged, and we started down the stairs.

I can't say why I did it. Maybe it was in the name of freedom, or as a memorial to our love; certainly it was a whim. But I sometimes wonder if those peach dyed-satin pumps are still there, and if anyone has seen them and wondered too.

No one at the reception noticed my bare feet.

CHAPTER NINETEEN

After I obtained my commercial flying license that spring, I was screened, along with about one thousand other applicants, to see if I was a precise enough flyer to become a skywriter. It amazed me that I was, and my two-month apprenticeship began. As it turned out, skywriting was taught by the oral tradition, handed down carefully, from one pilot to another, and even then, reluctantly.

My instructor, Joey, wasn't much older than I was, but he'd been flying since his thirteenth birthday.

'This is the plane you'll be flying,' he told me on my first day, pointing to a biplane with an open cockpit.

'This?' I asked, with a hint of shock in my

voice. The machine was beautiful, but ancient.

'Something wrong?' he asked.

'This thing's older than my daddy.'

'Then be good to it,' he said, patting its side.

I nodded and listened as Joey explained about the lightweight oil that I would load into the tank in the plane, how it was fed into the exhaust, heated by the large radial engine to become vapor, vapor transformed into words, words into money. We spent hours hovering over letters inscribed into the dirt and onto paper on the ground, rehearsing and timing the moves, using my body as the plane, pretending to soar a mile straight before turning sharply into a curve, timing it by counting the seconds, pulling hard against a drive that wanted to force me straight, always straight. He explained that I would lay the letters down flat in the sky, tilted to readability by the earth-bound viewer's angle and the universe's space.

Joey took me up in the old plane and I practiced what I'd done on the ground, squeezing the trigger on my control stick to release the oil, seeing only smoke behind, the letters mere puffs of white by landing time. Mr. Rig, our boss, watched from the ground, later clucking about what a natural I was.

That summer, while I was whizzing around

the sky spurting smoke, Eric began his third year clerkships, and he started with medicine. It was hard work and a difficult time; we didn't see much of each other.

One hot evening I took him dinner at the hospital, carting deli sandwiches and potato salad, soft drinks and brownies. He was on call every third night, working until three or four in the morning.

'Hi, Robbie,' I said, greeting the resident Eric worked with as I entered the small conference room on the Eight North Ward.

'Hey, Al.'

'Want a brownie?'

'No thanks. Eric's in room eight-eighty-four. Go ahead and interrupt him, he won't mind.'

'I can wait.'

'Better go get him. He'll be in there forever if you don't.' He laughed, shaking his head and walking down the hall, where he disappeared into a patient's room.

I put the sacks of food down on the table, wrote DO NOT EAT on them, and walked to room 884. The door was ajar and it was dim inside, lit only by a lamp. In the bed was a young woman, made deep-eyed and delicately beautiful by frailty, and beside her was Eric, sitting in a chair; he was holding her hand.

'Thank you for being brave,' she said. Her voice was raspy, hard to hear. I leaned closer to the doorway.

'Thank you for showing me bravery,' Eric answered.

My brow wrinkled; I held my breath.

'I'll be going now,' she murmured.

'I'll be here,' he answered.

She closed her eyes, letting her head fall back onto the pillow, and rested. Eric bowed his own head, brought her skeletal hand to his lips, and held it there for several long seconds.

I backed up, the unexpected intimacy of the moment driving me away. In my haste I bumped into Robbie.

'Whoa!' he exclaimed. His voice seemed too loud, destructive of some brittle tranquillity. 'Excuse me,' he added, 'isn't he in there?' He pointed toward room 884.

I nodded and hurried down the hall.

It wasn't long before Eric and Robbie joined me in the conference room, looking grim.

'I'll leave you two to your dinner,' Robbie said.

'Thanks,' Eric responded, and he reached out to hug me. 'Hi, Al,' he said.

'Hi,' I answered.

He released me and sat down, shielding his face with his hands. When he looked up, his eyes were bright, wet. 'My patient just died,' he said.

I gasped. She had appeared so peaceful and looked about our age—too young for dying. 'The woman in eight-eighty-four?' I asked.

'You saw her?'

'I came to the door, but you were talking . . .'

'About being brave.'

I nodded.

He went on, 'She said I was brave because I sat with her while she died. But she did the dying.'

'She showed you bravery.'

He nodded and smiled, splitting his face into what appeared to be sorrowful and joyful halves. We watched each other for a moment.

'You wanna eat?' he finally asked.

I shook my head.

'Fuck?'

'Eric!'

'What, Al?' He came to me, held me.

'She's dead,' I whispered.

'And we're not. We can eat and fuck, and if she could, she would.'

I nodded slowly and we kissed, moist, heated, alive. As we did, I couldn't help thinking about those who aid the dying, about how they must be constantly reminded of how fortunate they are for having life. Or perhaps they build a thick veneer, assembling reasons why they are unlike those who die, holding death at a distance.

That evening, I had, for the first time, held my eye to the keyhole that is death, sensing what a fleeting, tenuous hold we have on life, and in the process, gained the first layer of veneer.

CHAPTER TWENTY

In October of Eric's third year of medical school, a year before we were to be married, we flew to Chicago to invite his parents to our wedding. We hadn't been back since that long-ago Christmas, its sting now faded and smooth, like driftwood.

On the way, we avoided speaking of families, controversy, and conflict. Instead we read paperbacks, took naps, and played poker.

It seemed too soon when we arrived, taking a limo from the airport, this time in daylight, watching Chicago through tinted windows. The city seemed bare and worn, cold, with dry gray and brown replacing the dazzling orange, crimson, and yellow we had left in the east. We held hands in the car, but didn't speak, saving our words, our thoughts, our strength.

When we arrived, we again stood on the lawn, like we had almost two years before; we looked at each other.

'I love you,' I said.

'I love you, future wife,' he answered.

I smiled, and we walked to the door.

It seemed odd that he had to ring the bell, that he didn't have a key. And it was disconcerting, standing there on the porch with our suitcases, listening to a few brittle leaves rattling against the branches in the yard, watching birds fly, dark inkblots against the pale sky, out over the lake.

When it was obvious no one was home, Eric asked, 'You want to take a walk?'

I nodded and we started toward the shore. Eric was never more beautiful than that day, his eyes radiant, his skin retreating from color, leaving pink swatches high on his cheeks and the tip of his nose. Each detail of him was brilliantly outlined against the backdrop of his home, a place that once had been a refuge, and then a blank disappointment, where he had known love and then seemingly lost it. I held his hand and squeezed, wanting to deliver back to him what had been taken.

When we got back to the house, it was dark out and Mr. and Mrs. Moro were home; our suitcases were gone from the front porch. Eric rang the bell. His father came to the door.

'Hello, Dad,' Eric said.

'Eric, Alexandra,' Mr. Moro said, tipping his head toward each of us and holding the door open as we entered. 'Your mother has dinner prepared.'

'It's nice to see you again, Mr. Moro,' I said.

'The pleasure is mine,' he answered, leading the way to the dining room.

Mrs. Moro emerged from the kitchen, carrying a turkey. 'Hello, Eric, dear,' she said, 'and Alexandra.'

'Hi, Mama.'

'Hello, Mrs. Moro.'

'Sit down, children. The food will get cold.'

We sat. We ate. We talked about things that probably bored even the turkey. Eric saved our news for dessert, over cherry pie. That's when he said, 'Alex and I are getting married next October. We'd like you to be there.'

'Well!' Mrs. Moro exclaimed.

'I thought that might be the occasion of your visit,' Mr. Moro said.

Then there was silence, and nowhere to look. The pie grew dry in my mouth.

Finally, Eric said, 'The wedding will be near Philadelphia. Will you come?'

Again, silence. Mrs. Moro began to eat her

pie. Mr. Moro stared at Eric. 'I understand this to mean you are not asking our permission,' he said.

'No,' Eric answered.

'She's not Catholic,' Mr. Moro commented and took a sip of his coffee.

Mrs. Moro glanced up from her plate and examined me, slowly nodding.

'Neither am I,' Eric pointed out.

His mother gasped before clamping her mouth shut and watching her husband.

Eric and Mr. Moro were locked in a gaze that must've been common in years past.

'I'll convert,' I said.

'Good idea,' Mr. Moro said, just as Eric said, 'You will not.'

'I don't mind,' I said. 'We can marry in a Catholic church in Pennsylvania, or in your church, here.'

'I am not Catholic,' Eric said in a measured tone.

'But Eric,' I protested, 'what can it matter?'

'Goddammit, Al, I mean it.'

Eric had never spoken to me in that way, his tone stern, and it stunned me. 'These are your parents,' I said. 'Won't you at least listen?'

'Won't you?'

'Yes.'

'Then listen to this. As long as I live, I'll

never set foot in a Catholic church again.'

'I guess that settles it,' Mr. Moro declared, and for the first time since Eric had broached the topic, I looked at his father. He was smiling, but his expression was smug, not joyous.

We left that evening; our suitcases never made it upstairs. His parents didn't object to our departure, simply saying good-bye in the front foyer when our cab arrived, as if we had merely driven across town for turkey, pie, and a chat.

There were no flights out that night, so we stayed at a cheap hotel in town. I was exhausted and disappointed; Eric was intent on shrugging off the evening, shedding it along with his clothes as we sat on the bed.

'What did your father mean when he said "I guess that settles it?"' I asked. 'Are they coming or not?'

'He means it's settled for them. No Catholic church, no wedding.'

'So they're not coming.'

'From their point of view there's nothing to come to.'

'Proving you're both equally stubborn.'

'I learned it from him.'

'I don't get it, Eric. Do you resist Catholicism to defy your father?'

He stood and walked to the window, studying the blackness beyond, stuttered with flickering city lights.

'No,' he said. 'I'll never be a hypocrite. Not for him, not even for you.'

I remained sitting on the bed, studying the weave of the carpet. After several minutes, I walked up behind him, embraced him, and with him, watched the night.

With or without the Moros, our wedding would be at a small inn in Buck's County, about two hours north of Philadelphia. The ceremony was planned for outdoors, beneath red-orange sugar maples, yellow-clad elms, and the green of fir trees, or indoors if it rained, under beams of cherry wood, in view of a gray-green twisting river, symbolic of our ever-flowing love and union.

I was to wear gold silk, Eric a suit of Italian design, and we would dance, and sing, and drink, and go polar-bearing in that river at midnight. It seems fantasy-like now, two kids dreaming of what might be one day when they grow up. But at that time it was real, possible, and would take place as scheduled, to be far better than we could imagine.

We knew our love was invincible. We thought we were too. We were wrong.

CHAPTER TWENTY-ONE

Eric started his surgery clerkship, the most important one for his future, in January of his third year of medical school. He was up at 5:00 AM, home past midnight.

As for me, I didn't fly much in the winter, so I was sketching a lot, and teaching. I had time on my hands, and felt Eric's absence like a lost limb that still tickles and aches.

One day in the gray-white dusk of early February, I arrived home to find a man sitting in the dark on our sofa. I gasped, ready to back up and run, then I saw it was Eric. 'Oh, you scared me,' I said.

'Sorry,' he said.

'Why are you home so early?' I asked, switching on a lamp.

He buried his face in his hands and slowly shook his head.

I closed the door, walking toward him. 'What happened? What is it?'

He looked up, anguished, scared, a different Eric.

I sat down beside him. 'Did someone die?' I asked.

'No.'

'Eric, something's wrong.'

'I stuck myself.'

'Stuck yourself?'

'With an IV needle.'

'But why are you home?'

'I had to get tested.'

'Tested?'

'The needle was from a patient with AIDS.'

Suddenly, a lump of dread lodged stubbornly in my throat.

'Alex . . . there's no other way to say this . . .'

'What, Eric?'

'I'm HIV-positive.'

'You're what?'

'The virus that causes AIDS. I have it.'

I stopped breathing. 'No,' I said. 'There's some mistake.'

'It's been confirmed, Al. I'm positive.'

'That can't be true!'

'It is.' Again, he hid his face in his hands before going on. 'And it's not from that patient last week. It's from before.'

Before. I reeled, feeling as if I were falling from a high place, as if the earth had been pulled out from beneath me, plunging me into an eternal freefall with no possibility of ever stopping. With a word, my life was washed dark, stained permanently blood red. I slid off the sofa and squatted at Eric's feet, sobbing, trembling and small, hanging my head and clasping my hands behind my neck in the 'crash-landing' position.

'No!' I cried, over and over.

He studied his hands, motionless in his lap.

Finally, my sobs ran dry and I asked, 'Where did you get it?'

'I don't know,' he said, and looked at me. 'I can only guess where it came from.'

'Were there men?'

'No. But . . . '

'What?'

'When I was around seventeen, during the summer after my freshman year, I took that trip to New Orleans on Shadow Blaster, and . . .'

'Tiffany,' I said. 'She had it.'

'I'm not sure.'

'What are you saying?'

'I don't know how to say what I'm saying.'

I examined his face, finding no confusion or despair, only sincerity and regret. He said, 'We did heroin together.'

'You were a drug addict?'

'No, but she was. I can't explain why I did it with her that summer, maybe to show her I loved her, but it was stupid. I never did it again.'

'So you knew you were at risk.'

'No!' He stood and began to pace. 'No, I didn't know.'

'You're a medical student and you didn't—'

'We used clean needles that she stole from her father. He was a doctor.'

'Then you got it from sex with her.'

'No, we never did it. But we shared those needles. I sometimes went second.'

'They weren't clean after she used them.'

'You're right, but it never occurred to me that she could've been infected. Her father had been her only sex partner; she never used with anybody but me . . .'

'So maybe it wasn't her after all.'

'Al, Tiffany's father died of AIDS more than a year ago.'

'He did?'

He nodded.

'How do you know?'

'I called her mother when I found out about this, to see if Tiffany had been infected, to see if that's where I got it. She told me she thinks Tiffany's father may have given it to her.'

'Her own father infected her?'

'Probably.'

'My God.' I raked my hand through my hair, disbelieving, not willing to comprehend. 'Where did *he* get it?'

'From someone else who had it, who got it from someone else who had it, who got it from someone else who had it . . .'

My head began to whirl from the vision of this coupling web of contacts. I saw it like a net, woven from solid blood, connecting people diverse and nameless in a bond stronger than any other, one that would carry them to their graves and beyond, through history, forever linked. And Eric was part of it, married by blood to Tiffany, who dragged at him even now, years after her death.

He sat beside me and I watched him, realizing that something had slipped irretrievably away from us—not innocence, not hope, but confidence, youth's expectation of good luck.

'You need to get tested,' he said.

'Me? You mean . . . no . . . '

'All my partners need to be tested, Al.' His eyes filled with tears and he shook his head. 'My life will be ended if I've infected you.'

'You don't think I . . . ?'

'I don't know.' He took my hands in his.

'We've always used condoms, though,' I said.

'I know, but . . . '

'But . . . '

We shared a look, holding everything that life could be in our gaze, knowing that a piece of it had chipped, was tumbling inexorably away.

He began to cry. 'I love you,' he said.

I was silent, weeping, and we stood, clinging to one another.

Night came unnoticed as we lay on the bed above the covers, fully clothed, fear and despair chasing away hunger, sleep, routine.

'What was it like?' I asked into the darkness above us, shades of gray and shadow, our eyes open against it.

'What?' he asked.

'Heroin.'

'It was like being held close in your mama's

arms, back when she loved you best, when she kept you safe from the world.'

I nodded into the gloom, but didn't speak, knowing there was another place safe from the world.

Tiffany was already there.

CHAPTER TWENTY-TWO

In the next five days, waiting for my HIV result, I shed a gallon of tears. I loved Eric—his HIV infection hadn't changed that—but competing emotions had clattered to the surface, leaving the love, the foundation and the core, waiting patiently beneath. Terror, like heat, shot up highest of all, and beat with a pulse just under my skin. The terror was less about dying than it was about shame and degradation, being pushed below the crust of humanity.

The day came to go back to the testing center and get my results. Clutching the little paper with my 'anonymous' number on it, four random digits between me and destiny, I left for the bus. It was mid-February, gray and cold, frozen.

I got on the bus with the others, people whose hearts didn't hammer while tears threatened, who were headed for shopping or jobs. My mind rocked, stumbling from hope to despair. With all the passion Eric and I had shared, every kiss laced with death, every climax milky poison, I knew that I could not have escaped. Fumbling, I sat alone, thinking of what it meant to be HIV-positive. It meant my future was a hazy mirage, always just ahead, untouchable; it meant life would depend on medicines and doctors, that what had been natural would become 'bodily fluids,' transformed into medical waste disposal problems; it meant sex had been stolen, leaving a taunting memory.

Sooner than I wanted, I was off the bus and walking toward the clinic, to my sentence.

I took a seat in a blue plastic chair in the waiting room, glancing around, wondering. Was she . . . ? Did he . . . ? What about him? But in them I only saw myself reflected: horror, panic, desperate desire, and ultimately, defeat.

Eventually, my number was called and something in me stood up, walked through the thickness of time suspended, and followed a woman's brown ponytail, held by a red rubber band, up a flight of stairs. We entered a small room where around us swarmed posters of men and men, men and women, condoms and everybody, and words like AIDS, SIDA, HIV, Safe Sex.

The woman and I sat across from each other and she looked at me. I knew then that my life would be forever measured against the moment I was told, sorted into before and after.

'My name is Sandy Keller,' she said.

'Okay,' I said.

'I'm here to give you your results.'

'Okay.'

'What's your risk factor?'

'My fiancé has it.'

'HIV?'

'Yes.'

'Do you understand what HIV is?'

'Yes.'

'Do you know what a positive result means?'

'AIDS.'

'Not exactly. It means you're infected with the virus that causes AIDS . . .'

My world was silent after she said '*You're infected with the virus that causes AIDS.*' I was HIV-positive. My life was over, declared so by a simple blood test, in a little room with a round-cheeked woman who wore a red rubber band and would soon go to lunch and eat a salad with low-cal ranch dressing and iced tea, or maybe soup, or—

'Are you listening?' she asked.

I stood up mechanically. 'That's it?' I said.

'Yes, but just because you're not infected doesn't mean you shouldn't—'

'Not?'

'You're not infected. I just told you that. Are you okay?'

'I'm negative? I'm negative.'

'Yes. Look, here are your results.'

I stared into the manila folder she held open and onto a blue-and-white striped sheet. It said: 'HIV Antibody—Negative.' Suddenly everything was loud and twirling and too colorful. I closed my eyes briefly, bringing my hands together, my fingers pointing upward under my chin, and mumbled, 'Thank you, God.'

The woman looked at me, puzzled, then smiled, opening the door. There were others waiting.

My elation carried me to the bus stop. There I bent to feel snow with my bare hands, smiled at grumpy strangers, and let everyone board before me. Time was suddenly a gift; it made me feel generous. I wanted to sing, hug someone, dance, tell the world, especially Eric. I crashed. His name, what was ahead, brought gravity back to my world.

That week we found out Eric's T-cells were only around 200, that he had probably been infected for more than five years.

I envisioned us traveling the world for cures: secret herbs and rare potions, tree roots and snake spit, but Eric decided to see an AIDS specialist in town. He was prescribed AZT and ddI.

Around this time, I became aware of community organizations that had been in existence since the epidemic began. They offered support, information, services. But I stayed away from them, doing my own research, needing to make it hard, grasping for control.

Eric continued to attend school. His HIV results had been reported to a special committee there, made up of medical experts, infection control personnel, hospital lawyers, and the medical school dean. They decided that, with monitoring, Eric could proceed with his education without restrictions.

Besides Eric's previous sexual partners, we told no one about the HIV. We were reeling, resisting facts, recoiling from reality, nurturing faith, fanning the spark of hope. Coping required denial. Denial required secrecy.

Sometimes, we could almost imagine nothing had changed.

CHAPTER TWENTY-THREE

The first time I kissed Eric after knowing was like jumping off a high dive with my eyes closed. Of course I had kissed him before, and he had been HIV-positive then, but knowing that it was there between us, invisible and insidious, made it somehow different. And the trying. Trying not to think about it, trying not to show I was thinking about it, trying not to taste it, or feel it, or let it in, trying not to allow it to be a factor. It was work.

And then there was sex, what was left of it. I became intimately involved with phrases like 'safer sex,' 'mutual masturbation,' and 'infectious potential.' Orgasm was hazardous without latex. But for me, there was no sex without Eric.

He was stroking me, teasing me, making me forget about T-cell invasion and retroviruses by taking me out of my mind and into plunging, focused intensity, when I whispered, 'Let's make love.'

He didn't answer, so I opened my eyes and pulled him to me, kissing him in the old way. I pushed him to his back, his erection stiff, tight, and waiting, and mounted him.

'No!' he said, yanking me upward.

'Get a condom,' I said.

'No, darlin'.'

'Yes, Eric. It's my life too.'

'That's right, it's your life.'

I reached into the bedside table drawer and retrieved a condom that had been purchased before we knew, when condoms meant convenient birth control and nothing more.

'Look,' I said, tearing the wrapper, 'I love you. I'm with you and I'm not leaving. I'm a grown woman making my own decisions—'

'And I'm a grown man making my own decisions, and I've—'

'You can't do that. I can't do this.' I pinched my lips between my teeth to keep from crying.

He took the condom from me, and through tears that pooled over my vision, I watched him put it on.

'Come on,' he said.

I sat on him. It was like warm, full love inside me, better than I had remembered, maybe for what it represented between us, beyond sex, beyond pleasure, beyond commitment: an aching, unconditional love.

Through it I cried, while he fought the urge to protect me at all costs.

Sex had become sad.

CHAPTER TWENTY-FOUR

My sister Linda gave birth to a baby boy on May 13, a Monday. She named him Darcy, after his father. He was beautiful: small, curled pink hands, blond hair spiked into a fluffy halo. He cried and sucked, blinked and pooped, bringing tears to our eyes.

Eric was on pediatrics rotation that month, and when he was done with rounds, he knocked on Linda's hospital room door.

'Come in,' Linda called. I was holding Darcy.

'Hi, new mom,' Eric said, kissing Linda on the cheek.

'Eric, look,' I said, holding Darcy out to him. He smiled, Linda smiled, but although Eric came to stand beside me, he wouldn't take the baby. 'Here, hold him,' I said.

'No, thanks. He looks happy with you.'

'Come on, Eric,' Linda urged. 'What's the worst that can happen? Spit-up?' She laughed; we didn't.

Again, Eric smiled, but refused.

I stood up, holding the baby out to him. 'Here,' I repeated.

He shook his head, backing up.

Linda's brow creased. 'I thought you two were getting married this October. You'd better get this straight before then.'

Eric and I locked eyes over Darcy Junior. 'Take the baby,' I said.

'No.'

'Give him to me, Allie,' Linda said.

'He has to learn,' I said.

'Not on my baby, he doesn't,' Linda commented.

'She's right, Al. Give him back.'

'No,' I said. 'Take him.'

'He's beautiful, Linda. Congratulations,' Eric said, and turned to leave. I followed, still holding the baby.

'Allie!' Linda yelled. 'Come back here with him!'

I ignored her and kept walking, following Eric into the hall.

'Eric,' I said, 'you won't infect him by holding him, you know that.'

'It's too close to home, Al.' He walked away, into the stairwell. I followed. Darcy Junior began to howl. 'Take him back,' Eric said.

'I want to have children with you,' I said, beginning to cry.

'It can't happen.'

'Yes, Eric. Please.'

'It's too risky.'

'I want to . . . ' I sobbed.

'No. Take the baby back.'

'I want a life with you.'

'That can't include babies.' Eric took Darcy from my arms and back to Linda. I sat on the stairs, crying, and waited.

When Eric returned, he stood on the stairs below me. I had a sudden vision of other stairs, those at Linda's wedding, when Eric and I had escaped to the roof and made love, ignorant, happy. Only a year had passed since then, but knowledge had aged us, thrusting reality down our throats, forcing us to live alongside sorrow.

'What about our wedding?' I asked. 'Linda's right. We planned on October. That's only five months away.'

'I know. We should've talked about it before now.'

'So talk.'

'We can't get married.'

'I want to marry you.'

'Why?'

'You never would've asked that before.'

'This isn't before.'

'I love you the same. No, I love you more.'

'And I love you, Al, but I've seen what this virus can do to people.'

'I'm going to be here with you, married or not.' I took his hand, brought it to my lips, and held it there, feeling his life beating.

He sat beside me, cradling me in his arms. 'I know,' he said, 'but give yourself a way out.'

'I don't want a way out,' I said, tears flowing down my face. '"Together Forever," remember?'

He smiled sadly and nodded his head. 'I remember,' he said.

We sat that way for a long time, silent except for my sobs.

Finally, we stood and left the hospital, walking home through the spring evening, our hands linked, trying not to want all the things we could never have.

We postponed the wedding indefinitely.

CHAPTER TWENTY-FIVE

That autumn, Eric applied for residencies; it was his fourth and final year of medical school. Watching the leaves turn was magic again as we took our annual fall flight to Cape May, dipping low over the sand and water where we had played, and he had proposed, it seemed, in some other life.

On the way back, he said, 'I'm applying in psychiatry.'

'You are?'

'It's perfect for me.'

'You're a born surgeon, Eric.'

'I know.'

I stared at him and he looked away.

'Psychiatry's good,' I said.

'It's good.'

I reached for his hand, held it, a graceful surgeon's hand that dissected to perfection, creating works of art that could heal. Yet, a simple scalpel nick through a glove could turn that hand into dripping scarlet death. He didn't want that.

Eric's HIV had transformed our lives into a series of concessions and compromises. It was an invasive, intrusive, inculcating, in-your-face infection. We lived with it, and we bent. But when the next bend came, we weren't prepared for it.

National matching day, the day when future interns and residents are assigned their programs, comes in the spring. When graduation was only months away, several days before the match, the medical school dean called Eric into his office and told him there were no spots for him in psychiatric residencies in the United States. 'I'm sorry,' he added.

'He's sorry?' I shrieked when Eric told me. '*Sorry?*'

'I'll work something out,' Eric responded. He had driven a borrowed car to New Jersey, to my skywriting job, to tell me this.

'You're number one in the class, you scored

higher on the boards than anybody, and there's no place for you?'

'These things happen. I'll—'

'These things don't just happen, Eric. Plus, you already made one compromise by applying in psychiatry instead of surgery.'

'I know, but it'll be okay.' He looked at me for a long moment, the usual sparkle of his eyes eclipsed by sadness, and that's when I realized: the HIV wasn't just going to kill him. It was going to end his life.

I watched as he drove away, so willing to grit his teeth against one more hurdle, to take what was good and let the rest glance off him.

'Alex!' It was Mr. Rig. I was late for take-off.

'Coming!' I answered, and hurried to the runway.

'You know where you're going?' he asked.

'Philly. Westside.'

'Here's your message.' He handed me the paper. It read YOU ARE TWO, POOH.

'Pooh?' I asked.

'It's for a kid's birthday. Make sure the *h* is on there.'

'Okay. Bye.'

To reach my destination, I had to fly over Eric's medical school, massive and sprawling. I had flown over it many times before, but it looked different that day, transfigured into a place of pain, a home for endings. It twisted me inside. I climbed to altitude and started to write. When I was done, CURE AIDS was scripted in giant letters above the medical school, leaving nothing for Pooh.

A photo of my sky message made the front page of the *Philadelphia Inquirer* the next day. I was fired that afternoon.

'Isn't it supposed to be confidential?' I called to Eric from the living room several mornings later; he was still in bed, enjoying skipping his elective in GI radiology.

'What, darlin'?'

'Your HIV result.'

'Yes.'

'Who told?'

Silence. I walked to the bedroom door. He was lying on his back, still, his eyes fixed and unblinking. 'Eric?' I said, fighting panic. Silence. I moved closer. 'Eric!'

He blinked. 'Yes, darlin'?'

I closed my eyes against tears. He was alive. I went to him, to feel his warmth and breath, smell his hair, watch him move. He grinned. I climbed into bed with him.

'What is it, Al?'

'Nothing.'

'You were asking about my HIV test. What's up?'

'How did those programs know you were infected?'

'I'm not sure they did.'

'But you know that's why you didn't get a residency.'

'Easy to believe, hard to prove.'

'The dean knew. He was on that committee that discussed your status after you got tested.'

'Yes.'

'And he told.'

'Maybe. What does it matter?'

'It's not right.'

'Like a lot of things.'

'I'm not going to leave it like this.'

'You want revenge?'

'No. Just what's due you.'

He smiled, kissing me and climbing out of bed, heading toward the bathroom.

'Hey,' I said, following him, 'if the dean told those programs, he broke confidentiality. If they refused you entry based on your HIV infection, that's discrimination.'

He squinted, his face dripping from the water he had splashed on it, cold from the sink. 'Yes,' he said, 'but how do you prove it?' I shrugged. He pulled on sweats and I trailed him to the kitchen. 'You want coffee?' he asked. I nodded. We sat at the kitchen table, its surface sticky from Chinese take-out the night before.

As we sipped our coffee, he picked up the morning paper, then sighed, saying, 'I hear you, Al, but think about it from their point of view. A lot of people don't want an HIV-positive doctor.'

I remained silent, staring at him. He added, 'Can't you see that?'

'No. How can you see that?'

He didn't answer, but I knew what allowed him to see, to climb into another's skin. It's what had drawn his lips to the dying woman's hand, to murmur the words she most needed to hear: empathy. Its purity in him was so rare, its loss to humankind beyond measure.

'Ssshhh,' I whispered to the receptionist in the dean's office. She was blond, her lashes thick with blue mascara, and her name, according to the sign on her desk, was Sally.

'Listen,' I said, glancing around, 'I've got a surprise for my uncle—'

'Your uncle?' she asked, wrinkling her nose.

I must not have looked worthy of an uncle; my hair was unwashed, my denim jacket frayed, but I persisted. 'Uncle Dean . . . ' I glanced at his door. 'Uncle Dean Valois,' I said.

'That's *Val-wah*,' she responded, emphasizing the French silent *s*.

'Right,' I agreed, 'but back in North Dakota we always pronounced it *Vah-loys*.'

'Who are you?'

'Jenny Valois, from South Dakota.'

'You said "North" just a second ago. What do you want?'

'My uncle—'

'Go on, get out.' She stood up. She had an imposing build.

'I need—'

'I'm busy. Please—'

I started to cry. It was easy.

'Jeez,' she said. 'I didn't mean anything by it. Hey, it's okay.'

'No,' I sobbed.

She put a substantial arm around me, leading me to a chair. 'Here, sit,' she said. 'I'll get you a glass of water.' She left for the other end of the suite of offices, and instead of bursting into the dean's office to confront him as I had planned, I sat and watched her hips sway, listened to her stockings sing where her inner thighs rubbed together. She returned with the water in a coffee mug that said 'Have a Healthy Day' on the side. I sipped at it, blinking tears from my lashes. She stood watching me.

'What's wrong?' she asked.

'Sally?' I said.

'That's me, Solid Sal.' She slapped the side of her thigh.

'I'm Alex. Al, the pal.'

We laughed.

'Thanks for the water,' I said, standing up. I felt suddenly foolish for the uncle bit and embarrassed that I'd come. And then the dean of the medical school, Sidney Clayton Valois, came out of his office, and we both stared at him. He was tall and silver-haired, with a well-worn face.

'I'll be off now, Sal,' he said. 'I have that meeting.'

'Yes, Dean,' she said.

'Darn, I forgot my briefcase.' He turned and disappeared into his office for a moment.

Sally faced me. 'Go, now!' she whispered. 'Now's your chance to talk to him . . . your uncle.' She laughed.

I shook my head. In person, the dean appeared powerful, respectable, and untarnished, not capable of what I suspected he had done. I backed toward the outer door. Sally followed.

'Alex, come on, now's—'

'See you, then,' the dean said, and sailed by us and out the door.

'Go after him,' she urged, turning me around and pushing at my back.

'Forget it.'

She seemed to deflate, as if whatever I needed that was so important that it was worth lying for had kept her upright. 'Oh, Alex,' she sighed, shaking her head. 'I don't know when he'll be back, and—'

'Thanks, Sally. Thanks for the water and your help. It means a lot to me.'

'You're welcome. What . . . '

'It's too complicated to explain.'

'It's none of my business, anyway.'

Sally settled herself once more behind her desk and onto a chair on wheels, the seat of which did little to contain her buttocks. The casters scooted over a hard plastic mat on the floor, and as I watched her it struck me that my actions were probably the only thing that made her job interesting, providing a blip in an otherwise routine day. I was a reason for a soothing trip to the water cooler, a hooting laugh, an almost daring encounter with the dean as he stepped out of his office, a chance to catch a mispronunciation of a French name.

'Bye,' I said.

She nodded in my direction, now serious, Sally replacing Solid Sal. I hesitated and considered. Finally I pulled a chair to the front of her desk, a place where people usually only stood. Then I sat down, facing her. She shuffled some papers and looked at me.

'I'm busy,' she said.

'I'm in trouble.'

'I'm sorry, but—'

'My boyfriend is a medical student here.'

'Oh?' She brightened. 'Who is he? I know them all.'

'Eric—'

'Moro!' she exclaimed. Then her face grew heavy, and she said, 'My, you are in trouble.'

She knew. My body must've sagged, because she reached over and grabbed my hand. 'I didn't mean it like that,' she said. 'I'm sorry.'

'You *know*?'

'Oh gosh, everybody does.'

'Everybody?'

'Well, just about.'

'How does everybody know? It's supposed to be confidential.'

She blushed deep crimson. 'I'm sorry,' she said. 'He's a great guy. I feel real bad for him. It wasn't right what they did.'

'They?'

'Uh . . . you know, whoever told.'

'Who told you?'

'Danny.'

'Danny?'

'Danny Carvacchi. They were . . . ' Again, she blushed.

'I know,' I said. 'Who told the programs, Sal?'

'The programs?'

'The psychiatry programs Eric applied to.'

'I wouldn't know anything about that. That's real complicated and all.'

'The information must've leaked from here.'

'I don't know about any of it.' She let go of my hand, and of me.

'It isn't fair that he didn't get in,' I persisted. 'He's first in the class—'

'There's more to it than that. The dean had to weigh—' She clapped her hand over her mouth, to plug her own leak. 'Please leave,' she said, standing.

'So it *was* the HIV that kept him out of residency.'

'Do you want me to call security?'

'I want you to tell me what you know.'

She came around to my side of the desk; I followed her with my eyes. 'Go,' she said, 'now. I didn't tell you anything.'

'The dean told the programs, didn't he?' I said, and remained sitting.

'I don't know what you're talking about.' She started to drag at my chair with me in it; it scraped a plush growl across the mauve carpet.

'You do know,' I said.

'I do not!' She stopped pulling the chair and started to cry. 'Please,' she said.

'Please,' I repeated.

We looked at one another, but despite my continued urging, she would say no more.

I left.

'Eric!' I called as I entered our apartment, slamming the door behind me. 'I need the names of the programs you applied to!' I reached into the refrigerator for orange juice; I hadn't eaten all day. I drank greedily from the container; a cold trickle dripped down my neck to my chest, absorbed by my T-shirt. 'Eric?' I asked, walking into the bedroom. There was a note on the bed in Eric's writing: WENT TO THE HOSPITAL, CALL YOU LATER. I LOVE YOU.

The hospital. He must've decided to go to his elective this afternoon, I thought as I wandered back to the kitchen. I emptied tuna fish from a can onto a hunk of bread and began munching, thinking.

The phone rang, startling me.

'Hello?' I croaked. I cleared my throat and repeated, 'Hello?'

'Ms. Taylor?' a man asked.

'This is Alex,' I said.

'My name's Dr. Buchanan. Mr. Moro asked me to call to—'

'Mr. Moro?'

'Yes.'

'Malcolm Moro?'

'Eric Moro.'

'You mean Dr. Moro.'

'Oh, right.'

'Why didn't he call?'

'He's having a bronchoscopy. Didn't he tell you he was coming to the hospital? Is this Alexandra Taylor, Eric Moro's fiancée?'

'Yes, but I thought he was in the hospital for school, not, not . . . not . . .'

'He's okay, Ms. Taylor, really. The test is routine for what he has.'

'What does he have?' I asked.

'He hasn't told you?'

'I know about the HIV, if that's what you mean. But what's this . . . is he sick?'

He hesitated, then said, 'This is nothing serious. I'm sure everything will be okay.'

'It will?'

'Yes.'

'For how long?'

I listened to a dull silence before mumbling, 'Thank you' and hanging up. Of course he didn't know. He was just a doctor.

I went to look for Eric at the hospital.

'Hi, darlin',' he said from a stretcher in the hallway outside the bronchoscopy suite, looking very much like a patient.

'What's going on?' I asked, leaning over to kiss him, trying not to cry.

'Nothin'.'

'You're sick—'

'Who said that? Dave?'

'Dave?'

'Didn't he call you?'

'A Dr. Buchanan called. He said—'

Eric laughed outright. 'Is that what he called himself? That asshole.'

'What's going on? Tell me!'

He struggled to sit up, then fell back and laughed again. 'Dave Buchanan's a friend of mine, a third-year involved in this research project. Didn't I tell you about it?'

'No.'

'Sorry. I agreed to get a bronchoscopy every six months, to see if I'm infected with Pneumocystis before I have symptoms. They pay me.'

'But you're on prophylaxis. Bactrim.'

'They want to see how well it's working.'

He smiled and sat up. He was wearing a hospital gown. 'Come here, darlin',' he said. I moved closer; we embraced. 'I love you,' he murmured into my hair.

'You're done, Eric,' a young man wearing a short white coat said, walking up to the stretcher. I let go of Eric and took a step back.

'Thank you ever so much, Dr. Buchanan,' Eric said.

'Is this Alex?' Dave asked.

'Yes,' Eric said. 'Alex, this is Dave.'

'Hi,' I said.

'Sorry if I scared you on the phone.'

'Is he okay?' I asked. 'Does he have Pneumocystis?'

'No,' Dave answered.

'Do you have my prescription?' Eric asked.

'Here.' Dave handed Eric a piece of paper and then said good-bye. He walked down the hall, headed toward a bright future, where Eric couldn't follow. Eric and I looked at each other.

'I'll get dressed,' he said.

'Good.'

He disappeared into a dressing room off the hall as I waited, with my thoughts, smacking up against time. It had suddenly picked up speed, and seemed to be gobbling itself up.

Eric and I left the hospital arm in arm. 'What do you want to do?' he asked.

'What do you want to do?'

'How about going to the Bookstore/Coffeehouse?'

'Okay.'

We stopped on the sidewalk in front of the hospital, and I reached up and ran my hands through his black hair, remembering the time we had first gone to that coffeehouse, the morning after we had met, and his story about the wizard, about hope where there's a need.

Eric smiled that half-smile I loved so much. I smiled back. We started walking.

We didn't make it to the coffeehouse. We got distracted along the way by an early-season baseball game, scraped together by a bunch of kids in a neighborhood park. We sat on the grass and held hands.

'You coaching Little League this summer?' I asked.

'I don't think so.'

'Why not?'

He shrugged. 'Are you painting with your "kids"?'

'I don't think so.'

'Baseball's great,' he said, watching the game, listening to the shrill voices.

I noticed the moments passing; my heart beat quicker. He shielded his eyes with a hand, looked up at a pop fly, and whistled. 'That kid's got a future,' he mumbled.

'Do we?' I asked.

He looked at me and we stared at each other for a long minute, his eyes dry, mine smarting with tears.

'I want more time,' I said.

'You've got my forever,' he answered, taking my hand.

'It's not enough.'

'I know.'

'Why you, Eric?'

'I've wondered that, but there's no answer.'

'Are you scared?'

'Sometimes.'

I blinked hard to keep from crying.

He went on. 'It's not being dead I'm afraid of, Al. It's dying. And being away from you.'

My tears began to flow. 'Then we won't let it happen.'

He took my hand. 'Are *you* scared?' he asked.

'I'm trying not to be.'

'I won't ask you to do anything you don't want to.'

'Like what? What do you mean?'

'Nothing. Forget it.'

'No, what did you mean?'

He shrugged, looked away.

'Eric, we're going to save your life.'

He nodded, but didn't meet my gaze.

Our hope was hanging by a thread, a dangerously sheer thread. Eric at the hospital, on the gurney, in the gown, had thrown me, piercing the fabric of my denial, taking me beyond scared, teetering on the edge of terror.

CHAPTER TWENTY-SIX

We rode Shadow Blaster to my parents' house a few days later. They had never pressed us for an explanation when we told them we'd decided to put off the wedding. But now that Eric was getting sick we had decided to tell them about the HIV. On the way, I wondered if our news could obscure even the best love, casting a dank, persistent fog over our world, proving more painful even than death. But soon we were at the house, where everything appeared benignly the same, untouched, approximating permanent.

We were at dinner when I said, 'Um, Mom, Daddy . . . I, uh, I have something to tell you.' I glanced at Eric; he met my gaze. 'Uh . . . God, this is hard.' I sighed, trying not to cry as I looked them over: Mom, Daddy, Cindy, and Harry. They were expectant and eager, with a slice of worry in between.

'What is it, sweetie?' Mom asked, setting her fork down. 'Are you sick?'

'No, Mom. But . . . but . . . Eric has HIV, the AIDS virus.'

My words were like the invisible whiff of an airborne infection, spreading rapidly from my lips and into the consciousness of the people I loved most in the world. I watched as it registered on their faces, reflected in stages of bewilderment and pain, each one different, and yet the same.

I expected the circle; it didn't come. For the first time ever, my family could not think of an exaggeration to make it better, because they could not think of a single thing worse. Then Eric said, 'Al's not infected,' reassuring us that there's always something worse.

Daddy stood and went to Eric, holding him, weeping. Soon Mom did the same, and eventually the rest of us were standing, hugging, and crying.

After dinner we sat in the living room and all the questions were asked and answered:

'Is there a cure?'

'Is Alex at risk?'

'Are we at risk?'

'Is it fatal?'

'Does it hurt?'

'What's an opportunistic infection?'

Above all, though, they wanted to help, and the first thing they did was buy us a vacation. We chose Maine, for camping.

I pretended not to think this could be our final trip together, our first and last chance to go camping. Ever since that day at the hospital, it had become increasingly hard not to notice each moment, not to think of the end, or of Eric getting sick. I knew the best thing I could do for him was to enjoy the time we had, but the time we had was tainted by thoughts of the time we didn't have.

'What do you think of this as a camping hat?' he asked as we packed our rented Jeep in preparation for the trip.

'A pith helmet?' I said, laughing.

'It's a safari antitick thing.'

'Good idea.' I looked him over, still muscular and sexy, still a head-turner. To all appearances, nothing wrong.

He looked me over as well. 'I got you a hat too,' he said, pulling something out of a bag. He hid it behind his back.

'What is that?' I asked, trying to grab his arm.

'Your beret, mademoiselle,' he said, putting it on my head with a flourish, adjusting it so that it lay at the proper angle.

The beret was bright orange, bordering on hideous, but Eric knew what he was doing; it was hard to be serious in those hats.

We climbed into the Jeep and drove away, outlines of recent smiles lingering on our faces. It had been at least five minutes since I had thought of the HIV; I was beginning to appreciate that.

It was late afternoon when we started out, and the freeway was jammed: gritty asphalt radiating heat, the odor of melting tar. But as the light grayed, we made it to open road, where the wind swirled warm through our windows. We laughed, joked, and sang, my bare feet propped on the dashboard, Eric driving, each mile giving perspective to our world. And increasingly, our world was us.

It was eight-thirty by the time we stopped for dinner at a small truck stop along the highway. Its sign read AL'S GOOD FOOD in blinking red neon, the s lagging behind, several o's gone for good.

'It can't be too bad,' Eric commented as we got out. 'It's named after you, Al.'

I laughed. 'I'll bet Al's not a woman, though.'

We ate crispy fried chicken and french fries, coleslaw. We had a couple beers too, Samuel Adams. The first swig took me back to the beginning with Eric, the pub, the game we had played, my worries about Peter. I shook my head, wanting to rid myself of those old memories, already crowding the present. I wanted to bring myself to now, to what would too soon become new memories.

'Are you Al?' Eric called across the room to the bartender when we were finished eating.

'Who?' she said.

'Al, of "Al's Good Food".'

'Hell, no. That asshole split years ago. Can't afford a new sign, that's what,' she said. Several customers at the bar snickered; they must've been regulars, sporting dingy baseball caps advertising local businesses: Lanner's Diesel Parts, Feed and Grain That's Plain, Derrikson's Ford.

'Al's my *ex*-husband,' the bartender went on, 'with a capital *X*.' Laughter twittered around the bar.

Eric got up for more beer as I watched baseball on a TV at the far end of the bar. I think the guys in white were beating the guys in red, but I didn't care; I was tipsy in a way that makes everything seem friendly.

Eric came back. 'That's Jane,' he said,

cocking his head toward the bartender. 'Al's *ex*-wife. He was a dick.'

'Dick and Jane.'

We laughed. Jane came and took our plates, which were smeared with grease and ketchup. 'You kids enjoy it?' she asked.

'Yes,' we said in unison.

'Fine. That's fine,' Jane responded. She wiped the table with a frayed dishtowel, then stepped back and looked at us. 'You newlyweds?' she asked.

We shook our heads, trying to stay suspended by humor.

'Well, you oughtta be,' she declared. 'Fine-looking couple, you two. Have pretty kids, that's for sure.'

'Thanks,' we mumbled.

A guy from the bar chimed in without turning around, 'Now that's saying a hell of a lot, Jane recommending marriage and kids and all.' This brought hoots from the others at the bar and from Jane a firm snap of the towel against the guy's behind. He yelped; the others laughed louder. What a life, I thought. Another beer and it all looked that much better.

We were drunk and unfit to drive, having remained at Al's for hours, moving ourselves to the bar, Eric's pith helmet and my orange beret distinguishing us from the others there.

The bar closed at one; we bade our farewells and left for the parking lot. The May moon was full and bright, making Eric's skin dead white, and I slipped his hat off, marveling again at the striking blackness of his hair.

We smiled, dancing into the night, whispering, stumbling, and giggling, until we found a grove of sorts: green leaves made midnight black, trees with heavy trunks and thick roots. It was good.

We stripped and lay there staring up for some minutes, the sky light in contrast to the leaves, their silhouettes sharp and oval, single and multifingered. We were two breathing beings among others, and in that moment that yawned into the universe, nothing seemed important except loving Eric and being loved by him. Sex that night on the cool, damp grass was intimate and richly satisfying, defining the phrase 'making love.'

In the morning we awoke, naked, cuddled together for warmth, with dry mouths and headaches made worse by dawn in our eyes. Sunrise revealed our 'grove' for what it was: a few scattered trees along a residential street. We dressed hurriedly and headed for our Jeep.

With daylight and sobriety, the town's

shabbiness was stark, and Al's had been transformed into a grubby bar with rust stains on its
once white sides. We sped away and stopped up
the road for breakfast at a Howard Johnson's,
where grease was practically a side dish: fried
eggs with pools of yellow butter in dimples of
gelatinous white, sausages oozing clear, hot oil,
congealing as it cooled, and white-bread toast,
soaked with yellow goo.

'What do you want to do today?' Eric asked
as the waitress cleared our table and we drank
a fourth cup of coffee.

'I thought we were going to Maine,' I said.
'Where are we, anyway?'

'We're in love,' he said, laughing. I joined
him.

'Want to go exploring?' he asked, taking my
hands between both of his, turning them palm
up and kissing them while peering up at me.

'Yes.'

We made a plan to stop at any location we
fancied, either because it was beautiful, exceed-
ingly ugly, historically significant, or
inexplicably interesting. This led to a lot of
pauses, picnics, sleeping under the stars, and
sex in meadows, ditches, and on riverbanks,
with black and white cows as silent, cud-
chewing witnesses.

The ugliest place we beheld was a power

station, a complex gray latticework of pipes and nozzles, tanks and smoking stacks. Yet, the muted light of dusk turned it into twinkling silver splendor, transforming it into urban art, surpassed in beauty only by an orange-purple sunset we saw, the sun sinking behind a hill, a white farmhouse glowing pink in the distance.

Often, during those ten days, traveling through town after Pennsylvania town—Hebe, Walnut Bottom, Warriors Mark, Glen Campbell, Tire Hill—we would simply sit, shoulder to shoulder or arm in arm, and see. We were drinking in the world, drenching ourselves in life.

I remember a night in a cornfield on the outskirts of a town called Brave, where we pitched our tent in a low bare patch, building a fire against the night-damp. The stars were glittering holes in the sky, peeping through from a distant universe, the fire's smoke gray against the black air. We stared up for hours, our necks stiff from the strain, and I wondered if heaven was there, on our side or the other, through the holes made by the stars. I hoped it was near.

That night, in the dim glow of the tent, I listened to Eric sleeping, his breath warm on my hand, then my cheek, my neck. I studied his lips, slightly parted and almost blue in that light, his face yet uncreased, next to ethereal. I tried to imagine what he would look like at thirty-five, fifty, seventy, but as I watched he only grew younger, a boy, full of eager energy and compassion. I felt a stab of sorrow for not having had that time with him.

I thought of waking him, using the minutes we had to say something that time might steal, but he was peaceful, and I was glad.

I wiggled out of our sleeping bag and crawled through the flap of the tent. Standing naked in the cloud-sifted moonlight near the embers of our dying fire, I began to hum. It was low, simple vibration without tune, the sound carrying me into the field surrounding our campsite. I ran swiftly, the rough corn leaves rustling, abrasive against my skin. I ran until the air was hot in my lungs, rasping through my windpipe, and my hum had turned to a howl.

I crawled back into the tent, snuggling once again against Eric. I slept well, my feet caked black with fertile Pennsylvania earth.

Cincinnati. Time to go home. But before we did, we took a riverboat ride. It was a polished boat, its purpose entertainment, with a red-and-white striped awning, a shimmering, river-churning paddle wheel, and a small band consisting of a banjo player, a drummer, and an organist. Odd music, odd dancing.

The boat was barely half full, mostly with gray-haired couples, some tourists, and us. Later, as we tired of dancing, we walked along the painted rail, watching the sluggish water, a turbulent, muddy navy blue. I looked up for stars, but it was cloudy, forecast to rain. We would need a hotel that night.

'I love you,' Eric said.

'I love you,' I answered.

He looked at me, then at the water, and nodded idly. 'Love is worth it, isn't it?' he asked.

'Yes.'

It began to rain.

CHAPTER TWENTY-SEVEN

When we got back from our trip I begged Mr. Rig to rehire me, but he refused. As much as he loved publicity, my kind was too hot for him.

I looked for other flying jobs, but they involved a lot of time and distance from home, from Eric. So, desperate, I found work in a branch of the public library at the art reference desk.

I worked Tuesdays, Thursdays, and Saturdays, and on those days I wore bright red lipstick. It looked hideous, but it was a gauge; I was trying to limit my stress. If I had to reapply it within an hour of arrival at my desk, it meant my lips were undergoing vigorous licking, and that meant trouble. Unfortunately, many days were heavy reapplication days.

On my way out after work on such a day, I noticed a flyer posted on a bulletin board at the library's entrance. It read: 'AIDS SURVIVORS SUPPORT GROUP. Wednesdays 7:30 P.M., 244 W. Henley Street. Join us to bitch, cry, laugh, and raise hell!' I read it again, stared at it for a minute, and repeated to myself, 'AIDS survivors.' I jotted the address on a dusty travel brochure I plucked from the floor, stuffed it into my backpack, and left.

Wednesday night, 7:30 PM, 244 W. Henley Street. Eric and I approached a frame house set back from the street, its paint a peeling light blue, the trim a darker blue-gray. The windows on the first floor were open to the porch, emitting crackling laughter along with billowing white lace curtains and strident, passionate voices.

I glanced at Eric; he smiled and whispered, 'My name's Alex, and I'm an AIDS survivor.'

I smiled and we walked on, up the splintered wooden steps and onto a warped porch that creaked our arrival. An empty porch swing suspended by two delicate chains swayed gently beside us. The inner door to the house was open; through the filtered haze of the screen, we could see a collection of people, some beautiful, most slender, talking, sipping seltzer, standing around.

'Go on,' Eric urged. I hesitated, and he reached around me, opening the door, guiding me ahead, into the foyer. A man noticed us and waved us inside as he walked over.

'Hello, welcome. Come right on in,' he said. His upper lip was obscured by a wiry blond mustache. 'I'm Gary, and I'm living with AIDS.'

'Hi,' I said, 'I'm Alex. I'm living with Eric.'

'He can't be all that bad,' Gary said, and chuckled. Eric smiled.

'No, I mean, Eric—'

'I have HIV,' Eric interrupted.

'So do we,' Gary said, leading us deeper into the living room. It was blue beyond belief, from carpeting to couch to wallpaper to ceiling; even the books on the shelves had blue covers and were arranged according to hue. I couldn't help staring.

Gary said, 'Godot, my partner, redecorated one day when he had the blues. Painted the outside, too.'

'It's very nice,' I said.

'No, it's not,' Gary said. 'It's gruesome. But, since he died I haven't . . .'

'I'm sorry.'

'Me too.' A shadow passed over Gary's face, erasing small talk, forcing tears to his eyes. 'He was an amazing person,' he said, looking around. He pulled at his mustache and went on, 'He did this when he was into Picasso's blue period. It must've been more than five years ago.'

'He was an artist?'

'House artist, like this,' he said, indicating the room with a sweeping motion of his arm.

'I'm an—'

'Hey, Gary, are we starting?' a man called from a cluster across the room.

Gary excused himself and I joined Eric, who was examining photographs on the mantel-piece. We helped ourselves to Perrier, carrot sticks, water crackers, brie. The group began with Eric and me on the rug in front of an empty fireplace.

'I guess we should start with introductions,' Gary said. 'You're on, Virgil.'

The man next to me, an African American with skin like midnight and a clean-shaven head, said, 'I'm Virgil, I'm a PWA—'

'That stands for Person with AIDS,' Gary interjected.

'Right,' Virgil said. 'I've had the virus since the eighties. I'm a survivor. I need laughter tonight. I need to cry. And I need love.'

There were nods and 'um-hmms' around the circle.

The man next to Virgil was small and delicate, with a thin voice. 'I'm Anthony,' he said. 'I'm HIV symptomatic. I'm a survivor, and I'm pissed. I need action tonight.'

This brought nods from the group and a 'yes sir' from Virgil.

Next to Anthony was Darryl. His cheeks were inverted, his face blotted with purple lesions. 'I'm Darryl,' he said. 'I'm a survivor with full-blown AIDS. I need a cure.'

'That's right, yes you do,' Virgil intoned, rocking fluidly.

'Let's chant for a cure,' a woman, not yet introduced, said.

'Yes sir,' Virgil said, now louder, his swaying picking up speed.

'Wait,' Gary said. 'We have new members.'

'That's right, that's right,' from Virgil.

Eric squeezed my hand, then kissed it, rubbing it against his face, warmly familiar.

'My name's Cat,' the next man in the circle said. 'I'm not a fag, now, so don't get the wrong idea.' The others rolled their eyes, a few shook their heads. 'But I've got the virus. I got it from a whore—'

'Welcome back, Cat,' Gary said. 'What do you need tonight?'

'What I need is heroin. But don't get me wrong, now, I ain't been doin' the shit. I need friends who ain't on it, ya know?' He pulled at the heavy silver zipper on the front of his black leather jacket; it had an arching, hissing, red-and-white cat painted on it.

'We know, brother,' Virgil said, now rocking in full circles, within inches of me.

Gary was next. 'I've got AIDS and I'm a survivor. I own this place, me and Godot—'

'God rest his soul,' Anthony said.

'Amen. Yes sir, amen,' Virgil chimed.

Gary went on, 'I started this group with Godot seven years ago.'

'Amen.'

'This group is for us,' Gary said, 'for our survival.' He fell silent, suddenly saddened, and there was a momentary pause in the room, as if those gathered were considering this, scanning the past seven years, wondering if hope had been buried along with so many friends and lovers along the way. Then Gary smiled and looked to the person next to him, grasping her hand briefly.

'I'm Kirsten, or Kristine, I haven't decided,' she said in an airy voice. She was thin, with pink lipstick surrounded by coarse black facial hair, a coordinated knit pantsuit, and pink patent leather pumps with matching purse. She said, 'I'm a survivor with HIV, no symptoms—'

'Amen, amen,' Virgil said.

Kirsten/Kristine continued. 'Just call me KK until I decide. I haven't decided about the, you know, the surgery, either, so KK's better anyway, and since I was Karl Kibben before, I'm used to KK. Yes, I think—'

'Thanks, K,' Gary said.

'You're welcome.'

'What do you need tonight?' Darryl asked KK.

'Hmmm . . . well, I guess I would like that surgery. But then, I haven't decided about it yet, and—'

'Thanks, K,' Gary repeated, and looked to the next person, to Eric's left.

'I'm Kiki, not KK, Ki-ki. I've got AIDS, and I'm a hurtin' survivor. I need to scream.' Her voice was deep and she had short, slick black hair, bronze skin, and a wide face with a broad nose. She turned to Eric, as if to pass the baton, and glared. I thought she would scream right then, she looked so angry, but instead, he met her gaze, and she smiled, like a break in her face. She was missing a front tooth.

'Eric Moro,' Eric said. 'Glad to be here, glad to be a survivor. I have HIV, no symptoms, low T-cells. I need . . . ' He looked to me, and I suddenly realized I didn't know the answer. A warm, early June breeze riffled through the room, skating over exposed skin, lifting delicate hair, as he said, 'I need to make Alex happy,' and gripped my hand. A few eyebrows were raised; I noticed a sidelong glance. Virgil mumbled, 'Amen. Yes, sir. Amen,' almost continuously, like a hymn sung low.

'I'm Alex,' I said, 'I'm HIV negative . . . I . . . I'm sorry.'

Silence ensued, followed by knee-slapping laughter, howling, gut-wrenching laughter that spread like a wave through the ranks of the circle, from Gary and Virgil on around. Eric and I joined in, but not with gusto, just courtesy.

Amid this, Kiki screeched, 'The only place in the fucking universe where anyone would be sorry to say that!'

It took a few minutes for the laughter to die down.

Finally, Gary said, 'Okay, Alex. What do you need besides to rid yourself of survivor's guilt?'

Survivor's guilt . . .

'Alex?' Gary said.

'Oh . . . right. I need advice,' I answered.

'Okay,' Gary said. 'Let's start.'

Virgil began. 'I've been seeing so much death going down around me, I don't know what to do. Sometimes I cry, sometimes I try to laugh, but in the end, love is taken. There's no undoing that.'

Anthony took Virgil's hand as he continued to sway.

'How many friends have you lost, Gary?' Virgil asked.

'I've lost count, my friend.'

'Me too.'

'I haven't been able to keep up with the funerals, memorial services, cremations . . . ' Darryl said.

'I try to go to them all—'

'The dance card is fuckin' full,' Kiki said.

'How many friends have you gained?' Anthony asked.

'Too many to count,' Gary answered.

'And how many of them will die?' Darryl asked.

'Every fucking last one of them, without a cure,' Kiki said.

'Let's chant for a cure,' Virgil said.

'At the end,' Gary said.

'Anybody heard about any new treatments?' Kiki asked.

Anthony answered, 'I heard about this fungus that grows—'

'Fungus!' KK said. 'Fungus is bad for you.'

'Not this kind,' Anthony said.

'Anyway,' Cat said, 'friends is more important to me than treatments. It's hard findin' them when you kick the shit.'

'Were all your friends addicts?' Eric asked.

'Hell, yeah. Wouldn't nobody else hang.'

'You didn't want to hang with anybody else,' KK said. 'I remember when you first came here, you were still strung out—'

'All right, all right. Leave me alone,' Cat said, scowling at KK.

'I will not,' she said. 'Like it or not, you're my friend, Cat, till the end.' She smiled triumphantly; he grunted and shifted in his chair, looking away.

'What kind of advice do you need, Alex?' Gary asked.

'I want to sue the residency programs that discriminated against Eric.'

'You applying for citizenship, man?' Cat asked.

'No,' I said, 'Eric's graduating from med school this month—'

'Congratulations.'

'More power to you.'

'Amen.'

'But,' I continued, 'even though he's the best in the class, they wouldn't give him a spot, because—'

'They're assholes, that's why,' Kiki said.

'And,' I said, 'they must've found out about the HIV, and then they didn't accept him, and now we don't have enough money for a lawyer—'

'Welcome to the "HIV-Infected, We're Treated like the Scum of the Earth Club,"' Darryl said. 'No need for whites.'

'Ain't that the truth,' Virgil commented.

'Sorry, Virg,' Darryl said. 'I meant tennis whites. As in, tennis club.'

'I know. And I meant the scum of the earth thing.'

'Oh.'

'But,' I began, 'it's not legal—'

'You a doctor, man?' Cat asked Eric.

'Not yet. I'm graduating—'

'Like prescriptions and stuff?' Cat asked.

'Leave him alone,' KK admonished, reaching around Gary to hit Cat on the arm.

'I's just asking. Shit,' Cat said.

Eric said, 'We need to find a lawyer. Does anyone here know one?'

'How about the AIDS Project?' Darryl said. 'They have a legal department.'

'I volunteer there,' Anthony said. 'I can ask.'

'Great,' I said.

'What do you need, Gary?' Eric asked.

Gary smiled. 'I need to give.'

'You do, man. Every week,' Cat said.

'Amen. Yes, sir.'

'Are you ready?' Gary asked. They all nodded and stood; Eric and I did the same, looking at each other, wondering. 'Are you ready?' Gary asked again. The group nodded and everyone clasped hands.

We watched as the rest of the group closed their eyes and began to chant '*AIDS cure now, AIDS cure now, AIDS cure now.*' Then we joined in; I could hear Eric's distinctive timbre, his loving whispers forever fresh on my ears. I closed my eyes, the chant a mantra, and began to undulate with the others to the rhythm of our words.

Piercing, shocking, it skinned my eyes open: a scream the pitch and volume of a train whistle from Kiki's lungs to our hearts. I watched her in alarm, her face twisted, her mouth open, bottomless. Then I began to nod, faster, forcefully. She was right; it felt like that.

Virgil's laughter was a dark bubble beside me.

CHAPTER TWENTY-EIGHT

The phone woke me at eight the following morning. It was Anthony, his voice thin and silvery. 'Alex?' he asked.

'Yes, who's this?'

'Anthony, from the group.'

'Oh. Hi.'

'I'm at the AIDS Project. I've got a lawyer here. He wants to talk to you.'

I sat up with Eric still slumbering beside me. 'Fantastic,' I said.

'Ms. Taylor?' a deep voice asked.

'Yes, is this the lawyer?'

'My name is Hank Brown. I'm a legal consultant at the AIDS Project. Anthony tells me you have a discrimination suit.'

'Are you a real lawyer?' I asked.

'As real as they get,' he said with a laugh.

'I'll be there in fifteen minutes.'

'I'll look forward to meeting you.'

'Thanks. Bye.' I hung up and ran for the shower.

I parked Shadow Blaster, sprinting up the steps and through the front door of the AIDS Project building. It was solid concrete and glass, rigid, seemingly indestructible.

'I'm here to see the lawyer,' I told the receptionist. 'Hank somebody—'

'Hank Brown. Down the hall to the left, down the next hall on the right, second door on the right.'

'Thanks,' I said, and hurried away, my scuffed black motorcycle helmet beneath my arm.

The door to Hank Brown's office was slightly ajar. It had a sign on it that read LEGAL DEPARTMENT, and below that a round sticker, a little tilted, that someone had tried unsuccessfully to scrape off. It read: WE'LL SUE THE ASSHOLES!

I knocked.

'Come in, please,' a voice said.

I entered. An African American man in his early seventies sat behind a chipped brown desk. He reached over it to shake my hand. 'I'm Hank Brown,' he said.

'Hi, I'm Alex Taylor.'

'Pleased to meet you, Ms. Taylor. Have a seat.'

'Call me Alex,' I said as I sat.

'All right, Alex. And I'm Hank to you.'

'Thanks.'

'First, we need to get a few things straight. You can see I'm in a wheelchair. Most people don't mention it, polite-like, but it's there nonetheless, so let's get it out of the way right now. Ask me anything you want about it.'

'It's none of my business—'

'Ask.' He was firm, almost angry. He had a voice that rumbled; I could practically hear it in the courtroom, arguing Eric's case, forceful, convincing.

'Okay,' I agreed. 'I . . . I . . . well, what, I mean . . .' Hank stared at me as I stammered, his dark eyes direct, waiting behind gold-rimmed spectacles. His body was large, like a cube, his skin the color of rich caramel, his hair edged in gray. 'I mean,' I said, 'what . . . what happened?'

'Gunshot to the back.'

'Gunshot?'

'Attempted lynching.'

'You . . .'

'I escaped.'

'Barely.'

'It left its mark on me.'

'That's horrifying.'

'Yes.'

'I'm sorry.'

'Then let's make it better.'

'How?' I asked.

'Tell me what's happening with . . . ' He looked down at a yellow legal pad on his desk. 'With Eric Moro.'

'He's my fiancé. He's graduating from medical school next week. They've denied him a residency.'

'They?' Hank asked. I watched as he scribbled notes on the pad.

'The programs he applied to.'

'How do you know the rejections have to do with discrimination?'

'He's the best—'

'You're engaged to him.'

'Yes.' He stopped writing and looked at me over his glasses. I added, 'But he *is* the best.'

'Can you prove that?'

'Uh-huh. Board scores, grades, evaluations, class ranking—they're all in his file at school.'

'Dr. Moro is HIV-positive?'

'He tested positive during his third year of medical school after a needle stick injury at the hospital.'

'Was he tested at the hospital?'

'At Employee Health. They reported it to a special committee.'

'What committee?'

'A committee that decides if hospital personnel who test HIV-positive can keep working with patients.'

'And they concluded Dr. Moro could?'

'Yes.'

'Was someone on the committee in a position to tell the programs about Dr. Moro's HIV status?'

'The dean of the medical school. He's in charge of the students' residency applications. He was the one who told Eric he didn't get a residency.'

'So you think he informed the programs.'

'Yes, especially after the way his assistant, Sally, acted.'

'And how was that?'

'She said it was complicated why Eric didn't get a residency, and that the dean had to weigh . . .'

'Weigh what?'

'I don't know. After that she clammed up. Then she started crying.'

'Crying?'

'Uh-huh, weird. And before that she practically dragged me out of the office.'

'I see.'

'She knows something.'

'It would appear so. Go on.'

'I think the dean didn't want to harm his reputation with those programs. He didn't want to send them a student with HIV because that would make them reluctant to take students from his medical school in the future.'

'Hmmm . . .' Off came the glasses; Hank rubbed the bridge of his nose between a thumb and forefinger. 'Hmmm . . .' he repeated, his eyes closed, his head bowed.

'Can we sue those programs for discrimination?' I asked.

Hank opened his eyes, raised his head, replaced his glasses, and said, 'It won't be easy.'

'I know.'

'Does Dr. Moro realize that?'

'Eric. Yes, he does.'

'If this Sally knows something, she'll be a key witness. Discrimination will be hard to prove unless we can show the programs knew about the HIV.'

'Right.' I waited, watching him, holding my breath, hoping.

Finally, he said, 'Get me a list of the

residency programs, Eric's class ranking, board scores and evaluations, a release of medical records, and get the man himself in here—is he healthy enough?'

'Yes. Yes, he is. You're taking the case?'

'No, I'm winning the case.'

'Who are you?' I asked.

He laughed; it reverberated across the expanse of his desk. 'I'm not Ironside,' he said, and laughed again.

I stood as Hank rolled over toward me. We shook hands. 'Thank you,' I said. 'I can't—'

'That's something else we have to get straight. No money and no thanks. My job is to fight the bad guys. You just keep bringing 'em to me.'

I smiled, nodded, and left.

Eric met with Hank that afternoon, while I was at work, and by the following week the lawyer had obtained Eric's records and was ready to file the suit. According to Hank, cases like Eric's fell under the Americans with Disabilities Act, which declared it illegal to discriminate based solely on HIV status.

I met Eric at the Bookstore/Coffeeshop that evening, after I was through at the library; he was there when I arrived. It was 8:45, the sun had set, and he sat at our usual table by the window. Unseen, I stood in the doorway for several minutes, studying him like I had almost four years before, when we had first met. He was losing weight; although still handsome, he was thin. He coughed periodically, dry and raspy; I had noticed and ignored it over the past week. His intensity was the same, however, and the smile that broke it when he realized I was there was unchanged, revealing my Eric.

'Hi,' I said, kissing him and slipping into the chair across from him, where my espresso waited.

'Hi,' he answered. 'That lawyer's really something.'

'I know.' I touched my lips to the coffee.

'He almost makes me wish I could be a lawyer.'

'Funny,' I said, 'he made me feel that way too.'

'You'd make a good one.'

'You too.'

We held hands across the table and I skimmed my fingers up his arm, beneath the short sleeve of his white T-shirt, over the wizard.

Eric would've been good at a lot of things, but life had turned simple. He was getting sick. We both knew it.

CHAPTER TWENTY-NINE

AIDS is an illness that will creep or crush, but either way, it heads in a singular direction; we were pointed there. The week before his medical school graduation, Eric was admitted to the hospital where he had been groomed as the outstanding doctor of his class. That day we found out he had Pneumocystis pneumonia, or PCP, and MAI, an infection of the bloodstream. Lucky for us, both were treatable. For a time.

I lay beside Eric on his hospital bed that first night, his eyes sunken and bright with fever, his face angular, still beautiful. 'I love you, darlin',' he said.

I answered, 'I love you.'

He slept, crystal fluid dripping into a vein

in his arm, his breathing rapid and shallow. I listened to him living, tried to hold it in my hand.

Some hours later, my neck sore, my mouth tasting of sorrow and panic, I sat up and sighed, watching him. He slept the deep sleep of serious illness, no space for dreams, no need for nightmares. I kissed him, his lips dry and hot, an exaggerated pink-on-white.

When I stood, anguish ripped through the dark, hard against me. I stepped into the hallway to breathe, to walk, to escape, the light abrupt in my eyes. But worry trailed me, my problems looming into an unruly swarm, corpulent with demand. I sat on the floor outside Eric's room, and wept.

At around 3:00 A.M., I went back to Eric's bedside, stroking him in his sleep. He awoke, his fever gone, and it was almost like those early days, when nighttime was for making love, and excitement held fatigue at bay. I stripped by the light of the moon on that twelfth floor ward with the hum of the IVAC pump my serenade, the man of my dreams my audience of one.

After I had danced naked for him, making us giggle and gasp, I climbed into his bed and we played M&Ms, our shorthand for 'mutual masturbation.' Usually we played it with actual M&Ms, but that night we weren't prepared, so we used fingers, toes, knees, breasts and elbows, with explosive results. Then we slept, like our first night together, cuddled and content.

The next morning, vitals were at six and breakfast at six-thirty. It wasn't until seven that we noticed the stack of condoms some kind soul had left at our bedside while we dozed. But no M&Ms.

Eric had been hospitalized for five days, gaining weight, feeling better and better. I hadn't left his side during this time except to go home and change clothes or get something to eat, and I had thought of nothing but his fever curve, lessening cough, life-saving IV treatments, and clinging to seconds ticking into oblivion.

'Good morning,' he whispered on the fifth morning, waking me. It was unusual for him to awaken before me. The sun was just rising, infusing the hospital room with a hopeful pink warmth.

'Good morning,' I answered, rising off my cot to go to him. I kissed him, taking his hand in mine. 'How do you feel?' I asked.

'Okay.'

'Just okay?'

He glanced away, out the window. 'Look at the sunrise,' he said.

I followed his gaze. The sun lit the clouds with a copper rim of fire; it was heartwrenchingly beautiful. 'Um-hmm,' I said, then looked back at him. He continued to look out the window, his expression far off.

'What is it?' I asked.

'I almost got there,' he said.

'Where?'

'To graduation. I almost made it all the way through medical school.'

I gasped, twisting my head to see the calendar. It was June 13. How could I have forgotten? 'Eric . . . ' I said. We locked eyes.

'I got damn close, Al.'

'But you did finish. Graduation's only a ceremony.'

'You're right.' He glanced away again, tears filling his eyes. 'It's only a ceremony.'

We were silent for a few minutes. I didn't know how to make it better; my mind scrambled for words that could make a difference.

Finally, he said, 'When I found out about the HIV, I knew there'd be a lot of things I'd never do.' I started to cry. He continued. 'I accepted that, but at least I wanted to do an internship. When that fell apart, I set my sights on making it through medical school, hanging on till graduation.'

'You did, Eric. And we'll get you an internship. '

He turned toward me, bringing my hand to his lips. 'I love you, that's what matters, Al. As my strength starts to fade, you've been picking it up and using it.'

I sobbed. 'Your strength isn't fading, you're better every day . . . '

'I'm dying, Al.'

'No!' I stood. 'I'll find your doctor. You're going to graduation.'

'It's a quarter to six in the morning.'

'I don't care. I'll wake her up.'

'I don't have the strength . . . '

'Then I'll walk through the procession with you.'

We stared at each other. Suddenly, something I had carelessly forgotten seemed vital to his survival. Yes, it was a ceremony, but more importantly it was a mark on a page of his life, a life with so few pages remaining, where the possibility for achievement was sputtering under the weight of illness.

That was the hardest part for me, being close to him, understanding, sharing his dreams. Being there allowed me to see too clearly what he could not look away from. It felt like a flame held against my eye.

I had to go home to get clothes for Eric, and for me. I also had to shower.

'Alex!' a man sitting on our stoop called as I rode up on Shadow Blaster. He stood and waved.

My breath caught. The man was Eric five years younger, with shorter, thicker hair, no earrings, no ravages of pain or virus. It was Jerry, Eric's younger brother. Beside him stood a woman, her clean-shaven head shining in the early morning heat, three small silver rings identical to Eric's earrings piercing the side of her right nostril, her dark eyes plucked from Eric's face, and his mother's before him. She was Pammy, Eric's sister from Paris. We had invited them for graduation months ago, then forgotten.

'Hey, Alex,' Jerry said, approaching me as I parked the bike and took my helmet off.

'Jerry?' I asked.

'In the flesh.'

'You grew up,' I mumbled.

'I'm Pammy,' the woman said, extending her hand. 'Where the hell is Eric?'

They stared at me, waiting.

'It's the thirteenth, right?' Pammy said. 'Did we fuck up?'

'No,' I said. 'The graduation's today. I'm glad you're here. Let's go upstairs.'

They followed me into the apartment. It was stale, messy. Pammy sat on the sofa, Jerry took a chair.

'I have to shower,' I said. 'Do you want a drink?' I opened the refrigerator; a pungent blue-gray rim of mold had taken hold on its rubber seal. It was empty save for mustard, a desiccated hot dog, one aging beer. 'I have water,' I said.

'Water, that sounds good,' Jerry said.

'I don't have ice,' I said.

'That's okay—'

'Where is he?' Pammy asked.

I turned and faced her.

'Is he at a rehearsal or something?' she asked.

'How long have you been waiting?'

'I got in at two this morning,' Jerry said. 'Pammy was already here.'

'Sorry,' I said.

Pammy stood. 'Did you guys break up? 'Cause if you did, that's okay, but I'd like to see my brother. I came a hell of a long way to watch him graduate.'

I sat at the kitchen table, studying my nails. A single tear dripped down the side of my face. I watched it splash on the brown wood grain. 'You'll see him,' I said.

'What is it?' Jerry asked.

I looked up at him. He was handsome in the way Eric couldn't help being, even sick: dramatically dark, muscular, and casually sexy.

'I told him to tell you before now,' I said.

'What?'

'But he didn't want to. He was hoping you wouldn't need to know so soon.'

'He's not graduating?' Pammy asked, standing. Jerry stared, his brow wrinkling.

'I wish it were that.' I paused. 'He's sick.'

'Sick?' they said in unison.

'He's in the hospital. He has AIDS.'

'AIDS?' Jerry repeated, a look of horror crossing his face.

'HIV or AIDS?' Pammy asked.

Our eyes met. She looked so like her mother, delicate features, her head oval, perfectly smooth, but her face was set with resolve, rebellion. 'AIDS,' I said.

'My God,' Jerry said. 'Where'd he get it?'

'I'd rather he tell you,' I said. I sighed a shaky breath, sniffled. 'I have to get back to the hospital.'

'How bad is he?' Pammy asked.

'He has PCP. That's—'

'I know what it is,' Pammy said. 'I've seen a lot of this, in Paris.'

'You have?'

'Yes. So he has PCP, that's treatable.'

'And MAI.'

'Where?'

'The bloodstream.'

'Again, treatable.'

'For a while,' I said.

'It was the drugs that summer, wasn't it?' Pammy asked.

'When?' Jerry asked. 'What drugs?'

'You know?' I said.

'We only had each other. We didn't have many secrets,' Pammy answered.

'He did drugs?' Jerry asked.

'That little whore infected my brother,' Pammy said, her fists clenched.

'She wasn't a whore,' I said.

Jerry looked between us, confused, catching up by force.

'I'd kill her if she hadn't already done it for me,' Pammy said.

'There's no accounting with this disease, Pammy,' I said. 'There's nothing we can do but hold on—to ourselves, to each other.'

Pammy's hands relaxed. A couple of tears edged out of her eyes. She quickly wiped them away. Jerry stood and hugged her, holding her close. She was stiff for a few moments, then her shoulders slumped and she began to sob. 'He's my brother!' she wailed over and over. Then Jerry's sobs joined hers, and I watched them rock each other, having arrived to celebrate with and to honor their older brother, and instead being met by terror and grief.

Their sorrow brought my own to the surface and it spilled over for a time until I choked it down.

'I have to shower, get dressed and go back,' I said, standing.

They looked at me, their sobs having slowed, tears mottling their faces red.

'Is he graduating today?' Pammy asked.

I nodded. 'I'll carry him if I have to.'

Pammy walked toward me, placing a hand on my shoulder. 'And I'll carry you carrying him if I have to,' she said.

'I think I'm most qualified to carry him, and Alex, and you, Pammy,' Jerry said.

I wept anew, this time with relief. We would carry each other.

Pammy, Jerry, and I arrived at the hospital at eleven; Eric was having his IV capped with a Hep-lock in preparation for his shower; the graduation was at one. When Eric saw his siblings, his face lit up like a hundred floodlights; his smile was wider than I had seen it in weeks.

'Bro!' he yelled. 'And Pammy! You guys made it!'

They hugged, three-way, Eric's bare, thin buttocks exposed by the gap in the back of his hospital gown, the brothers' dark heads a contrast to Pammy's golden sheen.

'I guess Alex told you,' Eric said, pulling away to sit on the edge of the bed.

'Yeah,' Jerry said, gulping tears. 'But you look good, bro.'

'You too,' Eric answered. 'You look like me.'

Jerry tried to smile.

'We know about the PCP and MAI, Eric,' Pammy said, 'and we're gonna fight it every inch of the way. You sure you're okay to go to graduation?'

'Sure,' Eric said, taking my hand.

'It's only a ceremony,' Pammy said. 'Don't push yourself on account of us.'

'Right,' Jerry said. 'Your health is most important. We can celebrate right here.'

'I know it's only a ceremony,' Eric said, looking up at me. 'But I want you guys to see me graduate, to see that I made it.'

I smiled, trying not to cry again.

'Are Mom and Dad coming?' Jerry asked.

'Oh shit!' I said. 'Did we forget them too?'

'No,' Eric said. 'No to both questions.'

'Good,' Pammy answered.

'They couldn't make it,' Eric said in response to my questioning look. 'I guess it's just as well under the circumstances.'

'They don't know?' Jerry asked.

'No,' Eric said.

'When are you gonna tell them?' Jerry asked.

Eric shrugged.

'Why couldn't they make it?' Pammy asked.

'Some business meeting Dad had,' Eric answered, standing up. 'I guess I better get in the shower while I have the chance.'

'You need help?' I asked.

'No, thanks.' He kissed me, went into the bathroom, and closed the door.

'My God,' Jerry whispered, 'he's so skinny.' His eyes filled with tears, he sat and began to cry, trying to hold it back. He covered his mouth with his hand.

'He does look like shit,' Pammy said, 'but don't tell him that.'

'I won't,' Jerry said.

'Let's try to stay hopeful and upbeat,' Pammy said.

We all nodded. Jerry wiped his eyes.

'Don't you think he should tell your parents that he's sick?' I asked.

'No,' Pammy said.

'But they can help,' Jerry said.

'Help?' Pammy said. 'They've fucked up everything so far.'

'What do you mean?' I asked.

'I mean they're shitty parents. Parents are supposed to protect their kids and support them, but especially they're supposed to believe them.'

'They aren't perfect,' Jerry said, blowing his nose, gaining control, 'but they do love us.'

'They do?' Pammy said.

Jerry answered 'Yes,' but I wondered if the truth wasn't somewhere between the two.

'As far as I'm concerned,' Pammy said, 'they stopped being parents a long time ago.'

'Eric said your father lost interest in him,' I said.

'That's putting it mildly.'

'You don't know what you're talking about, Pammy,' Jerry said.

'*You* don't know what you're talking about, Jerry,' she answered.

'What *are* we talking about?' I asked.

But before either one could answer, Eric

emerged from the bathroom, wrapped in a towel, grinning. 'You want a show, stay,' he said. 'Otherwise, everybody except Alex scram while I dress.'

Pammy and Jerry left. I sat and watched Eric. He put on a crisp white shirt and brilliant tie—magenta, black, turquoise—his slacks now too big, almost comical. I bit back tears as he faced me, arms out, and turned slowly for my approval. I nodded, stood, and took his hand. We joined Jerry and Pammy in the hall and walked out of the hospital, the four of us, together.

At the graduation, Pammy, Jerry, and I sat close to the podium, just in case, and the others, my family mostly, sat high in the bleachers of the red-brick, ivy-covered stadium. There they waved and cheered, watching a sea of navy gowns with orange trim far below, trying to pick out Eric from beneath hundreds of flat, square caps.

Being in crowds had changed for me since Eric's diagnosis. Questions pushed forward: How many among us were infected with HIV, or had undiagnosed tumors creeping along our brains, up our colons? How many would be dead on this date next year? I tried to ignore such questions, but it was difficult. My innocence was lost, my blessed ignorance sullied, yanked out from beneath me.

We watched Eric as he walked steadily to receive his diploma from a smiling, graying patriarch. The crowd applauded, then provided a silent gap, for the following graduate. I don't suppose they noticed, their eyes on the next in line, how slowly Eric walked, and how delicately, as if his measured steps were balanced on the fragile surface of health, beneath which he dared not fall. We sweated; we held our breath; we tried to feel only pride, to shed only tears of simple joy.

When the ceremony was over, and we waited for Eric to join us, Danny, Eric's gross anatomy partner from four years before, brushed by me. At first I thought she didn't see me, or didn't recognize me, but when she was a few steps beyond where I stood, she turned and said, 'Alex?'

'Hi, Danny,' I said. She stepped toward me. She was even more stunning now that she had matured some; she seemed angular and serious, yet somehow yielding and gentle.

'How are you?' she asked.

'Okay, and you?'

'Fine.' She paused, awkward, before saying, 'If there's anything I can do . . . with the, you know . . . ' She glanced around quickly, looking over her shoulder, and added, 'The illness, just ask.'

'Thank you,' I said, trying not to cry. I searched the masses for Eric. He was chatting with some classmates, but I could see he was fatigued, wobbling a little. 'I have to go,' I said. 'Congratulations.'

'Are you sure you're okay?' she asked.

'As okay as possible.'

'You don't look sick.'

'I'm not infected, if that's what you mean.'

'You're not?'

'No.'

'But . . . I assumed . . . I mean, you stayed with him and everything.'

'I stayed with him because I love him.'

'Of course,' she said, embarrassed. 'I didn't mean—'

'There's Eric. I have to meet him.'

'Okay. It was nice talking to you.'

'You too. Good-bye, Danny.'

'Good-bye, Alex.'

I walked away from her, toward Eric, but she hesitated for a moment, unsure. She had escaped HIV infection, but not HIV; it had rocked her world as it had ours, just not as forcefully—she still had the option of turning her head and walking in the opposite direction.

Later, in Eric's hospital room, we poured champagne, made jolly, toasted his success. But although he smiled, he was exhausted, sleeping easily despite the throng of merry-makers who had come to wish him well, grateful to sip amnesia from a Styrofoam cup.

CHAPTER THIRTY

Like most predictions, the one about Eric's hospital stay was wrong; it stretched from two weeks into a month.

Eric and I had been going to the AIDS Survivors Group regularly after that first time, until he got sick. That's when I needed the group most, but I was overwhelmed, scrambling. I missed three weeks.

'Hello? Gary?' I called in the foyer of 244 W. Henley Street the next Wednesday evening.

'Is that Alex?' Gary's voice floated down from upstairs.

'Yeah. I'm early.'

He emerged at the top of the stairs, wet and naked except for a small white towel around his waist. 'I'll be right down,' he said, and turned away. His legs were muscular, the HIV yet invisible.

I sat in the blue living room for a while, then looked around, went to the mantel, and picked up a picture. It was Gary and another young man, with a tanned and sculptured body.

'Godot,' Gary said from over my shoulder. 'Way handsome, hunh?'

'How long . . . I mean . . . '

'Before he died was that taken?'

I nodded.

'Years,' he said, shaking his head. 'Years.'

'Sorry I haven't been around,' I said, replacing the photo.

'No apologies needed.'

'Hellooooo,' KK called from the foyer.

'Hi, KK,' we said.

'Where's your sexy hunk of man, Alex?'

'In the hospital,' I answered.

'What a shame,' she said, and in came Virgil with Kiki.

'Amen, amen, we're surviving,' chanted Virgil.

'Shit, I want a cure,' Kiki said, throwing her bicycle helmet on the couch; it made KK jump.

'Hey, dudes,' Cat said, striding in. He had spurs on his boots and they jingled as he walked.

We settled into the usual positions, finding

comfort in small routine while our whole world tilted, slipping.

'Where are Darryl and Anthony?' Gary asked. 'It's not like them to be late.'

And then we saw him—Anthony, silhouetted in the doorway, a narrow shadow. He grunted, like he'd just been pounded on the back. 'Darryl's gone,' he said. 'He died an hour ago.'

'Died?' Kiki said. 'He was gettin' that new treatment for KS, what the fuck happened?'

'He stopped breathing,' Anthony said, stepping into the light. His bloodshot eyes were huge in his face. 'He didn't want heroic measures,' he went on, 'and even though he had an advance directive, the doctors asked me—maybe 'cause they knew I was Darryl's surrogate, and I was standing right there—they asked me if they should resuscitate him.'

We waited, watching him, his heavy silence made more conspicuous by the sound of a fly buzzing against the glass of the front window.

'And . . . and . . . ' Anthony mumbled, trudging to the sofa, sagging into his place, 'and what did I say? My heart screamed yes! but my mouth said no.'

We exhaled a collective breath. Anthony began to cry. 'Why did I have to be the one to let him go?' he wailed.

Gary went to Anthony and held him, his sobs small bursts of sorrow against Gary's chest. Somehow Gary remained dry-eyed; his grief seemed beyond tears, more profound, in a distant, lightless place.

Darryl's death stunned more than saddened me. I found it overwhelming, the realization that he could be alive and then dead, without warning, without good-bye. That it could happen to someone I knew.

We were quiet, watching Anthony shake his small head, his tears falling onto his delicate hands, clasped in his lap; Darryl had sat next to him in the group for years.

'Chant, now!' Kiki shouted, and we rose, clasping hands around the circle. She started: '*Darryl lives, Darryl lives, Darryl lives, Darryl lives*,' and we all joined in. Then, '*AIDS cure now, AIDS cure now, AIDS cure now*.' I didn't notice myself crying until Kiki screamed and I opened my eyes to see that we all were. We let go and sat.

'Where's Eric?' Virgil asked.

'Hospital,' KK answered. 'It's a shame.'

'With what?'

'MAI, PCP,' I answered.

'I'm so sorry,' Virgil said.

'He's better,' I said. 'He's coming home soon.'

'Amen, amen.'

We were quiet except for the buzzing of the fly, the humming of Virgil's 'amens,' a soothing, rhythmic mantra hollowed of words.

Finally, I stood and walked to Anthony, taking his hand and sitting beside him in Darryl's place. It was my place now.

CHAPTER THIRTY-ONE

When Eric was discharged from the hospital it was mid-July; we tried hard to be normal. I was frantically assisting Hank with research for the lawsuit, scrabbling to get Eric that internship, to grant him what I was desperately denying to myself was his last wish.

'I got the job,' Eric said at dinner one night while a tired, oscillating fan pushed humidity around us.

'What's that?' I asked.

'You know, that job teaching the physician assistants anatomy, over at the college.'

'That's nice.' I stabbed at a salad as I pored over a thick stack of photocopies, my day's research from the law library.

'I start tomorrow,' he said. 'And I don't make

enough to disqualify for Medicaid.'

'Um-hmm.' I munched lettuce, a chunk of carrot.

'I need to work. Otherwise I'll go crazy.'

'Right.'

'I had to fuck three women to get the interview.'

'That's nice.'

'Dammit!'

I looked up. 'What?' I asked.

'What's happening, Al?'

'What do you mean?' I asked, standing and carrying my bowl to the kitchen, rinsing it methodically.

'This is the time I have,' he said. 'This is all.'

I stared into the porcelain sink, at years of circular brown-gray stains on its surface, evidence of shared intimacy by tenants unknown and unknowable. I wondered, was that all that would be left by us? I began to cry, tears so weak, so human, they would never stain.

I felt Eric's arms circle me from behind. 'Is it too hard just to live?' he asked.

I shook my head vigorously.

He held me close, my narrow back fitting too well against his chest. He said, 'I'm surprised how simple pleasure is. Patients told me, but I didn't know till now.'

I couldn't meet his eyes, the truth like slow

torture burrowing a hole through me.

He went on, 'Facing it changes you, Al. Objects are so bright, I could squint all the time.'

I wanted to be with him, to look through his eyes, but *he* was the bright spot in my life, and, like a shooting star, he was dimming.

'Now I can appreciate a shared salad,' he said, 'or a part-time job, even staying on Medicaid.'

He turned me around and I was forced to meet his gaze. He smiled and kissed my eyes, tasting my tears, savoring even sorrow. 'Appreciate, Al. That's about all I have left to give.'

'No,' I said, choking on the effort of the word. 'That's not all. I'm going to get you that internship if it kills me.'

I noticed what I had said too late to pull it back, and that's what he wanted, unleashed honesty, the most difficult gift. His smile turned into a grin as he kissed me again, this time on the lips.

We held each other for a long time at that sink, under humming fluorescent lights, filtered through a carpet of dead insects, and we appreciated what we could.

Eric and I had become in one small way like he and Tiffany had been, united by pain and neediness—only he had switched places with her and I with him. He needed unconditional love, while I needed to save him.

I couldn't let the outcome be the same.

CHAPTER THIRTY-TWO

Eric and I flew to Chicago in early September. Almost two years had passed since we had seen his parents, since we had been there to invite them to our wedding. It was excruciatingly sad to think of those two short years, to ponder simplicity lost, plans rendered meaningless.

We drove a rental car from the airport and rode in silence for most of the way, watching the gray–blue water of Lake Michigan glinting silver in the afternoon sunlight.

'This could be the last time I come home,' he said.

'Don't say that,' I said, biting my lip and looking out the window, tears stinging my eyes.

He took my hand. 'Then let's just say I come home every two years.'

'Okay. Every two years.'

Silence again, but not easy like before; grief had been given voice.

'How are you going to tell them?' I finally asked.

'About the HIV?'

'Yes.'

'I hadn't planned on telling them.'

'You hadn't?'

'No.'

'Why not?'

'Why?'

'They're your parents.'

'They'd be disappointed if they knew.'

'This isn't about letting anyone down, Eric. You have an illness.'

'It's not just an illness. It's AIDS.'

The truth of that statement shut me up. And perhaps he was right, that he'd disappoint his parents by dying, by rebelliously flaunting the natural progression of the species. And AIDS. The ultimate transgression.

We pulled into his parents' driveway; it made my heart race to see that house again, a home of such offhand neglect, secret heartache, and masked resentment. He turned off the ignition and we got out.

Eric's mother didn't come out to greet us, and his father wasn't home, but the front door was open, so we carried our suitcases in and took them upstairs without being noticed.

We went into Pammy's room. It was difficult to reconcile the woman with the room, it fitting more easily than she into the corners of conformity. 'Come here,' Eric said, pulling me onto the bed and grabbing a pack of peanut M&Ms from his jean-jacket pocket, where a condom would've once been.

'No,' I said, 'your mom might come up.' I struggled off the bed, glancing at the open door.

Eric lay there looking at me, his thin booted legs hanging over the side of the petite bed, his eyes smiling with the mischief of a little boy. I studied him for a minute and then smiled too, leaving the door ajar and stripping while he did the same, ripping open the pack of M&Ms with his mouth.

After we were done, we found Mrs. Moro out sunning herself in the backyard. She had fallen asleep, a sweating iced tea glass in her hand, her skin a tender, deep brown leather, gathered in folds over her belly, her neck. The sickening scent of coconut oil wafted from her, mixing with the smell of fresh-mown grass from a neighbor's yard. A bright green scarf covered pink rollers in her hair, and white-rimmed plastic sunglasses shielded her eyes.

Eric touched her forehead. She swatted at him, like a fly, but he dodged. He touched her cheek next and her eyes popped open.

'Who? Wha'?' she gasped, yanking her glasses off and sitting up, upsetting her iced tea; it poured evenly over her flat abdomen, dripping down her sides and through the slats of the lawn chair. As she sat up, her bikini top, the straps of which she had untied to tan her chest and shoulders evenly, slid down off her breasts, revealing their pale fullness and rich brown nipples.

'Mama, it's me,' Eric said as she frantically grasped the bikini straps, tying them into a bow behind her neck.

'Oh, Eric. Thank goodness it's only you, dear. Really, I wasn't expecting . . . oh, my. I'm sorry about, you know, all that.' She waved her hands around her breasts, clearly embarrassed, and sighed before looking at him. 'Oh,' she said, 'you're thin. So thin.'

'Mama, Alex is here.'

I stepped forward.

'Oh, of course,' she said, and stood, straightening her scarf and wiping at her belly. 'Hello, Alexandra.' She held out a hand slick with suntan oil. I shook it.

'Hello, Mrs. Moro,' I said.

'Let's go in, shall we?' she said, gathering her

paperback, beach towel, and glass. 'You'll have to excuse my appearance,' she commented, her hand again fluttering to her head, her cleavage, her belly. 'Just getting a little late-season sun.'

We smiled; we were as pale as two ghosts, having spent the summer at the hospital and in various libraries. We followed her into the kitchen.

'Eric,' she went on, 'I must see to it that you're fed. What on earth has happened to you? I have never seen you this thin.'

'Well, I—'

'What would you like, dear? I have roast beef, turkey, bologna—'

'Nothing for me, Mama. Maybe Alex—'

'I'll make you two some ham-and-cheese sandwiches with milk. Go sit in the dining room.'

'Okay,' Eric agreed, and winked at me as he led the way out of the kitchen. We sat at the dining room table.

'I didn't know your mom was so built,' I whispered when we were alone.

'Those,' he said with a smile, 'are silicone implants.'

'Oh.'

'I could've made a fortune doing them.'

'But you told me—'

'I wouldn't have, but I could have.'

'Here you are,' Mrs. Moro said, emerging from the kitchen carrying two plates piled high with potato chips and thick sandwiches. She set them down in front of us and left, returning momentarily with two tall glasses of milk.

'There,' she said, setting the glasses on the table.

'Thanks, Mama,' Eric said.

'Thanks Mrs. Moro,' I mumbled.

'You're welcome, dears,' she responded, standing at the side of the table, watching as Eric took a bite. She nodded, making little chewing motions with her jaw in concert with his.

'I'd better get dressed,' she said.

She gazed at Eric for several moments more, forcing him to eat a sandwich I knew he couldn't be hungry for. After all, we had just feasted on M&Ms.

Dinner with the Moros that night was just like every other dinner I had had with them. Most of the conversation was about what I was doing: flying, art, library work; Eric talked a little about his teaching job. Although Mr. Moro occasionally stared at his son quizzically, he never asked why he was so thin or why he wasn't doing an internship. When I brought up the subject of Pammy being in Philadelphia, it was simply ignored. All talk of whether we were married, living together, or Eric's obviously changed appearance was avoided. In short, it was a pleasant evening. It ended again with Scrabble. And again, Mr. Moro won.

The following day we went boating on Lake Michigan. As it was sizzling hot, we wore shorts. I watched Eric's mother stifle a gasp as we entered the living room and she saw Eric's bare legs, so painfully thin. But Mr. Moro didn't miss a beat, scolding us about being late and urging us out the front door.

I started to follow Eric and his father, but before I could, Mrs. Moro caught me by the shoulder, spinning me around, her eyes dark and sharp, probing.

'Alexandra, you must tell me about Eric,' she said.

I stared at her. 'What is it, Mrs. Moro?' I asked.

'Is he . . . is he sick?'

There it lay, the question asked. I hesitated, longing to say 'yes' and tell her about the virus, to toss the worst into the Moro family lap. There was only so much time. Time to reaffirm love, start anew, or maintain the eggshell facade.

'Ask him,' I said, practically pleading.

Her expression went through a series of changes, from apprehension to suspicion, finally resting on disbelief. She said, 'That was silly,' then giggled, adding, 'Let's go. Malcolm hates to be late.'

We walked outside and toward the car, where Mr. Moro sat behind the wheel drumming his fingers, and Eric lounged in the back, reading a book.

We went sailing, got sunburned, left the next day.

Every two years.

CHAPTER THIRTY-THREE

We skated on the surface of life, twirling when we could, speeding when we had to and falling when we had no choice. I was amazed that everything appeared to go on as usual in the world, as we started to sputter and grind to a halt.

Two months after we returned from Chicago, Eric suffered his second bout of PCP and was sentenced to another two weeks in the hospital. He lost his job and filed for disability income; I cut back my hours at the library to be with him. We shared a lot of late nights in that hospital room, but this time he had no energy for M&Ms, only sleep. I watched him wither, with no appetite for food, no lust for living. I thought he would die then, but we had many months to go.

It was the night before Eric's discharge from the hospital. I was having difficulty imagining him home, so weak and frail.

'Are you sure you'll be able to manage when I'm at work?' I asked.

'Manage what?' he said.

'You know, living.'

'Don't worry. How much is there to do? Eat cereal? Switch on the TV?'

I sighed. 'I'm not working every day,' I said.

He nodded and we sat in silence for several minutes before he said, 'Hank came to see me today.'

'He did?'

'Uh-huh, when you were out having lunch.'

'Did he talk to you about your testimony?'

'Some, but mainly he came to do my will.'

'Oh.'

'And he asked again if you'd agreed to be my surrogate decision maker.'

'Like what Anthony did for Darryl?'

'Yes.'

'But you don't need that, Eric. It's for people who are really bad off, who can't . . . it's for people who are dying.'

'It's in case.'

'You have the advance directive.'

'That deals with resuscitation and heroics, but there are lots of other things that can happen.'

'You're leaving the hospital tomorrow,' I said, standing, swallowing hard. 'Let's concentrate on getting you well.'

'Okay.'

I looked at my watch; it was seven-fifteen. 'I'd better go if I'm gonna make it to the group,' I said. 'I'll see you later, love.' I kissed him on the cheek and he smiled.

I held my tears until I made it to the elevator. There I squatted, my back against the wall, and let sorrow ravage me; it felt better than thinking. Heroics, end-of-life issues, surrogates, directives—I didn't want any of it!

Finally, the elevator came and I entered, thankful to be alone. Once inside, the doors hesitated before closing, so I banged the 'Close Door' button repeatedly, eventually rewarded by a stuttering, sluggish response. I noticed as I hit it that the 'Close Door' button's letters were worn invisible from so much use, while the 'Open Door' button remained unspoiled. Suddenly, it seemed crazy to me, being in a hurry, hoarding seconds, racing time. I was learning: time will go its way, where we can't follow.

I arrived late to Henley Street. The usual members were already gathered, along with a new one, a Latina named Maria.

'Hi,' I said. 'Sorry I'm late.'

'Amen, you're surviving,' Virgil hummed.

'No problem,' Gary said.

I sat next to Anthony; I squeezed his hand.

'This is Maria Hernandez, Alex. This is Alex Taylor, Maria,' Gary said.

'Hi,' I said, 'my fiancé, Eric, is in the hospital with PCP. I'm negative.'

Maria answered, 'I have full-blown AIDS. My husband is dead, my one-year-old is positive, but my other two kids are negative.'

I tried not to gasp. Somehow, up until then I had successfully avoided women with AIDS who had children.

KK said, 'Maria needs baby-sitting during her doctor's appointments.'

'The AIDS Project might know how to help,' volunteered Anthony. 'I can talk to them.'

'Thank you,' Maria said.

'What about Eric?' I blurted. 'He's on disability. He loves kids.'

'Isn't he pretty sick?' Kiki asked.

'He's better now,' I said. 'He can do it.'

'Try it,' Gary said. 'What do you need tonight, Alex?'

They looked at me, seven people sentenced to death by virus. Their loving goodwill opened the floodgates once again on my tears. Anthony held me, and when I could, I said, 'I want him to live. Will there be a cure?'

'I want a fucking cure!' Kiki yelled. 'Let's chant.'

'Wait,' Anthony said, holding up a slender hand. 'I know it's not much, but there's a new herbal treatment I heard about that increases T-cells.'

'Every time I hear about one of those snake oils it turns out to be bullshit,' Cat said.

Anthony responded, 'I know, but—'

'God, I'll try anything,' I said. 'God . . . maybe I should pray.'

'Let's chant.'

We rose and chanted; I can't explain why it helped, but it did. And later, before I left, Anthony pulled me aside and gave me the number of a herbalist; it was one step this side of prayer.

While Eric's discharge paperwork was being done the following morning, I went to the pay phone to arrange an appointment with the herbalist. I booked us for the next day at a cost of two hundred dollars, cash.

After I had delivered Eric home and tucked him into bed, where he promptly fell asleep, I left for the pharmacy to pick up his prescriptions. A woman there trundled over to the counter; her arm was bigger than both my thighs put together.

'May I help you?' she asked.

'Pickup for Moro.'

'How many?'

'Ten—no, eleven. Eleven.'

'Eleven?' she repeated.

'Yes,' I answered.

'I see,' she said, turning to a sequence of alphabetized bins behind her.

I wandered away as she searched, to a row of shelves nearby.

There I saw cans of liquid boasting weight loss within a week. Each can contained 220 calories. My eyes roamed to the adjacent shelf, on which cans of liquid for weight gain were stacked. I thought of buying some for Eric, and eagerly read the label: Calories: 220.

'Ma'am? Ma'am?' a voice called. 'You, there, with the eleven prescriptions for Moro!'

'Huh?' I turned around. 'Oh, yeah.' I replaced the can and went to the counter.

'I've only got seven ready,' she said. 'You'll have to come back later.'

'But they were called in.'

'It's a lot of prescriptions, lady.'

'And he's really sick, lady.'

'I'm sure.'

There was something about her, those massive arms, her tone, that hideous blue eye shadow, that made me snap. 'Goddammit,' I growled, 'give me the medications, all of them.'

'I told you, I only have seven. Do you want them?'

'Give them to me!'

'You need to purchase them, ma'am.'

'I know that.'

'That'll be one hundred fifty-seven dollars and twenty-three cents.'

'It's Medicaid.'

'It is?'

'They didn't tell you?'

'No. Now it'll have to be done over,' she said through an exaggerated sigh. 'Some of these aren't even on the Medicaid formulary. I'll have to call the doctor for a TAR clearance and the others will have to be changed to generic.'

'Aaaaaaaeeeeeeee!' I screamed.

Her eyes widened and she stepped back.

I screamed again, my fists balled into wads of frustration and anger. 'All I wanna know,' I hissed, 'is why do the weight-gain and weight-loss formulas have the same goddamned calories!'

Her eyes blinked. She started to run to the back, and as she did, I swept the cans of liquid that boasted both thinness and bulk to the floor, where they made an ear-numbing crash. I bolted away while everyone stared.

When I reached home, Eric was just as I had left him; I checked to see that he was still breathing. Then I phoned the hospital and asked the doctor to call the prescriptions in to a different pharmacy, reminding her that Eric was on Medicaid. 'And, by the way,' I said, 'do you recommend those weight-gain formulas?'

'Whatever works,' she said.

I thanked her and hung up.

It was time to go to work. Eric looked so helpless and delicate, so peaceful and vulnerable, I hated to leave, but I had to. I dragged the phone to his bedside, kissed him on the forehead, and left.

I drove Shadow Blaster too fast to the library, a habit that was getting worse daily. Stopping in the ladies' room, I applied my red lipstick and examined my reflection. I was ashen, with purple-gray patches beneath eyes that were now never golden, only the brownest green. I had sprouted gray hairs among the blond, and I badly needed a trim, but there was no time for maintenance of me.

'Hey, Alex,' a colleague of mine from the art reference desk greeted me in the mirror.

'Hi, Sherry,' I said, shoving my lipstick back into my backpack.

'I'm ready to go,' she said, 'so if you don't mind, I'll—'

'No problem,' I said.

'There's only one thing. A guy was looking for this book about sculpture and surface anatomy or something like that. The author's Kolpinski. I located it, it's behind the desk, so—'

'Got it,' I said, and scooted out the door. There I leaned against the wall, breathing fast. Kolpinski's book, here in the library. Kolpinski, the reason I had met Eric, the reason I had sketched Eric. Kolpinski, from a different life. My breath was rapid; I felt a tingling around my lips, my fingertips, as I forced myself to climb the flight of stairs to the art reference desk. As I walked, a feeling of extreme unreality descended upon me, making edges malleable, causing surfaces to undulate, muffling sound, and transforming all light into a monochromatic white. I made it to my chair near the computer, sat, and breathed evenly, trying not to cry out or shriek; I knew I walked a thin edge.

When I felt better and things had firmed up, I stood and went to the shelf where reserves were kept. There, among benign volumes on tapestry, Greek architecture, Rembrandt, and others, was Kolpinski's book. It had a red cover; I took it in my arms. It was oversized and weighty, as ponderous as the man himself, and I just held it, stroking it for a while. Dark had crept over the windows when the young man finally got my attention.

'Excuse me,' he said. 'Excuse me, Miss?'

'Yes?' I said, looking up.

'I'm sorry to disturb you, but I'm looking for a book by Kolpinski. It's titled—'

'Here,' I said, and handed it to him; it was warm on its underside where I had held it to my chest.

'Thanks,' he said with a smile that was alarmingly flirtatious. 'Thanks a lot.'

'You're welcome. Please return it to the desk when you're done.'

'Sure thing,' he said, and walked away.

Later, when I called Eric, he was munching on macaroni and cheese, watching an old movie on TV.

'I'm fine, go back to work,' he said. 'See you when you get home.'

'Okay. I love you,' I said.

'I love you,' he responded, and we hung up.

Eventually, it was eight-thirty, time to close. The young man with Kolpinski's book sauntered over and watched me organizing the 'To Be Shelved' cart before saying, 'Here,' and holding out the Kolpinski.

I turned around. 'Thanks,' I said. 'You can put it on the counter.'

He set it down, then hesitated, and said, 'You wouldn't be free for a cup of coffee or a drink, would you?'

I looked at him and managed a smile. 'Free is something I don't anticipate being for a very long time,' I said.

'My loss,' he said with a shrug, and left.

My section was empty; it was time to go home. I went to the Kolpinski where it lay on the counter and opened it, flipping to the sketches of Eric. I fixed on them one by one, turning the pages slowly, lovingly. It came back like vertigo: what Eric had looked like, felt like, smelled like, sounded like. I could see him twirling on that stool, wandering around my apartment, pulling jeans over his bare ass, challenging me to reach for passion, fun, my future, my life.

I cannot explain what I did next. I glanced around to make sure no one watched and then methodically ripped Eric out of the book, all twelve images of him, and put the pages carefully in my backpack. I could've bought the book, but I needed the pages then, that second. And somehow they felt like mine.

CHAPTER THIRTY-FOUR

The next day Eric and I went to see Anthony's herbalist in a dusty garden-level apartment in South Philly. There was no sign on the door and inside, no receptionist, only a few sad, faded chairs in an outer vestibule and a door with a button and a sign that read: RING FOR SERVICE, IF YOU PLEASE. I rang. We waited.

Eric sat and gazed out the half-window through the black security bars and years of grime to the hard brown dirt outside, watching pedestrians' feet scrambling through busy daytimes. I rang again.

'Coming, if you please!' an effervescent voice called. Then the door opened, revealing a withered brown man with a bald head and long white beard. Except for his attire, which consisted of jeans and a work shirt, he looked strikingly like Eric's wizard.

I backed away, my face flushed, as the little man grabbed my hand and began to stroke it, massaging it with his fingers. 'You are well in your body, if you please,' he murmured, his eyes now closed. 'But your soul, it is fractured, in need of repair.'

I pulled my hand away; Eric was chuckling behind me. 'We didn't come for me,' I said. 'He's sick.' I pointed to Eric.

'Ahhhh. Ahhhhhh,' the man said, approaching Eric's chair. Eric fixed the man with his eyes, now transformed opalescent-dark by disease, two animated jewels set deep.

'I am Torgin, herbalist and potionist, if you please,' the man said.

'I'm Eric.'

Instantly upon grasping Eric's hand, Torgin fell to his knees, his face contorting with worry and woe, his eyes sealed shut as he caressed Eric's hand between the two of his. 'Ahhhhhh, oh, it is bad,' Torgin mumbled. 'Oh, so bad.'

'We know that,' I said. 'Can you help us?'

'He has the AIDS,' Torgin responded, rocking back on his heels.

'We know that, too,' I said. 'Do you have an examining room?'

Torgin shook his head, his beard swaying.

He stood. 'I am not doctor. If you want to die, go to Western doctor. I am herbalist, if you please.'

'I know,' I said, exasperated. 'But don't you—'

Eric stood unsteadily and placed his hand on Torgin's shoulder. 'Let's go,' he said.

'Good,' Torgin said, and led the way.

We went through the door Torgin had emerged from and down an unlit hallway to a cramped, windowless room lined with shelves on which bottles and jars were crammed. Around the perimeter, tables supported rows and rows of plants with grow-lights hovering above them. In the dim reaches beyond sight, I could hear voices sputtering a foreign language and smell smoke and the aroma of meat cooking.

Torgin instructed us to sit on a hand-knotted rug on the floor amid a group of stained red-satin pillows, while he scurried to a wooden worktable on which lay scattered multitudes of vials and canisters of dried plants, flower buds, powders, and thick liquids. We watched as he took mortar and pestle in hand and began darting to shelves, grabbing jars in what appeared to be a random fashion. From the jars he took pinches of plant dust and dollops of goo, mixing, always mixing, and as he worked he grunted and snorted, pulling his beard and fondling his bare head like a little gnome.

'Ahhhhh, there, if you please,' Torgin said, delivering two small vials to Eric, one consisting of gray sediment suspended in dark oil, the other a powder, auburn-green. 'Ahhhhh,' Torgin repeated, 'for the AIDS.'

Eric held the vials up to the light admiringly and smiled. 'Thank you,' he said.

'Powder in soy milk, quarter teaspoon powder, you dissolve, see?' Torgin said, making a stirring motion with his hand into a make-believe glass formed by his other hand. 'No cow milk,' he admonished, shaking his head and wagging his finger. 'Cow milk no good.'

'Okay,' Eric said, 'no cow's milk.'

'Take quarter teaspoon, one per day, until come back next week see me again.'

'And the liquid?' I asked.

'Liquid,' Torgin said, 'very precious, very special. This you take dropper—you have dropper?' Eric looked to me. I shrugged. Torgin went on, 'Get dropper. One-half dropper in wormwood tea, boiled, two times a day, until come back see me.'

'All right,' Eric agreed, and I stood, bending to help him up and placing the vials carefully in my backpack.

'Come back see me,' Torgin said. 'Feel much better, if you please.'

'When do we come back?' I asked.

'Next week Friday.'

'That's the day after Thanksgiving,' I said. 'Are you open?'

Torgin cackled, revealing spongy purple gums, absent of teeth. 'Always open, no Thanksgiving, always thankful, if you please,' he said. 'Two-hundred-fifty-dollar charge, no check, no credit, no insurance, cash only.'

I pulled a bank envelope out of my backpack and handed it to Torgin. 'Two hundred. That's what I was told,' I said.

Torgin took the envelope and peered inside, sifting through the bills quickly with his dry, skilful fingers. 'Very good,' he said. 'For you, discount,' and he smiled and turned away.

We showed ourselves out.

CHAPTER THIRTY-FIVE

The herbs were working. Within two days of starting Torgin's potions, Eric's energy level and appetite were back to normal and he had started to gain weight. His T-cells had increased to fifty, from nothing, and his eyes were less glassy. The money was a stretch, but Torgin extended our 'discount' and I continued to work, borrowing when I had to.

I found myself in health-food stores frequently, buying wormwood tea, and one afternoon, as I stood gazing over vitamins and powders, waiting for my purchases to be rung up, a man approached me. He was tall beyond reach, his hair broom yellow with a sorrowful, matching mustache.

'Miss?' he said, tapping me on the shoulder.

I looked up. 'Yes?'

'The gentleman behind the counter says you seek treatments for the HIV.'

I nodded.

'There is something new, very new,' he went on. 'So new no one in America has heard of it. I have just returned from China. I can tell you where to get it.'

'What is it?'

'I can give you no further information unless I meet with you privately,' he said, glancing around. 'It will cost money, but you will be cured of the HIV.'

'Cured? It gets rid of the virus?'

'Yes.' He looked around again. 'I cannot talk here. Take my card.'

He handed me a business card and walked to the other side of the store. Trembling from the word 'cure,' I followed him. 'Sir?' I said. He turned around. 'How much?' I asked.

'You will have to travel to China. And there's my fee.'

My heart was fluttering; I had a wicked urge to pee. 'How much?' I asked again.

'My fee is fifty thousand.'

My mouth dropped silently open.

'How much is your life worth?' he asked. 'Call me.'

'Alex!' the cashier called. 'Your stuff is ready

318

over here.' I turned and told him, 'Just a minute,' and when I turned back, the tall man was gone. I squeezed his card, the closest thing I knew to salvation, in my hand.

'Eric!' I yelled as I bustled in the front door with my packages of vitamins, teas, supplements, and preparations. 'Eric!'

'In here, Al,' he called from the bedroom.

I went to the bedroom door. 'Did I wake you?' I asked.

'It's okay. Come here. Sit on the bed.'

I sat beside him; his hair was soaked with the sweat of sleep. 'I'll get a cool washcloth,' I said, and left for the bathroom. I ran the water and called out to him, 'Eric, you won't believe what happened today.' I returned with the washcloth and sat down, stroking his forehead, his cheeks, his neck. He closed his eyes. I continued, 'I met a guy who has a cure for AIDS.'

His eyes whipped open. 'What?'

'I know, I know. I didn't believe it at first either. But I've thought about it all the way home. It'll cost some money and we'll have to go to China—'

'China?'

'Yes, but I've always wanted to go there and

it's time we had a vacation anyway and for a cure anything would be worth it and I knew you'd—'

'No,' he said, sitting up. 'It's time to talk.'

'We are talking. We're talking about a cure—'

'We're talking about bullshit, Al.'

'It's a chance,' I said.

'I've never died before, but I know what I don't want.' He reached out, his thin fingers encircling my wrist, and continued, 'I don't want to spend what time I have left in hotels in a country where no one speaks my language. I also don't want to leave you destitute.'

'If you leave me, I will be destitute,' I said. 'I need you alive.'

'I need to talk about this,' he said. 'I love you—I can't imagine being without you, but you, Al, you'll be okay when I'm gone.'

'No.'

'Yes, and dying isn't as bad as everyone thinks. After a while you accept it. The scariest part is the panic that almost chokes me when I think of leaving everything I know and slipping into the unknown. But then that passes, and I get a little curious.'

'Curious?'

He nodded. 'People spend their lives pondering what's out there, selling their brand of heaven or hell. But I'm gonna know.' A smile crossed his face. Eerie, distant.

'I'm not letting you go, ever,' I said, clutching his hand.

'I've seen life stop long before someone dies. Don't let that be too long for me.' His smile was gone, replaced by fear, pleading.

'What do you want, Eric?' I asked, beginning to cry.

'Let me go when my pleasure's done.'

'"Together Forever." Your promise.'

He smiled again, this time like the old Eric. 'I'm not breaking that promise, Al, I'm just redefining "together."'

I couldn't smile with him. Whatever panic or fear he felt, I was sure mine was thousands of times worse.

'My parents will want to do some Catholic bullshit after I die,' he said. 'That's okay, but I want to be cremated.'

'Don't die,' I whispered.

'Scatter my ashes from the sky, over the beach where we played.'

I nodded, biting my lip.

He was tranquil. I had heard him.

CHAPTER THIRTY-SIX

Maria, from the AIDS survivors group, had a doctor's appointment one day, so I told her to bring her three kids by; Eric and I would watch them for a few hours.

'Hello,' Maria said as I opened the door. Immediately, the older children, Juan, seven, and Eneyda, five, scampered by me and into the apartment. 'You two behave!' Maria called, and handed me the one-year-old, little Maria. 'I have to hurry,' she said, 'I am late. Here,' she handed me a diaper bag, 'she will want her bottle in half an hour, then a nap, then I will be back.' She smiled; she looked weak and drawn. 'Thank you,' she murmured, and left.

I stood watching Maria descend the stairs. Her legs were spindly rods that barely sustained her fragile weight as she lowered herself from one stair to the next, leaning heavily on the banister. She turned once, looking up and smiling, and then she disappeared; I went inside. Eneyda and Juan were sitting on the sofa side by side, whispering; they looked up when I entered.

'Hi,' I said. 'You want a snack?' They shook their heads in unison, with the measured, identical cadence of siblings drawn close by necessity.

'Uh . . . how 'bout a game?' I asked. Little Maria, still in my arms, began to squirm. I bounced her on my hip.

'Who's that man?' Eneyda asked.

'What man?'

'The man in the bed,' Juan said.

'Oh, that's Eric. He wants to play with you.'

'He looks sick,' Eneyda commented.

They should know. 'He's not too sick to play,' I said. 'I'll get him.' I went into the bedroom. Little Maria's eyes were wide with curiosity, or terror, but she didn't cry. 'Eric,' I said, 'the kids are here.'

He sat up. 'Great,' he said, rubbing his eyes of sleep.

'You sure you're up for it?' I asked. 'I can handle them if you want to go back to sleep.'

'No way. I've been looking forward to it all

323

week.' He stood up, wavering for a moment. He caught himself and laughed, pulling on jeans and a sweater, tying his leather belt in a knot around his waist, now too skinny for the smallest hole.

We stood facing each other for a moment as he took little Maria from me and hugged her firm body close to his spare one. She recoiled from the stubble of his chin and then laughed as he made a face at her and rubbed his nose against hers. I had to gulp back tears watching her chubby arms encircle his neck. They were inextricably linked in that web that was HIV, and it seemed even little Maria knew it; she wouldn't let him go.

I clasped Eric's hand, both of us knowing, but not acknowledging, that this brief afternoon would be the closest thing to a family we'd ever get.

Walking to the outer room, we stopped and watched little Maria's older siblings, strong with youth and health, as they jumped, yelping, from the sofa, trying to bat at the model airplanes suspended from the ceiling. Eric and I exchanged a glance, and then he laughed. The sound startled the kids, immobilizing them.

'It's okay,' he said. 'I'll get them down for you. Which one do you want?' Little Maria clung to Eric with one hand, stretching toward the models with the other, while Juan and Eneyda waited and watched.

'Here,' Eric said, handing Eneyda a biplane that I must've built when I was ten. 'And one for you,' he continued, yanking a jetliner down and giving it to Juan, who didn't quite smile, but took it nonetheless.

I went to heat up little Maria's bottle in the kitchen. When I returned, Eric and the kids were building an airport from bricks, paper, picture frames, cups, paintbrushes, textbooks, a strip of the shower curtain? They were giggling and carrying on, too intent to notice me, and having too much fun to be afraid. Little Maria was on Eric's lap, patting his chin, resting on his shoulder, and he moved easily, balancing her as he leaned forward to fix a runway, construct a tower, or assist in a take-off.

'Here,' I said, handing the warm bottle to Eric. 'I hope you've done this before, 'cause I haven't.' He looked up, a smile on his face, as little Maria snatched the bottle and sucked eagerly on it. We laughed.

'I've gotta run to the drugstore,' I said. 'Can you handle these guys for fifteen minutes?'

'The real question is, can they handle me?' Eric said. I smiled and nodded, grabbing my jacket as Eneyda and Juan chirped, 'Ric, Ric!' annoyed that he had strayed from the game for an instant to talk to me. I stood at the door and took a long look back before I left.

Out in the December air, I was glad for the cold and solitude. The sky was overcast, the wind sniffed and rustled around my pant legs, but the walk was invigorating, and for once the prescriptions were ready. It was a good day.

I got back in twenty-five minutes, only slightly concerned that I hadn't told Eric about little Maria's nap. It was quiet as I approached the apartment door. As I turned the lock, I heard the sound of little Maria wailing. She screamed, 'Da-Da-Da-Da!' again and again; the older children were silent.

It took all my will to open that door, and when I did, I saw that Eric was on the floor, his body writhing, twisting, and jerking, his dark eyes a mere sliver of white. The airport and planes were scattered violently around him, and little Maria's bottle was splattered against the far wall where Juan and Eneyda cowered in a corner. Little Maria stood close to Eric, crying and howling.

I gasped and dropped my bag, running to him. 'Jesus!' I cried, my hands shaking with fear. I tried to do what I could to stop the jerking. I grasped his head, but it quickly got away. My hands burned from the heat of his body; he was drenched in sweat. I tried to still his arms, but they spiraled outward with a power beyond Eric, flailing at me, driving me away.

'Call nine-one-one,' a little voice said. It was Juan. I ran to the phone and dialed.

It seemed a long while between when I called the paramedics and when they arrived. The whole time, Eric convulsed on the floor. I tried to take the children into the bedroom, but they screamed when I left them and I didn't want to leave Eric alone either. So we all stayed and watched, just watched.

The blare of the siren was high-pitched relief, and soon the paramedics were injecting Eric with something that made him stop seizing. He was so motionless that I thought they had killed him. Then I saw his thin chest lifting and falling in an achingly smooth rhythm that said he lived.

They took him away, down the stairs. It was agony to let him go, but I couldn't leave the kids. I pulled my hair, I paced, I cried, I worried, and I waited. The kids finally slept.

The shrill ring of the phone startled me. 'Hello?' I said. 'Is he all right?'

'Alex?' a woman asked.

'Yes! Yes, this is Alex Taylor. Please tell me he's alive.'

'It's Maria.'

'Is he okay?'

'Are you okay?'

'Maria! Oh, Maria, with the kids. You're not calling from the hospital.'

'Yes, I am. They admitted me.'

'But, Eric—'

'I have CMV of the eye. I am going blind.'

Her words cut me. 'I . . . I . . . I . . . ' I stammered.

'Can you get Juan and Eneyda to my mother's house?' Maria asked.

'Eric had seizures,' I said, beginning to cry. 'The paramedics took him away. I've been waiting for someone to call me. I've been waiting for you to come get the kids. I'm so worried.'

'Put Juan and Eneyda in a taxi to my mother's house. Get a pen, I'll give you the address and phone number.'

'Okay. Okay.' I grabbed a pen and a scrap of paper. 'Ready,' I said. She gave me her mother's address and her own room number at General Hospital. When I hung up, I turned to see Juan and Eneyda watching me, silent and wise, knowing too much.

It wasn't until I had sent Juan and Eneyda

off to Maria's mother's house in a taxi that I remembered little Maria; she was still upstairs! I took the steps three at a time and burst back into the apartment. Little Maria slept soundly on the big bed, breathing noisily through her pea-sized nostrils, dried milk spittle on her plump cheek. I tried to phone Maria at the hospital, but there was no phone in her room and the nursing station phone simply rang and rang. Next, I tried Maria's mother, but she spoke no English and I no Spanish. I hung up with tears in my eyes and immediately the phone rang, twitching my heart into a nasty, fast rhythm.

'Hello?' I half-whispered.

'Alex Taylor?'

'What? What is it?'

'My name is Dr. Harland, I'm calling about Eric Moro. We're admitting him for a workup of brain lesions.'

'What's that?'

'We're not sure. Maybe toxoplasmosis, maybe something else.'

'Toxo? *Toxo-gondii*?'

'That's right. *Toxoplasma gondii*. Are you a doctor?'

'No, I used to help Eric with his exams when he was a med student. It's in his brain?'

'We think so.'

'Oh, God.'

'It's treatable in most cases . . . ' Dr. Harland kept talking, but I didn't listen. I had been learning to wish, banking on herbs, euphoric over ready prescriptions, trying to survive—and suddenly a parasite that Eric had committed to memory so many years before was chewing through his brain. What could this doctor say that would change any of it?

'Where is he?' I asked, interrupting Dr. Harland.

'Twelfth floor, AIDS Unit.'

'Thank you.'

'Sure thing. Good luck.'

I hung up, knowing my luck would have to be much more than good.

I didn't think about it, I simply dialed the number automatically. And when she answered, I said, 'Mom? I need a favor. Please, just say yes.' She did, and within thirty minutes little Maria was in her loving arms.

When I got to Eric he was still groggy, something his doctors were calling 'postictal.' I was so relieved to see him alive that I almost didn't care if he could speak or move, just so that blood still pumped through him and I could listen to him exhale. Nearly losing him made me realize that I'd settle for almost anything, clutching a translucent strand of hope from a mere flicker of life. I held his hand; I traced his profile with my finger. I tried to catalog every detail of him that hadn't changed: his skin, the arch of his nose, the curl of his ears, the color of his hair, the feel of his nipple against my cheek, the tuft of hair below his navel, his kneecaps. So many things the same if you bothered to look, so many things unique, so easy to lose.

'Don't go,' I whispered. He didn't respond.

I spied a 'Patient Belongings' plastic bag near the wall and reached for it. His clothes were inside, that pair of jeans and the sweater, the too-big belt, his jean jacket, no underwear, no socks or even shoes. I lifted the jacket, recalling how I had frantically thrown it over him as the paramedics prepared to lift the stretcher and descend the stairs, his face blank, pale as the winter air. I smelled the jacket; it was Eric. I buried my face in it, sobbing into the place that had rested over his heart for years, passively noting its beats, and realized it would outlive him. I hugged it close and sensed a bumpy crackle in the pocket: M&Ms! I ripped open the bag, lifted Eric's hospital gown, and placed a red candy on his navel. Then I covered him again with the gown and kissed him lightly on the lips. Carefully, I folded the top of the package and

331

replaced it in the jacket pocket. For the future.

When I finally left Eric's room, I was surprised to run into Kiki and Gary in the hallway near the elevator.

'Hello, Alex,' Gary said. We hugged and I began to cry. He rubbed my head and I heard Kiki say, 'So, I guess you heard.'

'You heard,' I said.

'About Anthony,' Gary added.

I pulled back and looked at them, wiping at my eyes. 'About Eric,' I said. 'About Maria.'

Their faces seemed to shrink away, to lengthen. 'I'm so sorry,' Gary said.

'He has seizures,' I said. 'Brain lesions.'

'And Maria?' Kiki asked.

'CMV of the eye at General.'

'Oh.' We looked at each other. We were young, all under thirty-five, meeting on a weeknight at eleven, by chance in a hospital corridor, discussing parasites and viruses, knowing words that should've remained on doctors' lips. While others our age sipped wine and danced to smooth rhythms, we learned death over and over, from the inside out.

'And Anthony?' I asked.

'He passed,' Kiki said.

'Passed?' I repeated. 'Not Anthony . . . '
They nodded, sadly, together. I cried abruptly, like a kick to my throat, for sweet Anthony with

332

the transparent voice and generous heart, who had given me advice and helped me survive, who didn't say good-bye. Kiki and Gary stood dry-eyed, their tears long since spent. With the passage of mere hours, our Survivors Group had been severed irreversibly in half; it wasn't the first time for them.

As we said our good-byes and I walked away, slowly, I was glad they hadn't asked about Maria's kids. I wanted little Maria to myself that night; I needed her body near me, to breathe warm hope into my ear.

At dawn the next day, little Maria awoke and cried for her bottle; an hour later I entered Eric's hospital room. He smiled when he saw me.

'You look better,' I said.

'Look.' He held up the red M&M. 'I saved it for you.'

I opened my mouth.

'Close your eyes,' he said. I did. I felt him unzipping my jacket, unbuttoning my shirt.

'Hey,' I said, opening my eyes.

'Keep 'em closed,' he said. I closed them and felt his fingers snake into my bra and over my breast. He pulled me closer and I sensed his warm lips and tongue on my nipple. With my eyes closed, I could almost imagine that we were anywhere but where we were: on a windy beach or in a hot meadow, a ragged hotel or a tent in an ice field. Tears made me open my eyes; he was watching me. I sighed and sat down on the side of the bed. He popped the M&M in his mouth and sucked on it. 'Maybe later,' he said. I nodded and buttoned my shirt.

Dr. Harland walked in. He had a chubby face, surrounded by tousled blond hair, and a protuberant belly that his white coat didn't quite fit around. 'Good morning,' he said. 'Any problems over-night?'

'None,' Eric answered. 'Dr. Harland, this is Alex Taylor. Alex, Dr. Harland.'

'Nice to meet you,' he said.

'Likewise,' I answered. 'What are his T-cells? They were up just a couple weeks ago.'

'They do tend to fluctuate,' he said, flipping through the chart.

'But he's been on treatment and—'

'Here they are,' Dr. Harland said. 'Uh, two. Yes, two.'

'Two?' I repeated.

'That's right. Now, about the brain lesions. We'll be treating you for toxo for four or five days. If there's no improvement or you worsen, we'll need a biopsy.'

'Biopsy?' I asked. 'Of what?'

'The lesions.'

'You'd open his head?'

'We'd have to.'

I looked to Eric, incredulous, but he just nodded.

When the doctor had left, I said, 'You mean the herbs and vitamins and . . .'

'We tried, Al. We did our best.'

'There is no treatment for this fucking disease, is there?'

He reached for my hand and kissed it. 'They can treat the infections.'

'For a while.'

'Yes.'

'Then what?'

'What we talked about.'

'What about the seizures?'

'I'm on medications for them.'

'Will you have them again?'

He shrugged and looked away, out the window at the colorless sky. I held him close, his bones sharp against me.

Later that morning I went back to my parents' house, packed little Maria's diaper bag, and headed for General Hospital. It was three bus transfers away in a part of town where graffiti

335

opened gashes in the buildings, bleeding them of dignity.

The hospital was impressive in size and age, the hallways filled with groaning indigents and grinding out-of-date machinery. I don't know how I found Maria, but I know I climbed a lot of stairs.

'Hey,' I said softly as I approached her bed, one of six in a brown-gray room with sagging, stained curtains and smudged windows.

'Is that Alex?' she asked, turning her head toward me, struggling to sit up.

'Yes,' I said, 'and little Maria.'

'Maria!' she cried, and reached for the baby. I handed little Maria to her and put the diaper bag down, dragging a dented chair over, thankful to sit after all the stairs.

'How's she been?' Maria asked, trying to nestle little Maria into a space beside her, away from IVs and bed rails.

'Great,' I said. 'What a sweet baby.'

Maria smiled and began playing with her daughter. I watched in silence for some time before she said, 'Thank you for taking care of her.'

'You're welcome.'

'My mother brought Juan and Eneyda in earlier. They're doing good.' I nodded as she went on, 'They say I will go blind from CMV. Then I will die.'

'Oh, Maria. I'm sorry.'

She didn't cry; she leaned forward to kiss little Maria, and said, 'I'll miss them.' Tears filled my eyes and began to spill over onto my hands, which were clamped in my lap.

'You're good with her,' she said. 'She likes you.' She handed little Maria back to me, closed her eyes, and fell back into her pillow. She whispered, 'Take care of her. She likes you.'

'But Maria—'

'My mother is adopting Juan and Eneyda. Their father will visit and send money. And baby Maria . . . ' She opened her eyes and looked at her child before continuing. 'Maria's daddy is dead. From AIDS.'

'But your mother will take care of her,' I said.

'Maria has HIV. My mother doesn't want her.'

'No,' I said, shaking my head. 'That can't be true.'

'It is,' she said. 'You take her. No one else wants her.' Her words, painful for me to hear, but much worse for a mother to have to say, produced a deep, penetrating sting.

I stood and lifted little Maria to my hip,

kissed her mama on the forehead, and walked to the door. Maria didn't grimace until she thought I couldn't see, from pain I could only begin to imagine.

I couldn't keep little Maria, although I didn't mind Maria thinking I would. I was in too deep already, and sinking fast. I called Gary for advice, and to my relief, he agreed to call Maria's caseworker and discuss his becoming a foster parent to little Maria.

As I dropped the baby off at Henley Street that afternoon, her curly round head lolling with sleep, my twenty-four hours of parenting coming swiftly to a close, I envisioned her peeing on Gary's bluer-than-blue carpet and spilling apple juice on his blue-green sofa. Little Maria would bring a brief, bright life into Gary's blue world. They would survive together, for a time.

After lunch, I went to see Hank Brown at the AIDS Project. He had been calling me incessantly to get Eric set to testify at the trial; it was to start the following week.

'Hi,' I said sheepishly, peeking my head through his open office door.

'Jesus, woman!' he responded. 'Where've

you been? We've got a trial here!'

'I know. I—'

'You giving up?'

'No. I . . . Hank . . . oh, shit.' I started to cry and cursed myself. It seemed I had a bottomless well of tears these days, ready to flood my life.

Hank rolled to the door and closed it. He turned toward me. 'Talk to me,' he said.

My speech was punctuated by gasps and sobs. I talked about Eric, Maria, little Maria, Anthony, Darryl, and everyone else I had met with HIV. Sadness lay heavily over my life, a suffocating weight that I couldn't imagine ever being rid of. Hank listened without comment, so quietly, in fact, that I thought perhaps he had fallen asleep. I glanced over at him, and he nodded the nod of shared suffering.

'Hank,' I said, 'three, fifteen, twenty-five years—these aren't lifetimes.'

'Not fair, is it?'

'No.'

'How much is enough?'

'It doesn't matter. Just more.'

'But the desire for more will always be there, whether you're six or ninety-six.'

'But ninety-six is enough,' I protested.

'If you're far from it.'

'So, what are you saying? That it's okay for them to die because no matter how long they live they'll never be satisfied?'

'No. What I'm saying is, forever doesn't exist for any of us. Like infinity, it's intangible, unreachable. No matter how much forever you want, loving someone forever, living forever, it inevitably cracks open before you get there, and you fall right through.'

'I'm not asking for forever, Hank. Only for what's reasonable, maybe seventy, eighty years.'

'And then you'd let him go?'

'Well . . . it'd be easier.'

He shook his head. 'No, it wouldn't. We can only live one second at a time. We can't live in the time that's past, or the time that's ahead. When you pick seventy, it's only because it's so far away you don't believe it'll ever come—it seems like forever to you.'

'I'd settle for fifty, or even thirty, right now.'

'But when you get there, you'll feel cheated, like you do now. You'll want another thirty, fifty, or seventy.'

'How do you know?'

He chuckled. 'I'm there.'

'So I should accept it?'

'Do you have a choice?'

'I guess not.'

'Dying and loss are always hard, Alex. It doesn't get easier with age. Neither does living, but it's all we've got.'

'If we're lucky,' I said.

'If we're lucky,' he agreed.

'I could use some luck right about now.'

'We'll need more than luck to win this trial. We'll need Eric's testimony. I think we'd better videotape it.'

'But wouldn't it be better to have him come to the courtroom so people can see him?'

'Yes, but it's not realistic at this point.'

'Oh.'

'Will you be in court next week?'

'I'll try.'

We shared a look through the shine of his glasses, two round lenses between me and wisdom.

The trial was scheduled to begin the day we found out Eric didn't have toxoplasmosis. He had something worse: lymphoma of the brain. AIDS wasn't enough; he had to have cancer, too.

Discrimination was the last thing on my mind that day; it was hard to get angry at a lost opportunity when Eric was being painstakingly eaten by parasites, viruses, mycobacteria, fungi, and now rapidly growing cells out of control. Nothing could make it right, or even better. Not the law, not medicine, East or West, not justice, not fairness, not God. Getting Eric that internship had been the same as hope for me, something for him to live and fight for, a future, but now the odds were so thickly stacked against us as to erase all hope from consideration. I showed up at the courtroom only out of respect for Hank Brown.

'Good morning,' he said.

'It's lymphoma, Hank,' I said softly. 'It's cancer.'

'There are treatments for that.'

'It's stalling.' I waited for him to tell me otherwise. He didn't.

'It won't matter to the case,' he said. 'We have Eric's videotaped testimony and we're going to win this one for him.'

I buried my face in my hands. 'We can't give him back his life. That's what I wanted, and that's what I've lost.'

I felt Hank's hand on my neck, strong, gentle. 'But by winning this case we can give life to someone else like him, another doctor with HIV.'

'I wanted Eric to have that internship.'

'But that's not why you're here now.'

'I don't know why I'm here now,' I said,

trying hard not to cry in front of so many people, in a room reeking of authority and power.

'Yes you do,' he said. 'Just watch.'

The trial began.

CHAPTER THIRTY-SEVEN

I wasn't sure if Eric's parents loved him, or if his death would be just another disappointment to them, but if we were going to find out the answers, the questions would have to be asked soon. And Eric wasn't asking.

I called the Moros from a pay phone at the hospital that night.

When Mr. Moro answered, I said, 'Hello, it's Alexandra.'

'To what do I owe this rare pleasure?' he asked.

'It's Eric. He's in the hospital.'

'Has there been an accident?'

'No.'

'What is it?'

'He's sick, Mr. Moro. He's been sick for a while.'

Silence, lifeless, desolate. I listened to it hum a moment and then added, 'He hasn't wanted to tell you, but he has AIDS.'

There was a pause before I heard the dial tone.

I slept in Eric's hospital room that night. Despite that hopeful package of M&Ms, he didn't have the strength for them, and he slept while I tossed restlessly and watched him living.

It was dark and confusing when the door opened, letting a sharp slice of blinding white light into the room, the two bodies in the doorway silhouetted into anonymity.

'Who's there?' I whispered.

'Come into the hallway, please,' a man said.

I fumbled off my cot and slid across the floor in my socks, squinting and shielding my eyes from the light. I closed the door behind me so as not to wake Eric.

'That's her,' someone said.

'What?' I asked. 'Oh!' I gasped when I saw Mr. Moro.

'I'm the hospital administrator, Mr. Cochran,' the man said, extending his hand to me. I shook it tentatively as he went on, 'Mr.

Moro called me late last evening to tell me he hadn't known his son was sick. He said it had been kept from him.'

They looked at me. I wore hospital pajamas, a pair of sweat socks; I couldn't remember if I had brushed my teeth before bed. 'Maybe you should talk to your son,' I suggested.

'Is the patient competent?' Mr. Cochran asked.

'No,' Mr. Moro said just as I said, 'Yes.'

'I'll get the chart,' Mr. Cochran concluded, and left.

Mr. Moro and I were left standing there, shifting our weight, with no place to put our hands.

Finally, he said, 'I suspected your kind that Christmas—'

'What kind?'

'Not clean.'

'Clean?' I gulped. 'You think I gave it to him?'

'Don't lie on top of all your other sins.'

I saw Mr. Cochran coming down the hall with Eric's chart. I was bursting to argue with Mr. Moro, but I kept quiet, determined that he wouldn't drag me into denying that I was filthy, contaminated—for to do so would be to say that Eric was.

'It appears from the chart,' Mr. Cochran

began as he joined us, 'that your son is mentally competent, Mr. Moro.'

'He's showing very poor judgment,' Mr. Moro said.

'Poor judgment?' I asked.

'He should have told us he needed help. We can take care of him,' Mr. Moro said.

'I suppose we could have a psychiatrist come by,' Mr. Cochran said.

'Why?' I asked. 'Eric's fine.'

They looked at me briefly before peering back into the chart. Finally, they closed it.

'Let's do that,' Mr. Cochran decided. 'We'll have the Psychiatry Service come on by in the morning. They'll tell us how to proceed.'

'Fine,' Mr. Moro agreed.

'Proceed?' I asked. 'What do you mean?'

'We'll talk in the morning. Go back to sleep,' Mr. Cochran said, and they walked away.

I reentered the room and sat beside the bed, waiting for my vision to adjust to the density of the dark. When it did, I watched Eric until his eyes opened. He blinked and turned toward me.

'Hi,' he said, reaching for my hand.

'I called your parents, Eric. Your father's here. I don't know about your mother.'

'My father came to Philadelphia? Why?'

'Because you're sick. I told him about the HIV.'

347

'What'd he say?'

'That you should've gotten help from them, that they can take care of you.'

'Take care of me?'

'Yes, and Mr. Cochran, the hospital administrator, was here. Your father's trying to say you're mentally incompetent. I think I really fucked up.'

'There goes my independence,' Eric said softly, like a final resignation. I could see the gray silhouette of his hand raking through his hair, scraping his scalp for a way out. I wondered how far below it the brain lesions were.

'I'm sorry,' I said.

'Don't be. I probably should've told them before. Maybe then they wouldn't be pulling this.'

'But what can they pull?'

'They're my next of kin, Al. If they get me declared incompetent, they can take me home, make my decisions for me.'

'But what about your advance directive?'

'It doesn't cover things like this. That's what I was talking about when I asked you to be my surrogate.'

'But you're not incompetent.'

'Not now.'

'I'm trying to be brave, Eric, but . . . being

your surrogate means I have to let you go. I don't want to lose you.'

'It's hard.'

I held his bony hand and wanted to be strong, to stand up and take control, but there was something I wanted more—and that was for Eric to live. Being his surrogate didn't allow miracles. A slim dream, true, but it was all I had left.

We watched as the first faint flush of white rinsed the sky beyond the ice-cold glass of the hospital window, making Eric's black eyes glow before they closed again and he slept.

I left his room silently, to walk the blank hospital corridors over thin, blue carpets linking rooms of illness. I wanted to race away from death, suffering, sorrow and grief, but I could feel them seeping beneath my skin, creeping up the nape of my neck, sinking behind my eyes and insinuating themselves in places deep and hidden. Darkness had started to fuse with me.

The hospital moved at early hours, and I wasn't alone in the halls. I passed phlebotomists and clerks, X-ray technicians and nurses changing shift, and by the time I returned to Eric, his breakfast had arrived. So had his mother and father.

Eric's door was open and I remained

unnoticed just outside it, where they could have seen me if they had looked. Mr. and Mrs. Moro stood on the near side of the bed where Eric lay, awake now, listening.

'It's important for you to get good care,' Mr. Moro said.

'I'm getting good care here.'

'I'm unhappy with these doctors and their diagnosis.'

'I have AIDS, Dad.'

'You have lymphoma. That's cancer,' Mrs. Moro said. She was holding Eric's hand, stroking it.

Eric sighed and his father went on. 'They're treating you as some sort of charity case, but don't forget you are our son. We know people, prominent people, in Chicago. The doctors there will take better care of you.'

'I'm staying here, with Alex.'

'You belong with me and your mother,' Mr. Moro said. 'Rest now, we'll talk later.' Mrs. Moro leaned down to kiss her son, while Mr. Moro turned to leave, involuntarily facing me in the doorway. He was startled for a moment; then he nodded to Eric and brushed past me.

'I'll get him to Chicago,' he muttered under his breath as he passed. 'Mark my words.' He left in a whisk of cold air. Mrs. Moro followed him, not meeting my eyes.

'They want to take me home,' Eric said, looking at me.

'I know,' I said. I moved to the side of the bed.

'I told them I wouldn't leave you,' he said.

I knelt on the floor, my lips against his hand, feeling the useless strength of the tendons there, made prominent by wasting.

'You won't ever leave me, will you?' I asked.

'Not for them,' he said.

Relief surged through me, giving me a moment's solace before he repeated, 'Not for them.'

'Not for anything,' I said. 'Say it.'

He caressed my hair and smiled a distant smile, saying nothing.

I climbed into the bed beside him, making him notice me, my body, my flesh, my beating heart. 'Take me with you,' I whispered in his ear. 'I won't stay here without you.'

I felt him shake his head, then I let my tears slide freely, slipping left, over the bridge of my nose, down the side of my face and onto his pillow. I wondered how many tears that pillow's life had already seen, and how many more were yet to come.

*   *   *

When the psychiatrist came to examine Eric that afternoon, I was asked to leave. I went to the courtroom to see Hank.

'Hi,' I said, sneaking up behind him during a break.

'Hello, Alex. How's our man?' he asked.

'His parents are here. His father requested a psychiatric evaluation to see if Eric's mentally competent to make the decision to stay with me rather than go with them to Chicago.'

'A care-giver tug-of-war?'

I nodded. 'How's our case?'

'We've got problems.'

'Oh?'

'Sally, Dean Valois' assistant, backed out.'

'I thought she had agreed to testify that she overheard the phone calls the dean made to the programs about Eric's HIV.'

'Yes, but that was off the record, and now she says she "doesn't recall" that.'

'Why?'

'I'm sure the dean threatened to fire her, although she wouldn't admit it to me.'

'But he can't fire her for that! He left his door open—'

'I told her if that's what she's worried about, she's protected, but you and I both know he'll fire her if he wants.'

'So what'd she testify to?'

'That the dean knew about the HIV from his position on the committee and that she knew through the medical students.'

'Which doesn't help us prove that the programs knew, and therefore discriminated based on the HIV.'

'Precisely. We need her testimony.'

'We're gonna lose, aren't we, Hank?'

'Not necessarily. You never know how the jury will interpret the weight of the evidence.'

There was a little pause, then I said, 'Sorry I haven't been here more. I—'

He held up a hand. 'No need, I understand. By the way, have you given any more thought to being Eric's surrogate?'

'I want to do it . . .'

'But?'

'It's hard.'

'All worthwhile things are.'

I stared at him and sighed. 'It means letting him go. I want him alive, with me, more than anything.'

'More than giving him what he wants?'

'He wants the same thing, to be with me.'

'Yes.' His brown eyes examined me, over the top of his glasses.

'I know what you're thinking. If I don't become Eric's surrogate, his parents could take him to Chicago.'

'The psychiatrist may find Eric competent now, but . . .'

'Couldn't you be his surrogate, Hank? You know Eric.'

'He's chosen you, not me.'

Before I could respond, court came to order with a bang, ramrodding through life and death, staying on schedule.

'See you,' Hank whispered.

'See you,' I responded, scooting away. I stayed in the courtroom for about thirty minutes after that, trying to forget heroics and hospitals, just listening to Hank's melodious voice, prodding, cradling, commanding. To see him was to see logic, brilliance, and mercy combined with a passion for justice. Hank fought for Eric, but he fought just as much for all those with HIV, those whose daily dose of energy was miserably doled out to the task of finding shelter, food, child- and medical-care, to staying alive.

I arrived back at Eric's room as the psychiatrist, Dr. Kilkea, was standing up to leave, shaking Eric's hand. 'Is this Alex?' she asked when she saw me.

I nodded.

'Good,' she said. 'I'd like to talk with you privately if I may.'

'Okay,' I said, glancing at Eric. He winked, looking as competent as ever.

I followed Dr. Kilkea out to the nursing station and into a little conference room that smelled of burned coffee and day-old cigarettes. She had to ask a nurse doing charting to leave so we could be alone.

'Please sit,' she said.

I sat in a chair across a cluttered table from her and we looked each other over. She saw an unshowered, uncombed, unironed mess. I saw a woman in emerald green silk with smooth dark hair to her waist and gray eyes edged with the beginnings of crow's-feet.

'So,' she said.

'You took the word right out of my mouth,' I said.

She laughed lightly, revealing a smudge of pink-red lipstick on her upper teeth. 'What do you think of Eric's father?' she asked.

'He's not considering Eric's wishes.'

'What do you see as Eric's wishes?'

'To be here, with me.'

'And?'

'And?'

'What about his illness?'

'It sucks.'

'Sounds like you're angry.'

355

'Wouldn't you be? Sometimes I think it'd be easier to be him.'

'Are you saying you'd rather be the one with HIV?'

'I guess not, but sometimes I wish I had his HIV, something to keep with me when he's gone . . . Oh, God, you're gonna think I'm crazy now, aren't you?'

'No.'

'Aren't you interviewing me to see who can take better care of Eric, me or his father?'

She smiled and shook her head. 'I interviewed Eric for that purpose. He asked me to talk to you.'

'Why?'

'He's concerned about you. He wants you to live—'

'I want him to live and he won't.'

'Are you resentful that he's dying?'

'That wouldn't be fair.'

'But it would be understandable.'

'It would?'

'Anything you feel is okay. The important thing is to feel it, not to deny it or let it come out in ways that would be damaging to you or to Eric.'

I began to weep. 'I would do anything for him. If only there was one little thing, anything I could do.'

Dr. Kilkea nodded. 'There is. Listen to him. And be safe.'

She was blurry and statuesque through the haze of my tears as she stood and handed me a Kleenex with one hand and her business card with the other. I could see her fingernails, pink and manicured below my chin.

'Call me if you like,' she said. 'For you.' She hesitated as I blew my nose, then said, 'Eric needs you, not me.' I felt her hand on my shoulder before she walked away.

Two psychiatrists at the hospital deemed Eric mentally competent, but the Moros still wouldn't quit. They wanted to keep seeking opinions until they got one that suited them, turning that into the justification and means to take their son to Chicago.

Eric and I both knew he was competent and that any psychiatrist would find him so. What we didn't know was that Mr. Moro had a friend who was a psychiatrist, a friend good enough that he was willing to fly all the way from Chicago to evaluate Eric.

It was this psychiatrist that I ran into the following morning when I went to the hospital to see Eric.

'Excuse me,' I said when I saw the doctor.

'Mornin', Al,' Eric said. 'This is Dr. Harper.'

He twisted in his chair to look at me. 'You must be Alexandra,' he said.

'Um-hmm,' I said. He watched me as I set my things down and leaned over to kiss Eric.

'Dr. Harper's a psychiatrist from Chicago,' Eric said.

I straightened up. 'Your parents want a third opinion?' I said.

Dr. Harper turned his notes over in his lap. He was tapping his foot rapidly. 'We should continue,' he said.

I remained standing by Eric, stunned by this turn of events, unsure of what it signified. 'Okay,' I said, 'continue.'

'This consultation is confidential,' Dr. Harper said, his foot picking up speed.

I looked at Eric; he smiled. I wasn't re-assured. 'Do you want me to stay?' I asked him.

'It's okay, Al,' he answered. 'We should be done when, Dr. Harper? Thirty minutes?'

'I'll need about forty-five minutes more today. I'll complete my evaluation tomorrow.'

'What do you want me to do, Eric?' I asked.

'Give me another kiss and wait for me in the visitors' lounge.'

'Okay,' I agreed, kissing him, glancing at Dr.

Harper, and heading for the door.

'Please close it,' Dr. Harper called.

I did, and then started down the corridor, dismayed. I was walking toward the lounge, but I had passed it when I heard a sound, something between a hiss and a growl. It turned me right around. I wasn't sure if it had emanated from Mr. Moro, but there he was, standing in the doorway of the lounge, watching me.

We stood like that for several moments, just staring. His eyes were hard, angry, but there was a hint of Eric in them.

'Mr. Moro,' I began, walking toward him, 'we both love Eric. Why can't we let him decide?'

'The two of you have created an awful mess. It's my responsibility to clean it up.'

'But it's not a mess, it's a disease. He needs treatment, but most of all he needs caring and affection.'

'He is my son.'

'Yes, but—'

'He's coming with me and his mother.'

'Why can't you do what's right, even now?'

'Right? What do you know of right?'

'I—'

'I should have enforced the rules years ago. Now we are all paying.'

'He's the one paying, don't you see? If you take him back, he'll be miserable! Don't you even love him that much?'

'You do not know the love of a father for his son.'

'Do you?'

Mr. Moro turned away and reentered the lounge, leaving me in the hall. I followed him to the door. He sat and began leafing through a *Time* magazine.

I watched him, his face set, without apparent emotion. I asked, 'Does Eric know the love of a father for his son?' My question was met by silence, the flipping of glossy pages. 'Does he?' I persisted.

Mr. Moro looked up with eyes that were now devoid of any glimmer of Eric, and said, 'My son is coming to Chicago with me. You are not welcome in my home.'

The words were like a slap, a sudden choking of air in my throat. 'But why?' I asked.

'I should have enforced the rules years ago,' he repeated. There was almost something like regret in his voice, in the slow shaking of his head, but it was just the sheerest trace of that before it disappeared and he went back to scanning his magazine.

I wasn't sure what he meant by rules, except that I knew they didn't include me, or probably anything that Eric wished for. But it wasn't the rules part that scared me the most, it was the 'years ago.' Eric was mentally competent, but rapidly becoming more and more dependent, slipping backward, undoing time. I worried that his parents would tuck him right back into the cradle.

I backed up slowly, then turned, running to the elevator, pounding the down-button with my fist, pounding and pounding. I sprinted for the stairs, down twelve flights to the lobby and out to the icy street without a coat, without boots or hat. I reached Hank's office wild-eyed and panting.

'Hank!' I yelled.

'What is it, woman?' he asked, seeing me. 'I'm due in court in fifteen minutes.'

'I'll do it.'

He closed the door and motioned for me to sit. I did.

'Take a deep breath,' he said.

'Give me the paper.'

'What's going on?'

'Mr. Moro got a psychiatrist out here from Chicago. He's going to say that Eric's not competent so they can take him away.'

'That can be contested in a court of law.'

'But in the meantime, can Eric's parents get him to Chicago?'

'Probably, but you can go to court to get him back.'

'How long will that take?'

'It could take a while.'

'I don't have a while.'

'So this is why you've finally agreed to be his surrogate?'

'What choice do I have? I'll do my best, that's all I can say. It's got to be better than what his parents would do.'

Hank studied me, removed his glasses and rubbed his eyes, already fatigued at the start of his day. 'There's only one small problem,' he said.

'What now?'

'If his competency is contested, anything he signs now will be also.'

'Then I'm too late.'

Hank replaced his glasses and watched me.

'Dammit,' I said, standing, pacing. 'Dammit.'

'You don't need a lawyer to complete the document.'

'I know. I should've done it months ago, Hank.'

'Would you like to see what it looks like?' I nodded. Hank handed me two papers, held together by a staple.

I studied them for a few moments, then

asked, 'He was competent when he signed the advance directive—there's no contesting that, is there?'

'No.'

'When did he sign it?'

Hank leafed through his file cabinet. 'July 2, 1992,' he said.

'That was right after he had his first episode of PCP.'

'Right.'

'Hank . . . '

'Yes?'

'What if—'

'If you had agreed to it then, you'd not be having these troubles now.'

'So, what if . . . if he signed it now and—'

'I don't hear what you're saying. I'm not hearing this,' Hank said, gathering his coat, his briefcase and his hat.

I followed him into the hall. 'What if . . . '

He covered his ears with his hands, but as he did so, I could swear he winked.

I ran all the way back to the hospital, those sheets like hope, held tightly to my breast. When I got to him, Eric was asleep, thin, pale and beautiful. I sat at his bedside and read.

The instructions said that the papers had to be signed and dated by Eric and two witnesses; only one could be related to him. I began to fill out the portion about me being his surrogate; there was no space for a date. When I was done, I stuffed the papers in my pack and leaned over, resting my head on the bed, closing my eyes, and thinking. I thought about honesty, integrity, and the law. I thought about justice and truth, about Mr. Moro's words, 'What do you know of right?' But I did know right. Right was what Eric wanted and needed, to be in Philadelphia, with me, at home.

I got up and went to the pay phone, to call Pammy. She had stayed in Philadelphia after the graduation, to be close to Eric, and was working at a jewelry store in the 'hip' part of town, where her nose rings and shaved head represented a different conformity.

'Hey, Alex,' she said. 'How's the bro?'

'Better. Listen, I have a favor to ask of you.'

'Shoot.'

'You know what a surrogate decision maker is?'

'Is that where you appoint someone to make decisions for you if you're incompetent?'

'Or incapacitated.'

'That was covered in the AIDS Project newsletter two months ago. Does Eric want me to do it?'

'He wants me to do it.'

'Okay.'

'Will you be a witness to his signature?'

'No problem.'

'That's not the favor, though.'

'I'm listening.'

'You have to date it July 2, 1992. Otherwise, your parents could—'

Pammy laughed. 'No big deal,' she said. 'When do you need me to sign?'

'Say, seven tonight? At my apartment?'

'I'm there.'

'Thanks. See ya.'

'Bye.'

I called Gary. He agreed to be a witness too and said he would meet us that night at seven.

Eric was awake when I reentered his room; a nurse was taking his blood pressure and temperature. I hid the papers behind my back.

'What's up?' he asked when the nurse had left.

'What makes you think something's up?'

'Your smile.'

'I smile all the time.'

'Not lately.'

I closed the door.

'Now I know something's up,' he said.

'I have the papers here for you to make me your surrogate.' I pulled them out from behind my back.

'The ones we never signed.'

'Sign.'

'Why now?'

'It's not now. You signed them last July, remember?'

'Alex . . .'

'Just sign and date the damned thing. It's July 2, 1992, in case your memory's a little impaired.'

'This is illegal.'

'No one will know.'

'What about the witnesses?'

'Pammy and Gary. They're not worried about it.'

'Look, Al, I'm competent. That Harper guy can't prove anything.'

'Do you seriously doubt your father will get what he wants?'

'Not forever.'

'For the forever you have left?' Tears had come to my eyes, despite my vow not to break down, not to make him doubt my convictions.

'The last thing I want is for you to get in trouble over something like this,' he said.

'The last thing I want is for you to be taken away.'

'Last week you said you didn't think you could do it.'

'I've matured.'

'You've been pressured.'

'Are you going to sign, or do I have to forge your signature?'

'You wouldn't.'

'Only if you make me.'

He hesitated, studying me before saying, 'Give me a pen.'

I took the document, signed, witnessed, and dated, along with Eric's copy of his advance directive, with me to the hospital the following morning, but I didn't want to use it. Despite my bravado over the two bottles of Chianti I had shared with Pammy and Gary the evening before, the morning light and my hangover made the handwriting on that date, July 2, 1992, waver and blink, calling attention to itself, causing the ink to look wet, too fresh. Anyone could see it was fake, and if the deed was discovered, my chances of convincing a court to let Eric stay with me should he become incompetent would be seriously damaged, not to mention what might happen to me. My knees were weak as I rode the elevator, the papers in my backpack.

I was surprised to find Dr. Harper finished with his evaluation of Eric by the time I arrived.

Mr. and Mrs. Moro were there too. I saw the three of them conversing over Eric's chart at the nursing station as I headed for Eric's room.

Eric was dressed, sitting on his bed. 'Where the hell have you been?' he asked. 'I've been calling you all morning.'

'I've been on my way here. What's happening?'

'What we were afraid of.'

'The hospital discharged you already?'

'Yes. My parents and Harper are making the arrangements to get me to Chicago.'

'But they can't do that!'

'How am I supposed to stop them?'

'Refuse. Just tell them no.'

'The psychiatrist can sedate me, you know.'

'Just like that? Without your permission?'

'My parents are in charge, Al. The hospital recognizes them as my next of kin.'

'They wouldn't—'

'Alexandra, I'll need to ask you to leave.'

I turned around. It was Dr. Harper, with Mr. and Mrs. Moro behind him.

'I'm not going anywhere,' I said.

'I have Eric's parents here, his next of kin—'

'I'm not going anywhere, either,' Eric said, trying to stand. I held on to him.

'Sit down, Eric,' I said.

'No,' he responded. 'Dad, Mama, why don't

368

you come in here instead of hiding behind Dr. Harper?'

Dr. Harper glanced over his shoulder as Mr. Moro stepped forward, gently easing the doctor aside. Mrs. Moro remained behind her husband, her eyes wide.

'I have nothing to hide,' Mr. Moro declared. 'It's time you stopped being childish, Eric. As your parents, and given your current mental state, we have every right to take you home with us. Don't make us take measures to force you to cooperate.'

'There isn't a measure you can take to make me leave Alex,' Eric said. He began to waver, leaning on me.

'Sit down, Eric,' I said. 'Please.'

'Let's not make a scene by getting hospital security involved,' Dr. Harper said.

'I'm not going,' Eric said.

'This is crazy,' I said. 'Can't you see he's too weak? Can't you hear he doesn't want to go?' I thought of the papers, glancing at my backpack on the floor, then quickly looking away.

'Can't you see that it isn't important what he wants, but what he needs?' Mr. Moro asked. Mrs. Moro nodded emphatically.

'But they're the same!' I wailed.

Everyone was speechless for a moment, the ring of my voice plaintive on the air of that

369

small room. Then, abruptly, Dr. Harper and Mr. and Mrs. Moro were gone, leaving a deeper silence in their wake.

Eric sat heavily, then lay on his back, his jeans ridiculously baggy, his T-shirt a tent over his emaciated torso.

I picked up my pack and pulled the papers from it.

'No,' Eric said. 'It's too risky.'

'What isn't?' I asked, my eyes welling with tears.

He grasped for my hand, pulling me to the bedside and pressing it to his lips. 'I love you,' he said. 'Don't fuck your life up over this.'

'I won't,' I said, hoisting my pack over my shoulder, kissing him, and leaving.

Dr. Harper was on the phone at the nursing station, talking, gesturing with his hand, periodically peering over his glasses at Mr. Moro, who listened intently. Mrs. Moro sat on a chair nearby, dabbing at her eyes. I approached them; never had my heart beat so fast, almost distractedly so, seeming to push me forward with each throb. As I walked, I smoothed the papers with my trembling hands until I passed Mrs. Moro and reached the two men, their backs turned to me, and stood listening to Dr. Harper on the phone.

'The young man is resisting. I have the

parents here with me. Their son has been released by the hospital. I think—'

I tapped Dr. Harper on the shoulder; Mr. Moro caught sight of me out of the corner of his eye and turned around, at first startled, then impatient.

'Just a moment, excuse me,' Dr. Harper said into the phone, covering the mouthpiece and looking at me. 'Alexandra, I realize your concern for Eric, but you are just making things—'

'This should settle it,' I said, handing him the papers.

'What? What's this?' Dr. Harper asked.

Mr. Moro snatched the papers from my hand, making me gasp; I hadn't had time to make a photocopy that morning and suddenly I realized he was holding the only copy.

He looked at it, flipping through the pages rapidly.

'Hang on,' Dr. Harper said into the phone, and then, seeing the title of the document, he added, 'I'll call you back,' and hung up.

'There's a surrogate decision maker?' Dr. Harper asked. 'Let me see that, Malcolm.'

Mr. Moro handed the papers to the doctor, saying, 'This is a ploy.' Mrs. Moro had stood, joining her husband, grasping his arm.

I waited while Dr. Harper pushed his glasses

up on his nose and looked at the papers, inspecting them carefully, particularly the signatures, the dates. He lifted his glasses from his eyes and brought the signature page close to his face. I thought he was going to smell the ink.

Seconds stretched into oblivion as I watched, my face hot, guilt burning a hole through my stomach. The longer it took, the more I wanted to grab the papers back and say, 'Forget it,' but I couldn't. I had stepped into the abyss.

Finally, Dr. Harper turned toward me and stared. He didn't give me the papers, instead handing them back to Mr. Moro, who folded them and put them in his inside breast pocket. I was sure my trickery showed on my face; Mr. Moro would surely see it, and Dr. Harper was a psychiatrist, just this side of a mind reader! I wanted to run, but before I could, Dr. Harper spoke.

He said, 'There should be a copy of these on the chart.'

I breathed.

Mr. Moro said, 'You're not saying they're valid, Dick?'

'They appear to be. Unless the witnesses are a problem, or your son's signature is a forgery.'

'Who are these witnesses?' Mr. Moro asked.

A vein popped out on his forehead as he pulled the papers from his pocket and handed them to the doctor.

'Pamela Moro is one,' Dr. Harper said.

Mrs. Moro gasped.

'She's off-balance, I can attest to that,' Mr. Moro said.

'And Gary Kane,' I said. 'I can get him here if you need. He's a friend of Eric's.'

'Malcolm,' Dr. Harper said, sighing and shaking his head. 'I'd like to help, but with this document . . . I mean, these other issues are not my area. If you'd like to get a handwriting expert and contest the witnesses' ability to sign, you can. But . . . I don't think it's contestable.'

'Of course it is!' Mr. Moro said. 'This is all too convenient. It doesn't smell good.'

'Maybe not,' Dr. Harper said, 'but you'll have to prove it. It's a legal document.' Dr. Harper handed me the papers. 'Get a copy on the chart,' he said.

I took the papers and began to walk away in disbelief. I kept going until I reached Eric's room, entering as if in a daze. He was sitting on the side of the bed, just waiting.

'Shit,' he said when he saw me.

I stared at him. 'No,' I said, 'it's okay. You're staying.'

'It worked?'

'Ssshhh. It's a legal document, that's all. They recognized that.'

'They accepted that I'm not going?'

'I don't know.'

'There's no way my father's giving up.'

'All he said is Pammy's off-balance, implying she doesn't qualify as a witness. And they wondered if your signature was forged.'

'Nothing about the date?'

'Quit talking about it.'

'He'll be in here making a stink any minute. Just watch.'

We waited. We watched. Eventually, Mr. and Mrs. Moro and Dr. Harper did come, but they didn't enter Eric's room. Instead, we saw them pause outside the door, confer briefly, and then walk down the hall to the elevators, where they disappeared.

Several hours passed before we left the hospital. We waited to see the social worker.

'It'll only pay for four hours a day,' the social worker explained.

'But I work and he needs constant care,' I protested.

'I do not,' Eric said. 'Don't worry so much, Al.'

'That's all Medicaid will pay for,' the social worker said. 'I know it's not much, but home care is expensive.'

'What if he has seizures while I'm at work?' I asked.

'It's not my decision,' she said. 'I can get you twenty-four-hour care, but you'll have to pay—'

'I don't want twenty-four hours, just twelve, or eight even.'

'It's the same. You'll have to pay.'

'Can't we apply for special circumstances?' I asked.

'Believe me, everyone's got special circumstances,' she said. 'And everyone's just making do.' She stood up.

'Thanks,' I said, and she left.

'Don't worry,' Eric said. 'I'll be a good boy.'

'That's what I'm worried about.'

He laughed, and then I laughed. Both of us laughing at the same time; it felt good.

I phoned Gary from our apartment that afternoon.

'Alex, hi,' he said. 'Wait, there's someone here who wants to talk to you.' I listened: silence, breathing, hot and quick. What was going on? Then I heard a mumble and burble. Little Maria!

'How'd you like that?' Gary asked. 'She knows your name.'

'I'll have to trust you on that. Hey, I need help again.'

'Problems with the surrogate and Eric's dad?'

'No, I think that's worked out for now, thanks to you and Pammy. But I'm afraid to leave Eric alone while I'm at work. What if he has another seizure?'

'What'd Medicaid give you, that four-hour bullshit?'

'Yeah, how'd you know?'

'How do you think?'

'Right.'

'Blow off the four-hour. The people they send are scraped from the bottom of the barrel anyway.'

'But we don't have—'

'We'll take care of it.'

'Who?'

'Those of us who've been through this before and a lot of others who've been luckier.'

'You mean people from the AIDS Survivors Group?'

'Beyond that. How many hours do you need?'

'Eight?'

'You need twenty-four?'

376

'No. Just eight or twelve on the days I'm working.'

'No problem.'

'No problem? Just like that?'

'Alex, people who can help, will.'

I began to cry, so much so that I couldn't say thanks or good-bye as I hung up. But Gary understood. He understood something else too. It wasn't seizures I was afraid of; it was death, cold and alone.

CHAPTER THIRTY-EIGHT

Stiff winter melted into spring and we had settled into a routine of sorts. I worked at the library while various people stayed with Eric. Between Pammy, Mom and Daddy, occasionally Cindy and Harry, and the sweet men and women Gary rounded up, Eric was never by himself. In between, he got massive doses of radiation that plowed a path through his brain, keeping him amazingly cognizant and, equally incredibly, alive.

It was the beginning of April, the ground still hard and brown with winter, the leaves mere light green buds on somber branches, when Hank stopped by with a casserole. I met him at the door downstairs; our building didn't have an elevator.

'Hello,' he said.

'Hank, it's good to see you,' I said, stepping forward to take the casserole. 'Thanks, we appreciate it,' I added.

'From my sister. She asked after Eric.'

'Did they meet?'

He shook his head. 'She follows all my trials. She tends to remember the ones I've lost.'

'It wasn't your fault. We still think you're great. I—'

He held up a hand. 'I've come to ask Eric something.'

'I'd invite you up, but . . . '

'I know, no access. I'm used to it.'

'I'm sorry—'

'No need. It helps to remind me there are still battles to fight.'

'You probably haven't lost many.'

'I came to ask Eric if I can sue the rest of the programs.'

'You've done enough, really. We don't hold it against you. Eric thinks—'

'As a favor to me, please.'

'Favor? We owe *you*.'

'You owe me nothing. I'm asking this as a friend.'

I sighed. The lawsuit had been pretty bad at the end. Twelve people, regular-looking folks, standing up and declaring that Eric wasn't worth fighting for, that they wouldn't want him as their doctor. Hank had explained that's not what losing meant, but he was wrong; I had watched the jury members' faces and they had condemned Eric, the same way the programs had. Eric had shrugged and kissed me when he heard, then ordered a pizza; he claimed it had always been more my fight than his.

'There are six other programs,' Hank said. 'Just because we lost this one . . . '

'You mean you're willing to go through this six more times?' I laughed. 'For no pay?'

'What's an old guy like me need with money?'

I stared at him, his eyes dark and intense; I recognized Eric in them. 'What keeps you going?' I asked.

He took my hand, his black wool glove rough against the pink chap of my skin. 'Anger, Alex,' he said. 'Anger at slipshod judgments that destroy talent and lives. Those programs decided how Eric's life would be lived when they denied him the chance to prove how great a psychiatrist he can be. I'm here to tell the world, no one can do that.'

'You really care about him, don't you?'

He laughed, and said, 'No, I do it for the money.'

I smiled; Hank was the second man in my life I couldn't say no to.

CHAPTER THIRTY-NINE

We made it to late June before Eric could no longer climb the stairs to our apartment; after that we carried him. His doctors said the radiation had stopped working; they talked of 'hospice,' 'respite care,' 'comfort measures.' I shook my head; the tears were hot behind my eyes. Eric could still talk; he was still mine.

'Darlin',' he mumbled one dark night as I sat on the edge of the bed watching the streetlamp paint a smeared light blue across our window.

'What is it?' I asked, bolting up and hurrying to his side of the bed. 'Are you okay?'

'Darlin' Al, I love you.'

'I love you,' I said. Was this it? Was this good-bye?

'There are so many books I haven't read.'

'You'll have time,' I said, fighting panic, tears, and despair.

His teeth glistened as he smiled. 'Stay an optimist, will you?'

'I'll try.' I gripped his hand, painfully tight.

He was quiet, so still that I rested my palm on his chest to make sure he breathed. 'I'm okay,' he said.

'Of course you are.'

'He never forgave me, that's my one regret.'

'Who?'

'My father.'

'You talked to your parents just yesterday on the phone, don't you remember?'

'My mother said she loved me, and my father told me again to come home. But he never forgave me for breaking his rules . . . so many rules, so much I still don't understand.'

'What rules?'

'Things that were important to him . . .'

'He doesn't hold anything against you, Eric. He loves you.' I was crying, trying not to sob, willing the words to be true so he could believe them.

'You're a better woman than I deserve, Al.'

'No—'

'Stick with Hank.'

'What?'

'I'm tired.' He sighed, and I knew then what he wanted, remembering the words of the patient he had cared for: 'I'll be going now,' and his words in response: 'I'll be here.'

'Don't go,' I said quickly, kissing his hot forehead. 'Don't ever go.'

'Okay,' he murmured, closing his eyes.

I went for a book and began reading aloud to him.

The following day I took an indefinite leave of absence from my job, borrowed money from everyone I knew, and read practically nonstop to Eric, day and night. Often he slept, but most times he stared, faraway but purposeful, like he was gazing at destiny. It was at those times when I most felt the loss of our union, that he was on a journey to somewhere without me, to have new experiences that I would not know. It was then that I would bring him back by clearing my throat, reading louder, or kissing him, caressing him; it was then that he would smile, briefly, before he was gone again.

Even when it was clear he was asleep, I would continue reading, cramming words into his ears, determined that he would hear the end of this book and then the next and the next. How could I let him go in the middle of a story, leaving so much unsaid, unheard? How could I let his pleasure be done?

Sometimes, in late afternoon with the sun low, hot, and blazing yellow, the dust motes suspended by the laziness of summer currents, I would simply watch him sleep and give in to regret. I would think of all the 'lasts,' and how ignorant I had been not to notice them: the last time he pitched a baseball, or kissed a kid, or wore his white coat, or threw a snowball, or drank espresso, or sang; the last time we made love. How oblivious I'd been not to hold it tight and care about it more; how I should have cherished each moment and clutched them close, what we had. I had ignored time and now I couldn't get it back for all the riches in the universe. And then, while I thought, Eric would stir, see me, and smile, signaling me to resume reading, and I would, feeling time like air, invisible, weightless and impossible to hold, but still not knowing how to spend it but one solid moment at a time.

By the beginning of July, it had gotten too difficult to care for Eric in our apartment, so we moved him to my parents' house, where he could live on the first floor and Mom and Daddy could help.

I watched as the attendants transferred Eric downstairs from our apartment to the ambulance, realizing that the next time I returned there I would be without him. That thought immobilized me until I heard the horn summon me from below. Then I took a last look before closing the door on our nest, glimpsing the airplanes suspended, the medical textbooks on the shelves, the little Shadow Blaster model, my artwork taped to the walls, and coagulated coffee pooled at the bottom of the glass pot. Turning the key in that lock was effortless, yet somehow it had become the hardest thing to do, creating a hollow noise, an echo, a sound like death.

When Eric was settled and slumbering in my parents' house, I went outside to the neighborhood. The fiery, sticky freedom of July engulfed me, recalling summers gone by, running wild in those childhood streets, my cheeks flushed, my knees dirty beyond scrubbing, before bras, tampons, boys, HIV, and sickness. Children frolicked where I once had, contesting rules, jumping rope, tumbling and playing. I watched them and began to walk, my senses filling with the scent of hot sidewalks, my eyes slits to the sunlight.

I looked down as I went, seeing my feet, steady, dancing in shadow, then light, then shadow, then light. I noticed cracks in the cement from aggressive tree roots and the earth's movement. Suddenly, I scrambled to avoid them, recalling Hank's words about forever cracking, about falling through. How foolish Eric and I had been to challenge that truth with words engraved in simple gold! Together Forever. It had sounded so right, so solid once. And now. Now it was beyond re-definition, revision, repair.

'Alex! Alex!' my mother yelled from the front porch. 'Alex! Come quick! Hurry!' she shouted.

I ran. Eric had been in my parents' house for less than an hour and he was seizing.

The crack widened.

I had Mom call everyone who needed to know: Pammy, Jerry, Hank, Gary, and the others. Everyone except Eric's parents. That was my job.

I called from the hospital.

'Mr. Moro,' I said when he answered, 'Eric's very sick.'

'Even more reason to bring him home,' he responded.

'He's really sick this time.'

'I'll pay for a nurse to escort him with me, then.'

'You don't understand—'

'I understand that you can't handle him.'

'He's in the hospital—'

'Better for him to be here with us. My attorney tells me we have a court date for next week, regarding that document you say my son—'

'Listen!' There was silence on the other end. 'Listen,' I repeated, 'he's sick. Are you and Mrs. Moro coming?'

'To bring him home?'

'No. To see him. To say good-bye.' I choked, my knuckles jammed to my lips.

'Let us bring him home and we'll come. Or, I can have my attorney call you next week.'

'He can't travel,' I sobbed.

'Good-bye, Miss Taylor.'

'Mr. Moro,' I said to the dial tone, 'I'll tell him you forgive him. I'll tell him good-bye . . .'

I cried into the phone; passersby stared.

I was sitting at Eric's bedside, one more room on the twelfth-floor AIDS Unit, my forehead pressed against the cool silver shine of the bed rail, when Hank rolled in. I felt his hand on my shoulder, and I looked up.

'Hi,' I said. 'We're at it again.'

Something in Hank's look: defeat, acceptance, understanding, or sorrow made my heart quicken.

'Your mother called me,' he said.

'Thanks for coming.'

'No thanks needed.'

'He's stopped seizing,' I said, looking at Eric.

'He looks comfortable.'

'Yes.'

'It may not last.'

'What does?'

We both watched Eric, his face, so thin and wasted, had peace written on it. I held his hand, warm, still living.

Hank said, 'Don't forget you're his surrogate.'

'I won't, but it's not like he's on the brink of anything. I mean . . . you know,' I bit back tears, 'his pleasure isn't done.'

'I hope you're right, but if it is, it is.' Hank rubbed my shoulder, and as he did, I felt a fist tighten around my heart, from sudden knowing.

'No,' I gulped, 'not yet, Hank.' I stared at Eric, so serene, immobile and dormant, so vulnerable.

'It will never get easier, Alex,' he said. 'I'm sorry.'

His hand was gone; I didn't look up to see him leave.

It must've been five minutes more before I rose to close the door. Alone with Eric, I asked him what to do, begged him to live, kissed his closed eyes, unwrapped him from the sheets and hospital gown and stared at the body that was not Eric, never would be again, but was closer than any other. Then I watched in horror as tranquillity metamorphosed into spastic agony, tossing and twisting him for countless hours.

'Isn't there anything you can do?' I asked as Eric entered his second day of seizures. The group of doctors, five in all, gathered around Eric's bed during morning rounds and stared with consternation at his contortions.

The older one turned to the one nearest him. 'General anesthesia is still an option,' he said.

'He'd have to be in the Unit,' the other one answered. This wrinkled the first one's brow, and his head bobbed in short little nods.

Eric kicked the bed rail violently, a purple welt immediately bulging on his left ankle.

'Please stop it,' I cried, running to his leg, trying to catch it, rub it, kiss it, anything.

'The Unit's not appropriate in this case,' the

older doctor said. The rest of the doctors in the group were younger, dressed in short white coats, with looks either distracted or horrified, each blink a blessed relief from the sight of Eric's misery. When I turned my back for a cold cloth they walked out, a clump of useless expertise.

'Damn you!' I shouted after them in the hall outside Eric's room, causing several nurses to turn and stare at me. The group disappeared into another patient's room. I stormed back into Eric's room. 'Damn you, damn you, damn you!' I fumed, slamming the door. 'Damn you!' I repeated, now facing Eric, and he grew still. 'No,' I said, rushing to his side. 'I didn't mean you, my love. Oh.' I sank into the chair at his side and watched him catch his breath.

I don't know when it went from morning to dark. Everyone came to visit, but I wouldn't let them spell me, and finally, it was just Eric and me, breathing each other's air, waiting. I didn't turn on the lights; I didn't note the time. I got in bed beside him. He had the strength yet to displace his chest against my own, to taste of the salt of his efforts, to move his breath against my cheek. I embraced him; he lay there. I kissed him; he lay there. I straddled him; he lay there. I sealed his mouth and nose with my hand, depriving him of oxygen; he lay there. I removed my hand, still straddling a body lighter than my own, more precious than any other, and he lay there.

'Eric,' I whispered. He lay there. 'Just tell me you love me,' I said. He lay there. I went on, 'I talked to your father. He told me there's nothing to forgive . . . he loves you.' He lay there.

Finally, I got off the bed, put down the bed rails and knelt on the floor, my lips to his ear. 'Thank you for showing me bravery,' I whispered with a choke. He lay there. 'I guess you'll be going now,' I continued, my voice wavering, thick with panic. He lay there. 'Eric? Eric?' I pleaded. He lay there. I watched. Nothing. 'Eric,' I said, 'am I right?' He lay there. Then I repeated, quickly, 'I guess you'll be going now.' I gave him seconds to answer, and when he didn't, I added, 'I'll be here.' I collapsed to the floor.

He seized again, twice. With each seizure I sat there, not moving. When he was still, I stood, and soon he exhaled, long and shallow, across forever, slipping through my fingers and into that crack, where another breath would never be needed. Before he went, I could swear he smiled.

I sat against the wall in the dark, fighting the

urge to save him, to tear through the halls and yell to the nurses, to pull the 'code' button, to scream down the tunnel of oblivion. Instead, I sat silently and waited until I was sure it was too late. I was the one to let him go.

After a time, I switched on a light, to hold Eric's image tight against my memory, and what I saw looking up at me was the wizard, brilliant in contrast to Eric's translucent skin. I realized then that the wizard, our wizard, was going with Eric, and with it, its mitigation of harm, its allowance of life, its hope where there's a need. I felt the calm of surreal, untouchable finality as I picked up a piece of paper from the bedside table and began to sketch, steadily, methodically; I needed to get it right.

Before I left I turned off the light and sat with Eric, holding his hand that had given such pleasure, and being glad. I looked death boldly in the face then, and what I saw was the price of life.

I didn't say good-bye as I closed the door on darkness.

With the sketch in my jeans pocket, I mounted Shadow Blaster and peeled out of the hospital parking lot, across streets black and alone with midnight. We rode to nowhere till dawn.

                    *   *   *

They were waiting for me when I returned to
my apartment: Pammy, Jerry, Hank, my
parents, their faces gray with worry. Seeing
them gathered near the stairs outside my
building terrified me; it made everything unde-
niable. I parked Shadow Blaster as my father
approached me.

'Sweetie,' he began, 'I don't—'

'I already know, Daddy,' I said, starting to
cry. We hugged. 'He's gone, just gone,' I
murmured.

'I'm so sorry,' Daddy said. He was weeping,
starting to sob, when my mother came over and
joined our embrace. I felt buried, suffocated
almost; it took minutes before I broke free and
stood erect.

My voice was syncopated by grief as I asked,
'Where is he?'

My mother answered, 'At the hospital.'

I shook my head vigorously, seeing Pammy's
bright scalp and black tank top, Jerry's dark
hair, Hank's twinkling spectacles blur by with
the movement. 'No, Mom, not where is his
body, where is *he*?' I asked.

She looked puzzled, reaching out to gather
my hair away from my face and into a ponytail.
I jerked free of her hands and walked away from

her and my father, their anguish sweltering and massive, thick on my back. And there was Pammy, her face streaked red by tears, her arms muscular, like Eric's had once been.

She said, 'He's where he's always been.'

CHAPTER FORTY

We headed for Hank's office, to talk. My mind was sodden, murky, and the sun was impossibly bright, too normal. People walked, drove cars; leaves grew, rustled by wind. I dully realized that these things would go on in some form forever. According to the world, according to the grand scheme of things, nothing had happened, or worse, what had happened was ordinary.

As I climbed into the backseat of my parents' Oldsmobile for the short drive to Hank's, I felt like shouting to passersby that I was crushed, devastated, no longer like them. Even the back of Daddy's head, and Mom's hand in mine, were alien. Eric's death had happened to me, transforming me into something outside, something other.

I led the way to Hank's office at the AIDS Project; Hank, Pammy, and Jerry had arrived before us.

'Well,' Hank said once we were seated, 'it's not very kind, but as Eric's lawyer, I have paperwork.'

'Of course,' Daddy said. 'We understand.' He grasped my hand.

Hank went on, 'There's the will—'

'What about Eric's parents?' I asked. 'Shouldn't we—'

'No,' Pammy said. 'I don't give a fuck what that thing says. My father deserves nothing.'

'We aren't talking about a great deal of money,' Hank said.

'I don't care,' Pammy protested, her anger propelling her out of her chair. 'That asshole gets nothing of Eric's!' She had nowhere to go, so she sat again, her face set, her eyes dark fire. I stared at her, the angry side I had rarely seen in Eric so near the surface in her, down the spectrum from passion.

'Maybe,' Hank began, 'the best thing to do is to just read through it, as Eric has requested. Anyone not present who is named in the will will be notified by mail.' Pammy crossed her arms, her booted legs spread into a stubborn stance, saying nothing.

'Are you okay with this?' Hank asked me. I nodded.

'All right,' Hank said, 'here we go: "I, Eric Lawrence Moro, being of sound mind and body, do hereby bequeath my worldly goods in the following manner: To Pammy Moro, little sister, best childhood companion and faithful keeper of secrets, I leave my leather jacket, every condom I haven't already used, and all my hats to keep her from sunburn and frostbite."' We looked at Pammy. Her face was contorted into a smile that fought against tears. Hank swallowed and continued, '"To Jerry Moro, kid brother, handsome Eric look-alike, and all-around sweet guy, I leave my baseball mitt, my medical books, and my vast collection of unused socks and underwear. Sorry, little buddy, my talent comes with me, but I'm not worried about you."' Hank looked up, for response. Jerry was crying silently, the way a grown man would, sorrow half-swallowed.

I nodded to Hank to continue, although my breath was fast and shallow, my skin tingly and tight around my mouth.

'"To the people who cared for me as only parents could, Wilma (Mom) and Milton

(Daddy) Taylor, I leave, to Mom, my basket-ball, to Daddy, my art books.'''

'He sketched in the margins,' I said. I felt Daddy's hand tighten on mine and watched as Mom cried.

'Am I next?' I asked.

Hank nodded.

I took a big breath and stood. 'I'm sorry,' I said.

'It's okay,' Hank said. 'We can skip that part—'

'No, I want to hear it. But I need to hear it alone.'

'Of course, sweetie, we understand,' Mom said.

'We should have thought of that,' Daddy commented.

When everyone was gone, I approached Hank at his desk. 'Do you mind if I read it to myself?' I asked.

He shook his head and handed the papers to me.

'I can hear him so clearly,' I said. 'I can see him like he was at first, when I drew him.'

Hank nodded.

I said, 'He's so clear to me now, even more than when he was alive.'

'I know,' Hank said. 'Hold on to it.'

'How?'

'You'll find your way.'

'I guess I should read it now.'

'If you want.'

'I want more than this,' I said, waving the papers and walking away, toward the window.

'You have more.'

I turned to face him, the will a simple piece of paper dry and light in my hand. Then I began to read, silently: 'For Alexandra Taylor, the sexy, sparkling, fiery love of my life, I leave my heart, my soul, my body, my passion, my forever. Because of you, Al, I am not sad or angry about leaving, or not having had enough, because you made it enough. I thank you. I leave you Shadow Blaster, my Harley-Davidson motorcycle that you named, all my worldly possessions not otherwise bequeathed, especially my shirts you love to borrow, my cowboy boots you look so cute in, my recipes you'll never be able to follow, my stethoscope you are so fond of playing with, my phone book you are so curious about, my jean jacket you've practically stolen already, my photos that are mostly of you, my camera to take more pictures of you, and anything else you want that is mine. I leave to you, Al, my pal, all my dreams of success and greatness, all my desire and commitment, all that I am, which you will not need, because you are so much more. I leave to you any cash you can connect with me and all proceeds from any settlement of lawsuits in my name. Knowing you, you'll know how to give it away. I love you always.

'To my parents,—' I looked up at Hank and breathed, my face wet with the knowledge that no new words would come from Eric beyond this, that now I would hear words only from conversations past or imagined.

'I'll bring them back in,' I said.

When we were settled again, Hank continued reading: '"To my parents, Malcolm and Patricia Moro . . ."' Hank hesitated and Pammy's jaw tightened, but she remained quiet as he went on, '"I leave memories, in any way they choose to use them. And love."' Pammy exhaled, Jerry held her hand. We were silent.

'That's the will,' Hank said. 'Now there's the issue of the remains.'

'His body?' I asked.

'Yes,' Hank responded. 'As the surrogate, Alex, you can speak for Eric in this regard.'

'He wanted to be cremated. He asked me to scatter the ashes,' I said, my words sounding metallic and unreal.

'He told me that also,' Hank said. 'Has anyone contacted Eric's mother and father?'

'No!' It was Pammy again. 'Forget them. They don't give a shit anyway.'

My parents looked startled, but didn't speak.

'That's not true,' I said. 'They tried to take Eric back to Chicago, to help him.'

'That wasn't about helping,' Pammy said. 'That was about possession, about Daddy Moro getting his way.'

'Maybe,' I began, 'but Eric didn't hate his father, or his mother. He told me once, "it's okay for my parents to do some Catholic bull-shit after I die."'

'He did?' Hank asked.

'Yes,' I said.

'Eric hated the Church, hated Catholicism,' Pammy said.

'He told me he wasn't Catholic,' I said, 'but he said to let his parents have a Catholic service.'

'I'll contact the Moros,' Hank said. He looked at me. 'I guess that does it,' he added.

We stood.

'Why don't you come home with us?' Daddy asked me.

I shook my head. 'Thanks, but I'd rather be alone.'

'You sure?' Mom asked.

'Yes, don't worry.'

'We love you,' Daddy said, giving me a hug.

'I love you too.'

They looked at me mournfully, hoping to

402

soak up some of my sadness, but there was too much to absorb, too much for all of us.

We began to file out.

'See you,' I said, and headed for the ladies' room.

As I walked back down the hall toward Hank's office, Pammy caught up to me.

'There's something I have to tell you, Alex,' she said. 'About Eric.'

'What?'

'I didn't want to say anything in front of your parents and Jerry, but there was a secret Eric kept his whole life.'

'A secret?'

'He wanted me to tell you after he was gone.'

'I don't know how much more I can take today, Pammy.'

'He trusted me. I promised I'd tell you.'

'Okay.'

'Can we talk here?'

I looked up and down the hall. It was empty. 'I guess,' I said.

'Okay. Here goes. Eric was molested when he was twelve.'

'Molested? Sexually?'

'By the priest in our parents' church. The one that's still there.'

'No,' I said.

She nodded. 'And Dad refused to believe

Eric, probably because he couldn't handle what had happened. He said Eric was filthy and a sinner to make up such a thing.'

'But he was telling the truth.'

'Of course, but the whole thing disgusted our father. He couldn't face it, so he turned away from it.'

'And your mother?'

'She never knew.'

'But why didn't your father confront the priest?'

'Because to believe what Eric said would've turned his whole world upside-down.'

'What about Eric's world?'

'It was sacrificed.'

I didn't want to hear, but only now things began to slide into place, to finally make sense: Eric's resistance to getting married in the Church, his father's 'rules' that Eric had never understood, but felt he had broken; his over-whelming need to rescue Tiffany, a battered, equally molested soul, a kindred spirit.

'But why did Eric blame himself for your father's rejection of him?' I asked.

'Eric took to heart what Dad said, that he was filthy. He felt filthy after what had happened, that somehow he had been to blame.'

'He was only a kid.'

'Yes, and in awe of our father. He didn't

think Dad could be wrong, so he blamed himself.'

'But the priest was to blame.'

'Eric knew that intellectually, but emotionally it was harder to accept. Either way, it didn't change how he saw himself through Dad's eyes. Eric never went to church after that. He renounced Catholicism, which enraged our father.'

'Eric told me he'd never be a hypocrite.'

'Like that priest is. Still, Eric wanted Dad's love so badly—'

'And his forgiveness.'

'Yes, but Dad never forgave Eric for telling the truth. After Eric got sick our father felt responsible, though.'

'Responsible?'

'That he had "let" his son flaunt his rules, values, whatever you want to call it.'

'You think your father felt guilty for not limiting Eric more, by choosing to ignore what he was doing?'

'At the time, he couldn't face it: Eric's humanity, his developing sexually, his *normality*, but in retrospect I think he felt he gave Eric too much freedom, and it was that freedom that allowed Eric to get AIDS. '

'But you can't keep your kids in prison!'

'If our father could have, he would have.'

'But by his attitude, he achieved the opposite.'

'You're right. He lost me way back, when I saw how he treated Eric.'

'And now he's lost Eric.'

'And therein lies the guilt. A far cry from love.'

'Eric loved *him*, though.'

'He needed to, to prove him wrong.'

'Why didn't Eric tell me about the priest?'

'Telling makes people think, like it made our father think.'

'He couldn't have thought I wouldn't believe him.'

'No, but it's a hard thing to escape from once you know about it. He didn't want it to contaminate what you two had.'

'Then why tell me now, when it's too late?'

'I guess he didn't think it was, that somehow you'd make it right.'

I nodded slowly, not really understanding, then sighed, recalling that long ago Midnight Mass, the beauty, the purity, the faith, the hope—and Eric's inexplicable stubbornness, his father's steely back-turning, the priest with his white and gold robes . . . I didn't want to think further.

*   *   *

It wasn't until afternoon that Hank located the Moros. I was still hanging around the office, avoiding going home, when Hank got through and put Mr. Moro on the speakerphone.

'Mr. Malcolm Moro?' Hank asked.

'Yes. Who is this?'

'Hank Brown, your son Eric's attorney.'

'Attorney? What's this about? Is there some kind of trouble?'

'I have Alexandra Taylor here with me—'

'Is this about my contesting the surrogate decision? Because if it is, my lawyer's—'

'Mr. Moro,' Hank said, 'Eric passed away early this morning.'

Silence. Not even static, breathing, or a gasp, just nothing. Hank and I looked at each other and then stared at the phone, expectant.

'Mr. Moro?' Hank said.

'Why are you involved with this?' Mr. Moro asked.

'Excuse me?'

'I would like an explanation for why I wasn't notified by the hospital, why his physicians did not contact me regarding his condition.'

'I cannot answer that.'

'Where is he?'

That question again.

'His remains are in the University Hospital morgue,' Hank said. 'I'm calling because Eric requested that you be notified in case you wished to have a service—'

'Wished? He's Catholic. He belongs in the fold of the Church.'

'I understand.'

'I'll make arrangements to have his body flown here, to Chicago.'

'There is one other matter, Mr. Moro.'

'What?'

'Eric specified to Ms. Taylor and to me that he wished to be cremated.'

'That's absurd.'

'Alexandra Taylor is the legal surrogate.'

'I don't give a damn. I tell you he's Catholic, dammit. We don't burn our loved ones.'

'His request is legally binding.'

'Who are you?'

'Hank Brown, I represent—'

'What religion are you?'

'Not that it's any of your business, but Baptist.'

'Well, you Baptists may burn your kin, but I will not have my son put in a furnace.'

'Mr. Moro,' Hank said, 'I have been retained as your son's attorney and he has specified that his remains are to be cremated and scattered by Ms. Alexandra Taylor. There is no legal reason that his body must be released to you in its current form.'

'We'll see about that,' Mr. Moro answered, and the next thing we heard was a dial tone.

Hank raised his eyebrows and clicked off the connection. 'How'd that produce Eric?' he asked.

I shook my head. 'I don't know, but Eric loved him.'

'Eric was like that.'

'Generous.'

Mr. Moro turned out to be right, he got Eric to Chicago. And then Eric was right, he never set foot in a Catholic church alive again. What wasn't right was the way Hank and Mr. Moro had to argue and argue about the body and the form and the ashes and the burning. I knew Hank would win—he had the law on his side—and I suspected Mr. Moro's arguing had more to do with parental turf and control than anything to do with religion, a ticket to heaven, or his son's desires.

It was eventually agreed that Eric's body would be released for the Catholic service, which would be held in Chicago, and cremated immediately afterward. I was to transport him home.

My role in the transport started me thinking about the commercial flight back to

Philadelphia with the urn holding Eric's ashes. The whole process unnerved me: the thought of putting the urn through the X-ray scanner, deciding where to put it on the plane—under the seat in front of me, or in the overhead? What about in my luggage? What if it spilled? The more I thought about it, visualizing the problems of being accompanied by the urn into the restaurant/bar at the airport, into the ladies' room, it sitting beside me at the gate, the more I realized Eric would've gotten a great kick out of it. I wished I could share it with him . . .

Share it with him. Suddenly, it occurred to me that we *could* share it. We would take a ride, the two of us, one long, last, terrific ride, over stomach-jolting hills, dipping low around smooth curves, rain pelting us, wind drying us, the smell of sunset and sweet, warm leather our companions, the sight of blinking orange and red neon our art.

With Eric in my backpack, I would take him home to the tune of Shadow Blaster's song.

CHAPTER FORTY-ONE

I was in borrowed black silk when I entered the church, wobbling on heels I rarely wore, my pantyhose pasted to my legs by the sweat of July.

Afterward, I stood on the steps, in scorching sunlight, having watched as the bald priest blessed Eric's body, touching him in a sanctioned way, for the final time, the wizard unseen under layers of T-shirt, dress shirt, navy blue suit. I had watched as Eric's mother, father, and brother cried, as the others prayed, sniffled, sighed, and shook their heads, as AIDS was never mentioned, only 'cancer,' 'lymphoma,' 'brain tumor.'

I stood alone. I had asked them not to come, my family, his friends, our friends. I didn't want comfort, or mourning, or goodbyes. Not like this.

I looked up finally and they were gone, the people that had been there, the people that I had not known. They raced away in cars to destinations more comfortable, controlled environments without the problems of humidity and decay.

'You didn't want to go either, huh?'

'What?' I said, turning to see a young man behind me, about Jerry's age, dressed in black, his hair slick with heat.

'I can't stand that part,' he went on. 'I hung back until they were gone.'

'Who?'

'The funeral procession.'

'Procession?'

'The burial,' he said.

'Oh, shit!' I gasped. 'He wouldn't.'

'Are you okay?'

'Do you have a car?'

'Sure.'

'You've got to take me to the cemetery. Now!'

'I told you, that stuff gives me the creeps.'

'Please, hurry.'

'What's with you?' he asked as I dragged him across the lawn by his sleeve to the only car left on the street; I had taken a cab to the service.

'I'm responsible for the body,' I said. 'It's supposed to be cremated.'

'In this heat it may spontaneously combust.'

'Just take me there, please.'

'Okay, but I'm not staying.'

'Fine.'

We climbed in and he started driving. He was a friend of Jerry's. He said they were in premed together, which he kept chattering about, but all I could think of was Eric in that coffin, being lowered into a hole of clay and covered with heavy earth and sheaves of flowers, fragrant and rapidly wilting.

When we got there, I bolted out of the car before the young man had stopped it, and rushed toward the cluster of people near the grave site. I stumbled in the soft earth, seeing them turn toward me, shocked: the priest, Mr. and Mrs. Moro, the others, their eyes widening, their shoulders pulling back at my approach.

'Stop!' I screeched, but they already had. 'You can't do this,' I panted, now in front of them.

'Excuse us, young lady,' the priest said, meeting my eyes. 'This is a burial. Please respect the deceased.'

'You didn't respect him in life. He trusted you.'

'Excuse us,' the priest repeated.

'God sees the truth,' I said.

The priest's eyes were steady, then they flickered, briefly, indicating that he suspected I knew what he'd done. He glanced at Mr. and Mrs. Moro to see if they'd seen.

'I'll proceed,' he said, clearing his throat.

'Please do,' Mr. Moro said.

'He's mine now,' I said.

The priest continued reading from the Bible. His voice was even, but his fingers trembled where they were spread beneath the book. The mourners turned their backs on me.

'NO!' I yelled. They turned to look at me again. Mr. Moro came at me.

'Get out of here,' he said, taking me by the arm and trying to lead me away.

'This is illegal and you know it,' I said, yanking my arm from him. He quickly grasped it again, forming a fist around it, pulling me with him.

'Continue,' he ordered the priest, and we started to struggle.

The priest's voice droned on but the onlookers gaped at us. Mr. Moro dragged at me and I dragged back. Suddenly, out of the corner of my eye, I saw the young man who had reluctantly driven me there and had vowed to leave immediately. Instead, he had remained to watch the drama, and was now out of his car and standing near us.

'Should I call the police?' he asked.

We stopped scuffling and stared at him.

'Good idea,' Mr. Moro said, and the young man hurried away.

We didn't know what to do then; the protocol had been irretrievably breached. Everything was still. Even the priest had stopped reading.

After about five awkward minutes, two uniformed police officers climbed the small hill to where we were gathered and asked what the problem was.

'She does not belong here,' Mr. Moro said.

'I have a copy of a surrogacy agreement. Here,' I said, handing it to an officer. 'I'm Alexandra Taylor, I'm responsible for the deceased's remains. He's to be cremated.'

The officers exchanged a glance and looked at the document for a long while; no doubt it was the first one like it they had ever seen. Then the larger one took off his cap and ran his hand through his hair, replaced his cap, and spoke. 'Can't you two come to some agreement on this here?'

We shook our heads.

'No form of compromise?' the other officer asked.

I wasn't about to ask what he had in mind. We shook our heads again.

'Well, sir,' the first officer said, 'it's the letter of the law I'm sworn to uphold. I see you've got a man of the cloth here, and I'm Catholic myself, but—'

'Goddammit, he's my son,' Mr. Moro said, but with less confidence than usual. The 'goddammit' made the officer look up hastily toward the priest, whose head was beginning to shine in the heat; he shifted his weight frequently.

'I'm sorry, sir, she's got a document here,' the officer said.

I expected Mr. Moro to again claim that it was fake, coerced, forged, and to insist on a hearing or some such legal maneuver, but he didn't. His shoulders sagged a bit, like the air had been let out of him, and he nodded, walking away and rejoining the others.

I wasn't close to the coffin, or to Mr. Moro, or the priest. I was perhaps ten yards away. But I saw it clearly, a memory emblazoned on my soul. Mr. Moro scrutinized the now silent priest, his gaze probing below the Church's finery, the layers of protective, sacred cloth, to the man underneath. I watched what Mr. Moro saw: flesh, humanity, the capability for bad deeds, the tip of evil. Knowledge crossed his face abruptly and he threw his head back, hurling a guttural roar from his belly toward the heavens.

'Go!' he ordered those gathered. They stared at him and he again bellowed, 'Go!' His fists were clenched as the confused group began to shake their heads, looking at one another, backing up.

'Malcolm,' the priest began, 'in this time of grief—'

'Damn you, go!'

The priest shut his Bible with a snap and walked down the hill, toward the hearse.

'Pat,' Mr. Moro said to Mrs. Moro, 'you stay.' He took her hand and they knelt by the side of the coffin. Mr. Moro rested his head on it and began to cry. Sobs convulsed his body, jerking his chest inward and out. The sound of his uncontrolled grief suddenly seemed the saddest I'd ever heard. Mrs. Moro joined him, her sorrow higher-pitched, more soothing, blessed by ignorance.

I witnessed what Eric had never seen, would never see: his father's profound and true love given voice, while regret, an eternal hangman's noose, descended upon him, never to be loosened.

Eric was at last believed. And at last forgiven.

* * *

The trip back to Philadelphia with Eric was as I had hoped: long, achingly hard, breathtaking. I talked with him, laughed with him, carried him on my back, and slept with him beside me. I didn't open the urn on the way, although I was tempted to run my fingers through him, to see if the two silver earrings had survived and if they had, to put them in my ears, alongside the one he had given me after our first night together.

I often wondered where he was, sensing him just beyond me, like the edge of a dream, the wisp of a cloud, somewhere, but nowhere. It was at those times, at night, with thick hotel curtains drawn, the flicker of the TV just a blink of human company, when I most longed to join him, fearing that time would take him to the far corner of oblivion. But I could see him too clearly to make him wrong about me, so I slept, my hand on the cool sheen of the urn, and awakened with daylight to ride again.

As Eric and I rode together into Philadelphia for the last time, past the bridges and river, around William Penn in his scaffolding high above us, over the narrow, cracked one-way streets, I realized that the city meant him to me, and my crying began, tears whipping backward into the stiff sides of my helmet, absorbed by my hair. I had never wanted to come home this way, without Eric's arms around me, without his hands to guide me, without a future.

I drove past the apartment we had shared, unable to raise my eyes to it, and continued to my parents' house.

CHAPTER FORTY-TWO

I'm not sure how I made it through the year following Eric's death, stumbling around town, seeing his soul in the sparkle and wink of so many strangers' dark eyes. For months I wandered around my parents' neighborhood, having given up the apartment, returning to live at home for a while. Occasionally I played basketball, or watched kids at baseball, or took Shadow Blaster on outings far into the countryside. Eric stayed home, in the closet.

I tried to work, and still attended the AIDS Survivors Group; I felt I had earned the name. I even started volunteering at the AIDS Project with Hank, doing what I could for the ones who would not survive.

While I was there one day Hank burst into the office.

'Yes!' he cried. 'Yes!' He began twirling around in his wheelchair.

'What?' I asked, laughing.

'We won!' he said. He stopped spinning and grabbed my hands. 'We finally won for Eric.'

'Won?' I said. 'Won?' I had long since stopped going to the trials, sick of hearing yet another jury condemn Eric.

'Yes, dear Alex,' Hank said, a huge grin on his face. 'We won.'

'You did it!' I said, hugging him.

'Persistence did it,' he said. 'And you'll be getting a bit of money soon, say around three and a half million dollars.'

'What?'

'That's right. Now you can afford to hire a "real lawyer"—or better yet, become one yourself.' He smiled.

'I wish Eric were here . . .'

'He's around, Alex. He'd be glad you got the money.'

'What made the difference this time?'

'Sally breaking down on the stand. I told you she was the key to this case.'

'But I thought you said the jury might not believe her once she admitted she'd lied on the stand before, about "not recalling."'

'That's right, but the truth eventually eats through the jury's doubt.'

'Why'd she decide to come clean?'

'She wouldn't say, but I think someone close to her was diagnosed with HIV.'

'Really?'

Hank held up a hand. 'I didn't tell you that,' he said, wheeling behind his desk.

I watched him. 'We got lucky,' I said.

His eyes met mine. 'But someone else didn't.'

'I guess you're right.'

'There's work to do.'

'I know.' I turned to leave, to let him get to the stack of paper on his desk, and as I did, I started to say 'thanks' before I remembered his prohibition.

Still, as I walked out, I heard him whisper, 'You're welcome.'

The money from the lawsuit was huge, obscene. And so typical of a culture that had turned its back on a gifted young man with AIDS to paste dollar bills to the wound, too late.

Yet, it was what the world had left of Eric, so I set up the Young Wizards Foundation to help foster parents who cared for children with HIV disease. Its logo was the wizard, which I had had tattooed over my left shoulder blade, behind my heart.

And I went to law school, hearing Eric's words through Pammy, to 'somehow make it right.'

CHAPTER FORTY-THREE

It was in the fall, more than a year after Eric had died, when I was riding Shadow Blaster and I noticed it was October, green turning to red, orange, yellow. I was reminded of the annual flights Eric and I used to take, to Cape May, of that beach, midnight swims and daring rescues, downpours, the lost ring. Autumn had meant hope and promise then.

The time had come to take Eric flying.

I called Joey that afternoon, at the place where I used to skywrite.

'Yeah?' he answered.

'Joe,' I said, 'it's Alex Taylor, remember me?'

'Hell, yeah. How are you?'

'Okay, and you?'

'Good. Why you calling, you need a job?'

'No,' I said, laughing.

'Good thing. Mr. Rig still hasn't forgiven you for that stunt you pulled.'

'I know.' I hesitated. 'I'm actually calling to ask—'

'Let me guess, you wanna ask me out.'

'Well . . .'

'Just kidding. What can I do for you?'

'The biggest favor, Joey. Please.'

'I'm not writing anything about AIDS, if that's what you want.'

'I want to borrow a plane tomorrow, if the weather's good.'

'Borrow? Sure!'

'Rent, then. I know Mr. Rig is never there in the mornings, and I only need it for a few hours. I'll pay.'

'There's no way—'

'This means the world to me, Joe. I can't tell you how much it means.'

'Are you gonna write something?'

'Yes.'

'What?'

'Do you have to know?'

'Listen, the only way I can swing this is if he thinks I took the plane up and a customer paid for a message. If you write some crazy shit, it's gonna be my ass—'

425

'I'm only going to write "I love you Eric."'

'You've still got that same boyfriend, eh?'

I was silent.

'It'd be a lot easier if you'd just let me do it, Alex.'

'It wouldn't be the same.'

'He'll never know the difference.'

'Believe me, he'll know.'

He waited; I could hear him considering. That job was Joey's life; he'd own the place one day. 'Okay,' he finally said, 'but on one condition.'

'I'll pay the usual amount, or more if you want.'

'Just pay for the message.'

'Okay.'

'But that's not the condition.'

'What, then?'

'Promise me if you ever break up with that guy, you'll give me a chance.'

'Promise.'

The next morning was sunny, perfect autumn, and I awoke with my heart beating fast. The sky was right: blue, clear, pink clouds on the horizon, fresh for flying, an untouched slate for writing. Today was the day.

Mom and Daddy had insisted that I come see

them on my way out to New Jersey. I brought the urn in with me, holding it under my arm.

They were at the breakfast table, finishing their coffee.

'Will you have breakfast first?' Daddy asked. 'Your mother made pancakes . . .'

'No thanks.'

'Sweetie,' Mom said, getting up, 'are you sure we can't come along?'

'I'm sure.'

Mom hugged me; pressing the urn into my ribs. Then she pulled away. 'I'm making brownies for the ceremony today.'

'Good.' Mom had planned a get-together that afternoon, to mark the day, to remember Eric. As if we'd forget.

Joey was nervous when I arrived, hustling me to the runway and practically shoving me and my backpack inside the plane.

'You're loaded and ready,' he said. 'You sure you're current?'

'Yes.' That was kind of a lie; I hadn't had my FAA physical in over two years, but I was healthy and I knew how to fly.

'Where you going?' he asked.

'Cape May,' I said with a smile.

'You didn't tell me that!' he shouted as I

started the engine, making him back up, his hair lashing around his face.

'You didn't ask me!'

'But it's post-season, no one's there!'

'I know!' I yelled, and waved. He remained on the runway, staring after me as I took off toward the ocean.

Flying again exhilarated me; I loved the cold wind at altitude, and as I reached the shoreline, I felt high and alive, ready. I flew over the beach a few times, remembering, wondering about the ring, buried or washed out to sea, approximating forever. I wondered why we hadn't spent more time there. I wondered if I'd ever be there again.

I looked at the urn next to me and said, 'I love you, Eric.' Then I started to write the message he would never see, maybe no one would, except me, and then only as it started to dissolve. It took more than twenty minutes to write and when I was done, I flew over the ocean, opening the urn and holding it high, out, and back, for the wind to take its contents. It seemed too confining to suspend him all in one place, even a place as big as the ocean, or as lovely as that beach, so I started back to the airport, letting him fly as I went, over farms, cities, streets, barnyards. While I did, I thought about the cremation, about what part of Eric had been dispersed then, over Chicago, and wondered if the wizard had painted that smoke as it rose to the heavens.

I knew then, like I'd always known, that Eric could never have been buried; he wouldn't have stayed down. He would have to be among it, all of it, a gray flake caught on the silver tip of a cowboy boot, a charred piece nestled between the forks of a basketball hoop, an ash resting lightly on a woman's breast. That was Eric.

He wasn't gone. He was everywhere now.

THE END

AUTHOR'S NOTE

Give of yourself to those in need: a meal cooked, a hand held, a back washed, a laugh shared. Give what is precious: your time, your compassion, your strength, for giving is the salve that heals humankind, the caulk that seals the crack.

THE NOTEBOOK
by Nicholas Sparks

The Notebook is an achingly tender story about the enduring power of love, a story of miracles that will stay with you forever.

Set amid the austere beauty of the North Carolina Coast, *The Notebook* begins with the story of Noah Calhoun, a rural Southerner recently returned from the Second World War. Noah is restoring a plantation home to its former glory, and he is haunted by images of the beautiful girl he met fourteen years earlier, a girl he loved like no other. Unable to find her, yet unwilling to forget the summer they spent together, Noah is content to live with only memories . . . until she unexpectedly returns to his town to see him again. Allie Nelson is now engaged to another man, but realizes that the original passion she felt for Noah has not dimmed with the passage of time. Yet the obstacles that once ended their previous relationship still remain, and the gulf between their worlds is too vast to ignore. With her impending marriage only weeks away, Allie is forced to confront her hopes and dreams for the future, a future that only she can shape.

Like a puzzle within a puzzle, the story of Noah and Allie is just the beginning. As it unfolds, their tale miraculously becomes something different, with much higher stakes. The result is a deeply moving portrait of love itself, the tender moments and the fundamental changes that affect us all.

A Doubleday Hardcover

0 385 40825 0

A SELECTION OF NOVELS AVAILABLE
FROM BANTAM BOOKS AND BLACK SWAN

THE PRICES SHOWN BELOW WERE CORRECT AT THE TIME OF GOING TO
PRESS. HOWEVER TRANSWORLD PUBLISHERS RESERVE THE RIGHT TO
SHOW NEW RETAIL PRICES ON COVERS WHICH MAY DIFFER FROM THOSE
PREVIOUSLY ADVERTISED IN THE TEXT OR ELSEWHERE.

99725 0	TALK BEFORE SLEEP	Elizabeth Berg	£6.99
99716 1	RANGE OF MOTION	Elizabeth Berg	£6.99
40803 8	SACRED AND PROFANE	Marcelle Bernstein	£5.99
40497 0	CHANGE OF HEART	Charlotte Bingham	£4.99
40890 9	DEBUTANTES	Charlotte Bingham	£5.99
40296 X	IN SUNSHINE OR IN SHADOW	Charlotte Bingham	£5.99
40496 2	NANNY	Charlotte Bingham	£4.99
40171 8	STARDUST	Charlotte Bingham	£4.99
40163 7	THE BUSINESS	Charlotte Bingham	£5.99
40895 X	THE NIGHTINGALE SINGS	Charlotte Bingham	£5.99
17635 8	TO HEAR A NIGHTINGALE	Charlotte Bingham	£5.99
50411 8	VERONICA	Nicholas Christopher	£6.99
40820 8	LILY'S WAR	June Francis	£4.99
40996 4	GOING HOME TO LIVERPOOL	June Francis	£4.99
50427 0	KITTY AND HER BOYS	June Francis	£5.99
99681 5	A MAP OF THE WORLD	Jane Hamilton	£6.99
99685 8	THE BOOK OF RUTH	Jane Hamilton	£6.99
40730 9	LOVERS	Judith Krantz	£5.99
40731 7	SPRING COLLECTION	Judith Krantz	£5.99
40206 4	FAST FRIENDS	Jill Mansell	£4.99
40612 4	OPEN HOUSE	Jill Mansell	£4.99
40938 7	TWO'S COMPANY	Jill Mansell	£5.99
40943 3	PROMISES, PROMISES	Patricia Scanlan	£5.99
40947 6	FOREIGN AFFAIRS	Patricia Scanlan	£4.99
40945 X	FINISHING TOUCHES	Patricia Scanlan	£5.99
40483 0	SINS OF THE MOTHER	Arabella Seymour	£4.99

All Transworld titles are available by post from:

Book Service By Post, P.O. Box 29, Douglas, Isle of Man IM99 1BQ

Credit cards accepted. Please telephone 01624 675137,
fax 01624 670923, Internet http://www.bookpost.co.uk
or e-mail: bookshop@enterprise.net for details.

Free postage and packing in the UK. Overseas customers: allow
£1 per book (paperbacks) and £3 per book (hardbacks).